BY BERWEN BANKS

a Novel

by

ALLEN RAINE

CHAPTER I.

BERWEN BANKS.

Caer Madoc is a sleepy little Welsh town, lying two miles from the sea coast. Far removed from the busy centres of civilisation, where the battle of life breeds keen wits and deep interests, it is still, in the opinion of its inhabitants, next to London, the most important place in the United Kingdom. It has its church and three chapels, its mayor and corporation, jail, town hall, and market-place; but, more especially, it has its fairs, and awakes to spasmodic jollity on such occasions, which come pretty often —quite ten times in the year. In the interims it resigns itself contentedly to its normal state of lethargy.

The day on which my story opens had seen the busiest and merriest fair of the year, and the evening found the little town looking jaded and disreputable after its few hours of dissipation, the dusty High Street being littered with scraps of paper, orange-peel, and such like *débris*. The merry-go-rounds and the "shows" had departed, the last donkey-cart had rattled out of the town, laden with empty gingerbread boxes.

In the stable of the Red Dragon three men stooped in conclave over the hind foot of a horse. Deio, the ostler, and Roberts, the farrier, agreed in their verdict for a wonder; and Caradoc Wynne, the owner of the horse, straightened himself from his stooping posture with a nod of decision.

"Yes, it's quite plain I mustn't ride him to-night," he said. "Well, I'll leave him under your care, Roberts, and will either come or send for him to-morrow."

"Needn't do that, sir," said Roberts, "for I am going myself to Abersethin on Friday; that will give him one day's complete rest, and I'll bring him up gently with my nag."

"That will do better," said the young man. "Take care of him, Deio," he added, in good, broad Welsh, "and I will pay you well for your trouble," and, with a pat on Captain's flank and a douceur in Deio's ready palm, he turned to leave the yard. Looking back from under the archway which opened into the street, with a parting injunction to Roberts to "take care of him," he turned up the dusty High Street.

"Pagh!" he said, "it has been a jolly fair, but it hasn't sweetened the air. However, I shall soon have left it behind me," and he stepped out briskly towards the straggling end of the street, which merged into a wild moorland country.

"*There's* a difference between him and his father," said Deio to his companion, as they led Captain back to his stall. "See the old 'Vicare du' hunting between his coppers for a threepenny bit! Jâr i man! you would think it was a sovereign he was looking for."

"Yes," said Roberts, "the old Vicare is a keen man enough, but just; always pays his bills regularly; he is not as black as they make him out to be."

"No, I daresay! They say the devil isn't, either," said Deio.

It was very evident the person in question was no favourite of his.

Meanwhile Caradoc, or Cardo as he was called all over the country side, the "Vicare du's" only son, had begun his tramp homewards with a light heart and a brisk step. He was a tall, broad-shouldered man, with health and youthful energy expressed in every limb and feature, with jet black hair and sparkling eyes to match. His dark, almost swarthy face, was lighted up by a pleasant smile, which seemed ever hovering about the corners of his mouth, and which would make itself evident in spite of the moustache which threatened to hide it.

The band of the local militia was practising in the open market hall as he passed, and an old Welsh air struck familiarly on his ear.

"They'll wonder what's become of me at home," he thought, "or rather Betto will. I don't suppose my father would notice my absence, so long as I was home to supper. Poor old dad!" he added, and a grave look came over his face.

In truth it was not a very cheerful home to which he was returning, but it *was* home, and had been his from childhood. It had been the home also of his ancestors for generations, which, to a Welshman, means a great deal, for the ties of home are in the very roots of his being. Home draws him from the furthermost ends of the earth, and leaving it, adds bitterness even to death.

His mother had died at his birth, so that the sacred word "mother" had never been more than a name to him, and he had taught himself to banish the thought of her from his mind; in fact an indescribable uneasiness always leapt up within his heart when her name was mentioned, and that was very rarely, for his father never spoke of her, and old Betto, the head servant, but seldom, and then with such evident sadness and reticence, that an undefined, though none the less crushing fear, had haunted him from childhood upwards. As he stepped out so bravely this soft spring evening, the look of disquietude did not remain long on his face. At twenty-four life has not lost its rosy tints; heart, mind, and body are fresh and free to take a share in all its opening scenes, more especially if, as in Cardo's case, love, the disturber, has not yet put in an appearance.

As he reached the brow of the hill beyond the town, the white dusty road stretched like a sinuous snake over the moor before him, while on the left, the sea lay soft and grey in the twilight, and the moon rose full and bright on his right. The evening air was very still, but an occasional strain of the band he had left behind him reached his ears, and with a musical voice he hummed the old Welsh air which came fitfully on the breeze:

"By Berwen's banks my love hath strayed,
For many a day in sun and shade;
And while she carols loud and clear,
The little birds fly down to hear.

"By Berwen's banks the storm rose high,
The swollen river rushing by!
Beneath its waves my love was drowned
And on its banks my love was found!"

Suddenly he was aware of a cloaked figure walking about a hundred yards in front of him. "Who's that, I wonder?" he thought, and then, forgetting its existence, he continued his song:

"I'll ne'er forget that leafy shade!
I'll ne'er forget that winsome maid!
But there no more she carols free,
So Berwen's banks are sad to me!"

By and by, at a curve in the road, he again noticed the figure in front of him, and quickened his steps; but it did the same, and the distance between them was not lessened, so Cardo gave it up, and continued his song. When the strain came to a natural ending, he looked again with some interest at the grey figure ever moving on, and still seeming to keep at the same distance from him. Once more he quickened his steps, and again the figure did likewise. "Diwss anwl!" he said. "I am not going to run after an old woman who evidently does not want my company." And he tramped steadily on under the fast darkening sky. For quite three miles he had followed the vanishing form, and as he reached the top of the moor, he began to feel irritated by the persistent manner in which his fellow-traveller refused to shorten the distance between them. It roused within him the spirit of resistance, and he could be very dogged sometimes in spite of his easy manner. Having once determined, therefore, to come up with the mysterious pedestrian, he rapidly covered the ground with his long strides, and soon found himself abreast of a slim girl, who, after looking shyly aside at him, continued her walk at the same steady pace. The twilight had darkened much since he had left the town, but the moonlight showed him the graceful pose of the head, the light, springy tread, and the mass of golden hair which escaped from the red hood covering her head. Cardo took off his cap.

"Good-night to you," he said. "I hope I have not frightened you by so persistently trying to catch you."

"Good-night," said the girl. "Yes, indeed, you have, whatever, because I am not used to be out in the night. The rabbits have frightened me too, they are looking so large in this light."

"I am sorry. It is very brave of you to walk all the way from Caer Madoc alone."

"To Abersethin it is not so far," said the girl.

"Do you live at Abersethin?"

"Yes, not far off; round the edge of the cliffs, under Moel Hiraethog."

"Oh! I know," said Cardo; "the mill in the valley?"

"No, round the next shore, and up to the top of the cliff is our house."

"Traeth Berwen? That is where *I* live!"

"Well, indeed!"

"Yes, I am Caradoc Wynne, and I live at Brynderyn."

"Oh! are you Cardo Wynne? I have heard plenty about you, and about your father, the 'Vicare du.'"

"Ah! poor old dad! I daresay you have not heard much good of him; the people do not understand him."

"Well, indeed, the worst I have heard of him is that he is not very kind to you; that he is making you to work on the farm, when you ought to be a gentleman."

"That is not true," said Cardo, flushing in the darkness; "it is my wish to be a farmer; I like it better than any other work; it is my own free choice. Besides, can I not be a farmer and a gentleman too? Where could I be so happy as here at home, where my ancestors have lived for generations?"

"Ancestors?" said the girl; "what is that?"

"Oh! my grandfather and great-grandfather, and all the long dead of my family."

"Yes, indeed, I see. Ancestors," she repeated, with a sort of scheduling tone, as though making sure of the fresh information; "I do not know much English, but there's good you are speaking it! Can you speak Welsh?"

"Ha! ha! ha!" laughed Cardo, and his voice woke the echoes from Moel Hiraethog, the hill which they were nearing, and which they must compass before reaching the valley of the Berwen. "Ha! ha! ha! Can I speak Welsh? Why, I am Welsh to the core, Cymro glan gloyw![1] What are you?"

"Oh! Welsh, of course. You can hear that by my talk."

"Indeed no," said Cardo. "I did not know anyone at Traeth Berwen could speak English as well as you do."

He was longing to find out who his fellow-traveller was. He saw in the dim light she was slim and fair, and had a wealth of golden hair; he saw her dress was grey and her hood was red. So much the moonlight revealed, but further than this he could not discover, and politeness forbade his asking. As if in answer to his thoughts, however, her next words enlightened him.

"I am Valmai Powell, the niece of Essec Powell, the preacher."

A long, low whistle escaped from the young man's lips.

"By Jove!" he said.

The girl was silent, but could he have seen the hot blush which spread over her face and neck, he would have known that he had roused the quick Welsh temper. He was unconscious of it, however, and strode on in silence, until they reached a rough-built, moss-grown bridge, and here they both stopped as if by mutual consent. Leaning their elbows on the mossy stone wall, they looked down to the depths below, where the little river Berwen babbled and whispered on its way to the sea.

"There's a nice noise it is making down there," said Valmai. "But why do you say a bad word when I tell you my uncle's name?"

"A bad word? In your presence? Not for the world! But I could not help thinking how shocked my father and your uncle would be to see us walking together."

"Yes, I think, indeed," said the girl, opening a little basket and spreading its contents on the low wall. "See!" she said, in almost childish tones, and turning her face straight to the moonlight.

Cardo saw, as he looked down at her, that it was a beautiful face.

"See!" she said, "gingerbread that I bought in that old street they call 'The Mwntroyd.' Here is a silver ship, and here is a gold watch, and a golden girl. Which will you have?"

"Well, indeed, I am as hungry as a hunter," said Cardo. "I will have the lassie, if you are sure you have enough for two."

"Anwl! anwl! I have a lamb and a sheep and some little pigs in my basket." And she proceeded to spread them out and divide them; and they continued to chat as they ate their gilded gingerbread.

"Suppose your uncle and my father knew we were standing on the same bridge and looking at the same moon," said Cardo, laughing.

"And eating the same gingerbread," added Valmai.

"My word! There would be wrath."

"Wrath?" said the girl, looking thoughtfully up in her companion's face; "what is that?"

"Oh, something no one could feel towards you. 'Wrath' is anger."

"My uncle is angry sometimes with me, and—too—with—with—"

"My father, I suppose?" said Cardo.

"Yes, indeed," said the girl; "that is true, whatever. Every Wednesday evening at the prayer-meeting he is praying for the 'Vicare du,' and Betto told me last week that the Vicare is praying for my uncle on Tuesday evenings."

"Oh, Lord! has it come to that?" said Cardo. "Then I'm afraid we can never hope for peace between them."

They both laughed, and the girl's rippling tones mingled musically in Cardo's ears with the gurgle of the Berwen.

"It is getting late," she said, "we had better go on; but I must say good-night here, because it is down by the side of the river is my way to Dinas. You will be nearer to keep on the road till you cross the valley."

"No, indeed," said the young man, already preparing to help his companion over the stone stile. "I will go down by the Berwen too."

"Anwl," said Valmai, clasping her hands; "it will be a mile further for you, whatever."

"A mile is nothing on such a night as this."

And down to the depths of the dark underwood they passed, by a steep, narrow path, down through the tangled briers and bending ferns, until they reached the banks of the stream. The path was but little defined, and evidently seldom trodden; the stream gurgled and lisped under the brushwood; the moon looked down upon it and sparkled on its ripples; and as Valmai led the way, chatting in her broken English, a strange feeling of happy companionship awoke in Cardo Wynne's heart.

After threading the narrow pathway for half-a-mile or so, they reached a sudden bend of the little river, where the valley broadened out somewhat, until there was room for a grassy, velvet meadow, at the further corner of which stood the ruins of the old parish church, lately discarded for the new chapel of ease built on the hillside above the shore.

"How black the ruins look in that corner," said Cardo.

"Yes, and what is that white thing in the window?" said Valmai, in a frightened whisper, and shrinking a little nearer to her companion.

"Only a white owl. Here she comes sailing out into the moonlight."

"Well, indeed, so it is. From here we can hear the sea, and at the beginning of the shore I shall be turning up to Dinas."

"And I suppose I must turn in the opposite direction to get to Brynderyn," said Cardo. "Well, I have never enjoyed a walk from Caer Madoc so much before. Will they be waiting for you at home, do you think?"

"Waiting for me?" laughed the girl, and her laugh was not without a little trace of bitterness; "who is there to wait for me? No one, indeed, since my mother is dead. Perhaps to-morrow my uncle might say, 'Where is Valmai? She has never brought me my book.' Here it is, though," she continued, "safe under the crumbs of the gingerbread. I bought it in the Mwntroyd. 'Tis a funny name whatever."

"Yes, a relic of the old Flemings, who settled in Caer Madoc long ago."

"Oh! I would like to hear about that! Will you tell me about it some time again?"

"Indeed I will," said Cardo eagerly; "but when will that be? I have been wondering all the evening how it is I have never seen you before."

They had now reached the open beach, where the Berwen, after its chequered career, subsided quietly through the sand and pebbles into the sea.

"Here is my path, but I will tell you," and with the sound of the gurgling river, and the plash of the waves in his ears, Cardo listened to her simple story. "You couldn't see me much before, because only six weeks it is since I am here. Before that I was living far, far away. Have you ever heard of Patagonia? Well then, my father was a missionary there, and he took me and my mother with him when I was only a baby. Since then I have always been living there, till this year I came to Wales."

"Patagonia!" said Cardo. "So far away? No wonder you dropped upon me so suddenly! But how, then, did you grow up Welsh?"

Valmai laughed merrily.

"Grow up Welsh? Well, indeed, I don't know what have I grown up! Welsh, or English, or Spanish, or Patagonian! I am mixed of them all, I think. Where we were living there was a large settlement of Welsh people, and my father preached to them. But there were, too, a great many Spaniards, and many Spanish girls were my friends, and my nurse was Spanish, so I learnt to speak Welsh and Spanish; but English, only what I learnt from my father and from books. I don't know it quite easy yet, but I am coming better every day I think. My father and mother are dead, both of them—only a few days between them. Another kind missionary's wife brought me home, and since then I am living with my uncle. He is quite kind when he notices me, but he is always reading—reading the old books about the Druids, and Owen Glendwr, and those old times, and he is forgetting the present; only I must not go near the church nor the church people, then he is quite kind."

"How curious!" said Cardo. "You have almost described my father and my home! I think we ought to be friends with so much in common."

"Yes, perhaps," said the girl, looking pensively out to sea, where the seahorses were tossing up their white manes in the moonlight. "Well, goodbye," she added, holding out her hand.

"Good-bye," answered Cardo, taking the proffered hand in a firm, warm grasp. "Will we meet again soon?" he said, dropping it reluctantly.

"No, I think," said Valmai, as she began the steep path up the hill.

Cardo stood a moment looking after her, and as she turned to look back, he called out:

"Yes, I hope."

She waved her hand, and disappeared behind a broom bush.

"Valmai! Valmai!" he said, as he tramped off in the opposite direction. "Yes, she is *Valmai*!" [2]

[1] "A pure Welshman." A favourite expression in Wales.

[2] "Like May."

CHAPTER II.

THE HOUSE ON THE CLIFF.

The Rev. Meurig Wynne, "y Vicare du," or "the black Vicar," as he was called by the country people, in allusion to his black hair and eyes, and also to his black apparel, sat in his musty study, as he had done every evening for the last twenty-five years, poring ever his old books, and occasionally jotting down extracts therefrom. He was a broad-shouldered man, tall and straight, about sixty-five years of age. His clean-shaven face was white as marble, its cold and lifeless appearance accentuated by his jet-black hair, strongly-marked eyebrows of the same dark hue, and his unusually black eyes; his nose was slightly aquiline, and his mouth well shaped, though wide; but the firm-set lips and broad nostrils, gave the whole face an expression of coldness and hardness. In fact he had a peculiarly dour and dark look, and it was no wonder that when he walked through his parish the little children left their games in the road, and hurried inside their garden gates as he passed.

He was perfectly conscious of this, and it pained him, though no one guessed it except his son, who felt a tender pity for the man who led so isolated and solitary a life.

The cause of his cold reserve Cardo had never been able to discover; but he somehow connected it with his mother's name, and therefore shrank from inquiring into his father's past life, preferring to let old memories sleep, rather than hear anything which might bring sorrow and pain into his life.

The Vicar was evidently uneasy, as he looked up listening, with one thin finger marking the place on the page he was reading. Cardo was later than usual, and not until he had heard his son's familiar firm step and whistle did he drop once more into the deep interest of his book.

As Cardo approached the house he saw the light in his father's window, and pictured to himself the cold, pale face bending over the musty books. "Poor old dad!" he murmured. Some sons would have tapped playfully at the window, but Cardo did not, he turned round the corner of the house, passing by the front door, which was closed, and did not look inviting, to the other side, where the clatter of wooden shoes and a stream of light from the open doorway made some show of cheerfulness. And there was Betto, his old nurse and his father's housekeeper, in loud, angry tones, reproving the shepherd boy who stood leaning against the door-post.

"Hello! what's the matter, Betto?" said Cardo in Welsh; "what mischief has Robin been up to now?"

"Machgen bach i (my dear boy!), is that you?" said Betto; "there's glad I am! You are late to-night, and I was beginning to puzzle."

"Has my father missed me?"

"Well, indeed, he hasn't said anything," said Betto, hunting for the frying-pan, and beginning to prepare the ham and eggs for supper. "But where's that Robin?" she added; "a clout or two with the frying-pan would not hurt his addle pate."

"He has been wise, and made himself scarce; but what has he done, Betto?"

"What has he done? the villain! Well, you know the sheep are grazing in the churchyard this week, and that 'mwnki' is watching them there. Well—he seated himself yesterday on a tombstone when we were in church, and whit, whit, whitted 'Men of Harlech' on his flute! and the Vicare praying so beautiful all the time, too! praying against the wiles of the devil and of Essec Powell!"

"Essec Powell! What has he been doing?"

"Well, machgen i, you will not believe! the boldness of those 'Methots' is something beyond! And the impidence of Essec Powell! What do you think, Caradoc? he is *praying* for your father—out loud, mind you!—in the prayer-meeting every Wednesday evening! But there! the master is beforehand with him, for he is praying for Essec Powell on Tuesdays!" and she tossed the frizzling ham and eggs on the dish. "Come to supper, my boy," and Cardo followed her nothing loth into the gloomy parlour, lighted by one home-made mould candle, for he was hungry in spite of the ginger-bread.

"Ah, Caradoc! you have come," said the Vicar, as he entered the room punctually at the stroke of ten, "what made you so late to-night?"

"Well," said Cardo, "when Deio, 'Red Dragon,' led Captain out of the stable, I found the swelling on his leg had risen again, so I left him with Roberts, the farrier. He will bring him home on Friday."

"You have ridden him too soon after his sprain, as I told you, but young men always know better than their elders."

"Well, you were right anyway this time, father."

"Yes," said his father; "as the old proverb says, 'Yr hên a wyr yr ifanc a debyg." [1]

"Shouldn't wonder if it rained to-morrow, the wind has veered to the south; it will be bad for the 'Sassiwn,' won't it?" said Cardo, after a pause.

"The what?" said the Vicar, looking full at his son.

"The 'Sassiwn,' sir, as they call it; the Methodist Association, you know, to be held here next week."

"I don't want to hear anything about it; I take no interest in the subject."

"Won't you go then, father? There will be thousands of people there."

"No, sir, I will not go; neither will you, I hope," answered the Vicar, and pushing his plate away, he rose, and walked stiffly out at the door and along the stone passage leading to his study.

His son listened to his retreating footsteps.

"As bigoted as ever, poor fellow!" he said; "but what a fool I was to mention the subject." And he continued his supper in silence. When Betto came in to clear away he had flung himself down on the hard horse-hair sofa. The mould candle lighted up but a small space in the large, cold room; there was no fire in the grate, no books or papers lying about, to beguile the tedious hour before bedtime. Was it any wonder that his thoughts should revert to the earlier hours of the evening? that he should hear again in fancy the soft voice that said, "I am Valmai Powell," and that he should picture to himself the clustering curls that escaped from the red hood?

The old house, with its long passages and large rooms, was full of those nameless sounds which fill the air in the quiet of night. He heard his father's footsteps as he paced up and down in his study, he heard the tick-tack of the old clock on the stairs, the bureau creaked, the candle spluttered, but there was no human voice to break the silence, With a yawn he rose, stretching his long legs, and, throwing back his broad shoulders, made his way along the dark passage which led into the kitchen, where the farm servants were seated at supper. Betto moved the beehive chair into a cosy corner beside the fire for the young master, the men-servants all tugged their forelocks, and the women rose to make a smiling bob-curtsey.

"Have some cawl,[2] Ser!" said Betto, selecting a shining black bowl and spoon.

"Not to-night, after all that fried ham; but another night I want nothing better for supper."

"Well, there's nothing will beat cawl, that's certain," said Ebben, the head servant, beginning with long-drawn noisy sups to empty his own bowl.

"Finished the turnips to-day?" asked Cardo.

"Oh, yes," said Ebben, with a slight tone of reproof in his voice; "the work goes on though you may not be at home, Ser. I consider there is no piece of land on this earth, no, nor on any other earth, better farmed than Brynderyn. Eh?" and he looked defiantly at Betto, between whom and himself there was a continual war of words.

"Well, I suppose so, indeed," said Betto; "*you* say so often enough, whatever, and what you say must be right."

There was such an insidious mixture of flattery and sarcasm in her words that, for a moment Ebben was at a loss what to answer, so Malen, the milkmaid, took the opportunity of changing the subject.

"There's tons of bread will be baked on Monday," she said, "ready for the Sassiwn. Jini 'bakkare' has two sacks of flour to bake, and there's seven other women in Abersethin will bake the same quantity."

"At Morfa," said Shanw, "they have killed a cow and a sheep; and the tongues, and fowls, and hams will fill every oven in the parish."

Betto sniffed and tossed her head scornfully. "They may well give them bread and meat," she said, "for I don't see what else they have to give them."

"What else, indeed," said Shanw, ready for the frequent fray. "They won't have your hum-drum old church fregot[3], perhaps, but you come and see, and hear Hughes Bangor, Price Merthyr, Jones Welshpool. Nothing to give them, indeed! Why, Price Merthyr would send your old red velvet cushion at church flying into smithireens in five minutes. Haven't I heard him. He begins soft and low, like a cat purring on the hearth, and then he gets louder and louder, till he ends like a roaring lion. And our own preacher, Essec Powell, to begin and finish the meeting. There's busy Valmai must be. Marged Hughes is there to help, and she says—"

"Oh, be quiet," said Betto, "and go along with your Valmai, and your Price Merthyr, and your hams, and lions, and things. Ach y fi! I don't want to hear about such things in a clergyman's house."

"Valmai is a beauty, whatever," said Dye, the ploughboy. "I kiwked[4] at her over the hedge this morning when she was going to Caer Madoc; she's as pretty as an angel. Have you ever seen her, Ser?"

"Valmai," said Cardo, prevaricating, "surely that is a new name in this neighbourhood?"

"Yes, she is Essec Powell's niece come home from over the sea. She is an orphan, and they say the old man is keeping her reading and reading to him all day till she is fair tired, poor thing."

"Well, it is getting late," said Cardo, "good-night." And his rising was the signal for them all to disperse, the men servants going to their beds over the hay loft or stable; while the women, leaving their wooden shoes at the bottom, followed each other with soft tread up the creaking back stairs.

In the study the Vicar poured over his books, as he translated from English into Welsh the passages which interested him most. He was, like many of the inhabitants of the South Wales coast, a descendant of the

Flemings, who had long ago settled there, and who have left such strong and enduring marks of their presence.

Their language has long given place to a sort of doggerel English, but they have never learned to speak the language of the country except in some of the straggling border villages.

Pembrokeshire, in particular, retains a complete separateness, so to speak, from the rest of the country, and is often called "Little England beyond Wales." Thus it was that the English language seemed always more natural to Meurig Wynne than the Welsh. His sermons were always thought out in that language, and then translated into the vernacular, and this, perhaps, accounted in some degree for their stiffness and want of living interest. His descent from the Flemings had the disadvantage of drawing a line of distinction between him and his parishioners, and thus added to his unpopularity. In spite of this, Cardo was an immense favourite, his frank and genial manner—inherited from his mother, who was thoroughly Welsh—making its way easily to the warm Welsh hearts. There was a deep well of tenderness, almost of pity, within him for his cold stern father, a longing to break through his reserve, a hankering after the loving ways of home life, which he missed though he had never known them. The cold Fleming had very little part in Cardo's nature, and, with his enthusiastic Welsh sympathies, he was wont to regret and disclaim his connection with these ancient ancestors. His father's pedigree, however, made it very plain that the Gwynnes of Brynderyn were descended from Gwayn, a Flemish wool merchant who had settled there in the reign of Henry I.—these settlers being protected and encouraged by the English king, who found their peaceable, industrious habits a great contrast to the turbulence and restlessness of the Welsh under their foreign yoke. Time has done but little to soften the difference between the Welsh and Flemish characters; they have never really amalgamated, and to this day the descendants of the Flemings remain a separate people in language, disposition, and appearance. In Pembrokeshire, Gower, and Radnorshire, we find them still flourishing, and for some distance along the coast northwards from Pembrokeshire there are still families, and even whole hamlets, descended from them, exhibiting traits of character and peculiarities of manner easily discernible to an observant eye.

Before the Vicar retired to rest he took down from a shelf an old Bible, from which he read a chapter, and, closing the book, knelt down to pray. As he rose from his knees, the last words on his lips were, "Caradoc, my beloved son!"

For the next few days the turnips and mangolds seemed even more interesting than usual to Cardo Wynne. He was up with the lark, and striding from furrow to furrow in company with Dye and Ebben, returning to a hurried breakfast, and out again on the breezy hillside before the blue smoke had begun to curl up from the thatched chimneys which marked the cluster of cottages called "Abersethin."

Down there, under the cliffs, the little village slumbered, the rising sun just beginning to touch its whitewashed walls with gold, while up above, on the high lands, the "Vicare du's" fields were already bathed in the morning sunlight.

As he crossed from ridge to ridge and from furrow to furrow Cardo's thoughts continually flew across the valley to the rugged hill on the other side, and to the old grey house on the cliff—the home of Essec Powell, the preacher. In vain he sought for any sign of the girl whose acquaintance he had made so unexpectedly, and he was almost tempted to believe that she was no other than a creature of his own imagination, born of the witching moonlight hour, and absorbed again into the passing shadows of night. But could he have seen through the walls of that old grey house, even now at that early hour, he would have understood what kept the preacher's niece so busily engaged that neither on the shore nor on the banks of the Berwen was there a sign of her.

In the cool dairy at Dinas, and in and out of the rambling old kitchen, she was busy with her preparations for the guests who would fill the house during the Sassiwn. She bustled about, with Marged Hughes in attendance, looking very different, but every bit as charming, in her neat farm dress as she had on her visit to Caer Madoc. The sleeves of her pink cotton jacket, pushed up above the elbows, showed her white, dimpled arms; while her blue skirt or petticoat was short enough to reveal the neatly-shod feet, with their bows of black ribbon on the instep.

Every house in the neighbourhood was busy with preparations of some sort. At the farmhouses the women had been engaged for days with their cooking. Huge joints of beef and ham, boiled or baked, stood ready in the cool pantries; and in the smallest cottages, where there was more than one bed, it had been prepared for some guest. "John, my cousin, is coming from 'the Works,'" [5] or "Mary, my sister, will be home with her baby."

Everywhere hearts and hands were full of warm hospitality. Clergymen of the Church of England, though generally looking askance at the chapels and their swarming congregations, now, carried away by the enthusiasm of the people, consented to attend the meetings, secretly looking forward, with the Welsh love of oratory, to the eloquent sermons generally to be heard on such occasions.

Cardo, ruthlessly striding through the dew-bespangled gossamer of the turnip field, heard with pleasure from Dye that the adjoining field, which sloped down to the valley, had been fixed upon for the holding of the Sassiwn. On the flat at the bottom the carpenters were already at work at a large platform, upon which the preachers and most honoured guests were to be seated; while the congregation would sit on the hillside, which reached up to the Vicar's land. At least three thousand, or even four, might be expected.

All day Cardo looked over the valley with intense interest, and when the day's work was over, unable to restrain his curiosity and impatience any longer, he determined to take a closer survey of the old house on the hill, which for so many years he had seen with his outward eyes, though his inner perception had never taken account of it. At last, crossing the beach, he took his way up the steep path that led to Dinas. As he rounded a little clump of stunted pine trees he came in sight of the house, grey, gaunt, and bare, not old enough to be picturesque, but too old to look neat and comfortable, on that wind-swept, storm-beaten cliff. Its grey walls, marked with patches of damp and lichen, looked like a tear-stained face, out of which the two upstairs windows stared like mournful eyes.

Downstairs, in one room, there was a little sign of comfort and adornment; crimson curtains hung at the window, inside which a few flowers grew in pots. Keeping well under the hedge of elders which surrounded the cwrt or front garden, Cardo passed round to the side—the pine end, as it is called in Wales—and here a little lattice window stood open. It faced the south, and away from the sea a white rose tree had ventured to stretch out its straggling branches. They had evidently lately been drawn by some loving hand towards the little window. A muslin curtain fluttered in the evening breeze, on which came the sound of a voice. Cardo knew it at once. It was Valmai singing at her work, and he longed to break through the elder bushes and call her attention. He was so near that he could even hear the words of her song, softly as they were sung. She was interrupted by a querulous voice.

"Valmai," it said in Welsh, "have you written that?"

"Oh! long ago, uncle. I am waiting for the next line."

"Here it is then, child, and well worth waiting for;" and, with outstretched arm marking the cadence of its rhythm, he read aloud from a book of old poems. "There's poetry for you, girl! There's a description of Nature! Where will you find such real poetry amongst modern bards? No, no! the bards are dead, Valmai!"

"Well, I don't know much about it, uncle; but isn't it a modern bard who writes:

"'Come and see the misty mountains
  In their grey and purple sheen,
When they blush to see the sunrise
  Like a maiden of thirteen!'"

That seems very pretty, whatever."

"Very pretty," growled the man's voice, "very pretty; of course it is—very pretty! That's just it; but that's all, Valmai. Pwff! you have put me out with your 'blushing maiden' and your 'purple sheen.' Let us shut up Taliesin and come to 'Drych y Pryf Oesoedd.' Now, you begin at the fifth chapter."

There was a little sigh, which Cardo heard distinctly, and then the sweet voice began and continued to read until the sun sank low in the west.

"It's getting too dark, uncle. Will I go and see if the cakes are done?"

"No, no!" said the old man, "Gwen will look after the cakes; you light the candle, and come on with the book."

How Cardo longed to spring in through the lattice window, to fling the old books away, and to draw the reader out into the gold and purple sunset—out over the breezy cliffs, and down to the golden sands; but the strong bonds of circumstances held him back.

The candle was lighted, and now he could see into the room. Old Essec Powell sat beside the table with one leg thrown over the other, hands clasped, and chin in the air, lost in the deep interest of the book which his niece was reading.

"He looks good for two hours longer," thought Cardo, as he saw the old man's far-away look.

There was a little tone of weariness in her voice as, seating herself at the table by the open window, Valmai drew the candle nearer and continued to read.

Outside in the dusky twilight Cardo was gazing his fill at the face which had haunted him ever since he had seen it on the road from Caer Madoc. Yes, it was a beautiful face! even more lovely than he imagined it to be in the dim evening light. He took note of the golden wavy hair growing low on her broad, white forehead, her darker eyebrows that reminded him of the two arches of a beautiful bridge, under which gleamed two clear pools, reflecting the blue of the sky and the glint of the sunshine, the straight, well-formed nose, the pensive, mobile mouth, the complexion of a pale pink rose, and added to this the indescribable charm of grace and manner which spread through her personality.

The evening shadows darkened, the sunset glow faded, and the moon rose in a cloudless sky. The distant sound of the regular plash of the waves on the beach reached Cardo's ears. He thought of the long reaches of golden sand lying cool and grey in the moonlight, and all the romantic dreams of youth awoke within him.

Was it right that Valmai should be bending over a musty book in a dimly-lit room? while outside were the velvet turf of the cliffs, the plashing waves, and the silver moonlight.

But the reading still went on, the gentle voice growing a little weary and monotonous, and the white eyelids falling a little heavily over the blue eyes.

Long Cardo watched and gazed, and at last, turning away, he walked moodily home. He knew his father would expect him to supper at ten o'clock punctually, and hurried his steps as he approached the house. Just in time, for Betto was placing on the table an appetising supper of cawl and bread and butter, which the two men were soon discussing silently, for the Vicar was more pre-occupied than usual, and Cardo, too, was busy with his own thoughts.

Suddenly the former spoke.

"Is the long meadow finished?" he said.

"Yes; Dye is a splendid fellow to work, and Ebben and he together get through a good deal."

"To-morrow they can clear out the barn. The next day is the market at Llanilwyn; they must go there and buy a cow which Jones Pant y rych is going to sell. I have told Ebben he is not to give more than 8 pounds for her, and that is one pound more than she is worth."

Cardo was silent. To clear out the barn next day was easy enough, but to get Dye and Ebben to the market on the following day would be impossible. It was the opening of the Sassiwn, and he knew that neither of the men would be absent on that occasion, even though disobedience should cost them their place. They were both Methodists, and it had gone hard with the Vicar before he had taken them into his service; but the exigencies of farm life had compelled him to do so, as there was absolutely not one young man amongst his own congregation.

To do him justice, he had forgotten for the moment that the market day at Llanilwyn would also be the Sassiwn day.

"Do you remember, father, the Sassiwn begins the day after to-morrow?"

"I had forgotten it, but I don't see what difference that can make to my buying a cow."

"But Ebben and Dye will want to be at the meetings."

A shadow crossed the old man's face. He made no answer, but continued to eat his supper in silence, and at last rose, and with a short "Goodnight, Cardo," went into his study. He knew as well as his son did that it would be useless to try and persuade his servants to be absent from the meetings, and the knowledge galled him bitterly, too bitterly for words, so he was silent; and Cardo, knowing his humour, said nothing to Dye and Ebben of his father's wishes.

"Poor old dad!" he sighed, as he finished his supper, "it is hard for him to see his congregation dwindled away to a mere handful, while the chapels around him arc crowded to overflowing. By Jove! there must be something wrong somewhere."

As usual after supper he followed Betto into the old kitchen, where the servants were assembled for supper, and where Shanw was again holding forth, to her own delight and Betto's disgust, on the coming glories of the Sassiwn.

"To-morrow evening will be the first meeting."

"Will it be in the field?" asked Cardo.

"Oh, no, Ser; the first is in the chapel always, and no strangers are there.

Essec Powell will have to shut up his old books for a few days now, and poor Valmai will have rest. Marged Hughes says she is reading to him for hours every day, but once she can get out of his sight he forgets all about her, and goes on reading himself."

"When does he prepare his sermons?" said Cardo.

"Prepare his sermons!" said Shanw indignantly. "Do you think Essec Powell would write his sermon out like a clergyman and read it out like a book? No, indeed! Straight from the 'brist'—that's how Essec Powell preaches!"

"What time is the first meeting next day?"

"Oh, early, Ser—eight o'clock. Are you coming? Anwl! there's glad they'd be. You shall go on the platform with Price Merthyr and Jones Abertawe and all the rest."

"Saul among the prophets," said Cardo, laughing, and picturing himself among the solemn-faced preachers. "No, no; that wouldn't do, Shanw. What would my father say?"

"Well, well!" said Shanw, clicking her tongue against her teeth; "'ts, 'ts! 'tis pity indeed. But, there, everybody knows it is not your fault, Ser."

Cardo frowned, and fell into a brown study. It wounded him to hear his father blamed, and yet in his heart of hearts he wished he would so far temper his zeal with Christian charity as to attend the meetings which were moving the hearts of the people so much.

[1] "The old know, the young appear to know."

[2] Leek broth.

[3] Rodomontade.

[4] Peeped.

[5] Glamorganshire.

CHAPTER III.

THE SASSIWN.

The Sassiwn day dawned bright and clear, and as the time for the first service drew near, the roads and lanes were thronged with pedestrians and vehicles of every description.

The doors of the houses in all the surrounding villages were closed for the day, except in a few cases where illness made it impossible for the inmates to leave their beds. Everybody—man, woman, and child, including babies innumerable—turned their faces towards the sloping field which for the day was the centre of attraction.

Already the grass was getting hidden by the black throng, and still the crowds arrived, seating themselves row behind row on the wild thyme and heather. The topmost corner of the field merged into a rocky wilderness of stunted heath and patches of burnt grass, studded with harebells, and this unapportioned piece of ground stretched away into the adjoining corner of the Vicar's long meadow. In the afternoon Cardo, who had virtuously kept away from the morning meetings, sauntered down to chat with Dye, who had condescended to absent himself from the third service, in order to attend to his duties on the farm.

"You sit here, Mr. Cardo," he said, with a confidential wink, "on your own hedge; the Vicar can't be angry, and you will hear something worth listening to."

Soon the sloping bank was crowded with its rows of human beings, all listening with intense interest to a pale, dark man, who stood on the front of the platform at the bottom of the field, and with sonorous voice delivered a short opening prayer, followed by an impassioned address. In the clear, pure air every word was distinctly heard all over the field, the surging multitude keeping a breathless silence, broken only by the singing of the birds or the call of the seagulls. Sometimes a baby would send up a little wail of fatigue; but generally the slumberous air soothed and quieted them into sleep.

The prayer over, the preacher gave out the words of a well-known hymn, and with one accord the people stood up, and from those hundreds and thousands arose the swelling tones of one of those old hymns which lay hold of every Welshman's heart, its strange reminiscences, its mysterious influences swaying his whole being, and carrying him away on the wings of its rising and falling melody. His fathers and grandfathers sang it in their old thatched cabins—and, farther back, the warriors and bards of his past ancestry breathed the same tones—and, farther back still, the wind swept its first suggestions through the old oaks of the early solitudes.

"Is it this, I wonder, this far-reaching into the past, which gives such moving power to the tones of an old Welsh hymn?" Thus Cardo mused, as he sat on the hedge in the spring sunshine, his eyes roaming over the dense throng now settling down to listen to the sermon, which the preacher was beginning in low, slow sentences. Every ear was strained to listen, every eye was fixed on the preacher, but Cardo could not help wondering where Valmai was. He saw Essec Powell with clasped fingers and upturned chin listening in rapt attention; he saw in the rows nearest the platform many of the wives and daughters of its occupants. Here surely would be the place for the minister's niece; but no! Valmai was nowhere to be seen. In truth, she had been completely forgotten by her uncle, who had wandered off with a knot of preachers after the hospitable dinner, provided for them at his house by Valmai's exertions and Marged Hughes' help; but he had never thought of introducing to his guests the real genius of the feast. She had snatched a hurried meal in the pantry, and, feeling rather lost and bewildered amongst the crowd of strangers, had retired to rest under the elder bushes, until called upon by Marged Hughes to help at the table, which she did at once, overcoming her shyness, and keeping as much as possible in the background.

The guests had been at first too intent upon their dinners after their morning's exertions to notice the slim white figure which slipped backwards and forwards behind them, supplying every want with quick and delicate intuition, aiding Marged Hughes' clumsy attempts at waiting, so deftly, that Essec Powell's dinner was a complete success.

Towards the end of the meal a young and susceptible preacher caught sight of the girl, and without ceremony opened a conversation with her. Turning to his host he asked:

"And who is this fair damsel?"

"Who? where?" said Essec Powell, looking surprised. "Oh! that's my niece Valmai; she is living with me since Robert my brother is dead."

"Well, indeed! You will be coming to the meetings, I suppose?"

"Yes," said Valmai, "I have been there all day; the singing was lovely!"

"And what did you think of the preaching?" said a very fat man, in a startlingly bass voice. He was carving a fowl. "That is the important point," he said, and the wing came off unexpectedly. "Young people are apt to think most of the singing," here he re-captured the wing and landed it safely on his own plate. "Did you hear my sermon?" he asked, between the mouthfuls of the fast disappearing wing, fixing his eyes upon poor Valmai, who began to wish herself under the elder bushes again. "My text was—" but fortunately here the company rose.

After a long grace they dispersed, and turned their faces once more towards the sloping field.

No one noticed Valmai—no one remembered her in the hurry to return to the preaching field—no one, she thought, would know or care whether she was present or not; and as she drew on her gloves and tied on her broad-brimmed straw hat, there was a little sadness in the curves of her mouth, a little moisture in the deep blue eyes, as alone she took her way after the preachers to the hillside. As she went she recalled the last open-air meeting she had attended, nearly two years ago, in that far-off land, where her father and mother had walked with her in loving companionship, when she had been the centre of their joys and the light of their home, and as she followed the winding path, hymn-book in hand, her heart went back in longing throbs to the father and mother and the old home under the foreign sky, where love had folded her in its warm embrace; but now—she was alone! no one noticed whether she came or went, and as groups and families passed her, wending their way to the hillside, she answered their nods and greetings with pleasant kindliness, but still found herself alone!

"It will always be like this now; I must learn to go alone. What can I expect when my father and mother are dead? there is no one else to care for me!"

She reached the crowded field, and ought to have made her way into the front rows near the platform where she might easily have found a seat, but Valmai was shy and retiring, and seeing there was no settled place for her, kept on the outskirts of the crowd, and at last found herself on the piece of uncultivated ground which bordered the corner of the Vicar's long meadow. She seated herself on the heather at the top of the bank, the sea wind blowing round her, and tossing and tumbling the golden curls which fell so luxuriantly under her hat.

All feeling of loneliness passed away as she sat there among the harebells and heather, for Valmai was young, and life was all before her, with its sweet hopes and imaginings. She was soon listening with deep interest to the eloquent and burning words which fell from the lips of the preacher; and with the harebells nodding at her, the golden coltsfoot staring up into the sky, the laughing babies sprawling about, was it any wonder that sadness fled away, and joy and love sang a paean of thankfulness in her heart?

It was at this moment that Cardo caught sight of her. Unconsciously, he had been seeking her in every square yard which his eye could reach, and here she was close to him all the time. The discovery awoke a throb of pleasure within him, and with a flush upon his dark face he rose and made his way towards her. She was absently turning over the leaves of her little Welsh hymn-book as he approached, and smiling unconsciously at a toddling child who was making journeys of discovery around the furze bushes. A quick, short "Oh!" escaped her as she saw him approach, her face brightened up—yes, certainly she was glad. Cardo saw it in the mantling blush and the pleased smile as he found a seat on the grass beside her. She placed her hand in his with a whispered word of greeting, for it would not do to speak aloud in that quiet concourse of people.

"Where have you been?" he asked, at last.

"At home," she whispered. "Why?"

"Because I hoped you would be out—"

Valmai shook her head as a farmer's wife looked round at her reprovingly. Cardo attempted another remark, but she only smiled with her finger on her lips.

"This is unendurable," he thought; but he was obliged to be satisfied with the pleasure of sitting beside her until the long sermon was over, and the crowd rose *en masse* with ejaculations of delight at the moving eloquence of the preacher.

"As good as ever he was!" "Splendid!" "Did you hear that remark about the wrong key?" "Oh! telling!" And amongst the murmer of approval and enthusiasm Valmai and Cardo rose. For a moment the former looked undecided, and he read her thoughts.

"No—not home with the crowd, but down over the beach;" and she fell in with the suggestion, turning her face to the sea breeze and taking the path to the shore.

Here the Berwen was running with its usual babbling and gurgling through the stones into the sea, the north-west wind was tossing the foam into the air, and the waves came bounding and racing up the yellow sand like children at play; the little sea-crows cawed noisily as they wheeled round the cliffs, and the sea-gulls called to their fellows as they floated over the waves or stood about the wet, shining sands.

"There's beautiful, it is," said Valmai, pushing back her hat and taking long breaths of the sea wind; "only six weeks I have been here and yet I seem to have known it for ever—I suppose because from a baby I used to hear my father talking of this place. It was his old home, and he was always longing to come back."

"Yes," said Cardo, "I can imagine that. I don't think I could ever be thoroughly happy away from here."

"Nor I too, indeed," said Valmai, "now that I know it."

"I hope you will never leave the place—you seem to belong to it somehow; and I hope I may never leave it, at least—at all events—" and he hesitated as he remembered his father's wishes—expressed many times, though at long intervals—that he should go to Australia and visit an uncle who had for many years lived there. The prospect of a voyage to the Antipodes had never been very attractive to Cardo, and latterly the idea had faded from his mind. In the glamour of that golden afternoon in spring, in Valmai's sweet companionship, the thought of parting and leaving his native country was doubly unpleasant to him. She saw the sudden embarrassment, and the flush that spread over his face.

"You are going away?" she said, looking up at him.

There was only inquiry in the tone. Cardo wondered if she would be sorry, and was tempted to make the most of his possible departure.

"I may have to go away," he said, "though I should hate it. I never liked the idea, but now I perfectly dread it. And you," he added, "should you miss me? It is not very lively here, so perhaps even I might be missed a little."

Valmai did not answer; she looked out to the horizon where the blue of the sky joined the blue of the sea, and the white breakers glinted in the sunshine.

"Yes," she said presently, "I will be sorry when you go, and where are you going to? Far away? To England, perhaps?"

"To Australia," replied Cardo.

"Australia! Oh! then you will never come back to Traeth Berwen!"

"Indeed, indeed I will, Miss Powell—you laugh at that—well—may I say Valmai, then?"

"Yes; why not? Everyone is calling me Valmai, even Shoni our servant."

"I may venture, then; and will you call me Cardo?"

"Yes, indeed; Cardo Wynne. Cardo Wynne, everybody is calling you that, too—even the little children in the village; I have heard them say, 'Here is Cardo Wynne coming!' See, here is the path to Dinas, I must say good-bye."

"Can't we have another walk along the beach? Remember, I, too, have no one to talk to!"

"Oh, anwl, no! I must hurry home and get the tea for the preachers."

"And then back to the meeting on the hillside?"

"No; the meeting is in the chapel to-night."

"But when it is over you will come back along the shore?"

"Indeed, I don't know. Good-bye," she said, as she began her way up the rugged homeward path.

When Cardo reached home, he found his father sitting at the tea-table. The old parlour looked gloomy and dark, the bright afternoon sun, shining through the creepers which obscured the window, threw a green light over the table and the rigid, pale face of the Vicar.

"You are late Cardo; where have you been?"

"In the long meadow, sir, where I could hear some of the preaching going on below, and afterwards on the beach; it is a glorious afternoon. Oh! father, I wish you would come out and breathe the fresh air; it cannot be good for you to be always in your study poring over those musty old books."

"My books are not musty, and I like to spend my time according to my own ideas of what is fit and proper, and I should not think it either to be craning my neck over a hedge to listen to a parcel of Methodist preachers —"

"Well, I only heard one, Price Merthyr I think they call him. He was—"

"Cardo!" said his father severely, "when I want any information on the subject I will ask for it; I want you to set Dye and Ebben on to the draining of that field to-morrow—"

"Parc y waun?"

"Yes; Parc y waun."

"Right, father," said Cardo good-naturedly. He was devotedly attached to his father, and credited him with a depth of affection and tenderness lying hidden behind his stern manner—a sentiment which must have been revealed to him by intuition, for he had never seen any outward sign of it. "It's no use," he muttered, as his father rose and left the room; "it's no use trying to broach the subject to him, poor fellow! I must be more careful, and keep my thoughts to myself."

Later on in the evening, Valmai sat in the hot, crowded chapel, her elbows pressed tightly in to her sides by the two fat women between whom she sat, their broad-brimmed hats much impeding her view of the preacher, who was pounding the red velvet cushion in the old pulpit, between two dim mould candles which shed a faint light over his face. Valmai listened with folded hands as he spoke of the narrow way so difficult to tread, so wearisome to follow—of the few who walked in it and the people, listening with upturned faces and bated breath, answered to his appeal with sighs and groans and "amens." He then passed on to a still more vivid description of the broad road, so smooth, so easy, so charming to every sense, so thronged with people all gaily dancing onwards to destruction, the sudden end of the road, where it launched its thronging crowds over a precipice into the foaming, seething sea of everlasting woe and misery.

Valmai looked round her with awe and horror.

"Did these innocent-looking, simple people belong to that thronging crowd who were hurrying on to their own destruction? was she herself one of them? Cardo?—her uncle?"

The thought was dreadful, her breath came and went quickly, her eyes were full of tears, and she felt as if she must rise suddenly and rush into the open air, but as she looked round the chapel she caught sight through one of the windows of the dark blue sky of night, bespangled with stars, and a glow of purer and healthier feeling came over her. She would not believe it—outside was the fresh night wind, outside was the silver moonlight, and in the words of the poet of whom she had never heard she said within herself, "No! God is in Heaven, it's all right with the world!" Her joyous nature could not brook the saddening influences of the Methodist creed, and as she passed out into the clear night air amongst the crowd of listeners, and heard their mournful sighs and their evident appreciation of the sermon, or rather sermons, for there had been two, her heart bounded with a sense of relief; joy and happiness were its natural elements, and she returned to them as an innocent child rushes to its mother's arms.

Leaving the thronged road, she took the rugged path down the hillside, alone under the stars, and remembering Cardo's question, "Will you come home by the shore?" she wondered whether he was anywhere near! As she reached the bottom of the cliff and trod on the firm, hard sand below, she saw him standing in the shadow of a rock, and gazing out at the sea over which the moon made a pathway of silver.

The fishing boats from Ynysoer were out like moths upon the water. They glided from the darkness across that path of light and away again into the unknown. On one a light was burning.

"That is the *Butterfly*," thought Valmai, "I am beginning to know them all; and there is Cardo Wynne!" and with a spirit of mischief gleaming in her eyes and dimpling her face, she approached him quietly, her light footstep making no sound on the sand.

She was close behind him and he had not turned round, but still stood with folded arms looking out over the moonlit scene. Having reached this point, Valmai's fun suddenly deserted her. What should she do next? should she touch him? No! Should she speak to him? Yes; but what should she say? Cardo! No! and a faint blush overspread her face. A mysterious newborn shyness came over her, and it was quite a nervous, trembling voice that at last said:

"Mr. Wynne?"

Cardo turned round quickly.

"Valmai! Miss Powell!" he said, "how silently you came upon me! I was dreaming. Come and stand here. Is not that scene one to make a poet of the most prosaic man?"

"Yes, indeed," answered the girl, standing beside him with a strangely beating heart, "it is beautiful! I saw the sky through the chapel window, and I was thinking it would be very nice down here. There's bright and clear the moon is!"

They were walking now across the beach, at the edge of the surf.

"It reminds me of something I read out to uncle last night. It was out of one of his old Welsh poets—Taliesin, or Davydd ap Gwilym, or somebody. It was about the moon, but indeed I don't know if I can put it into English."

"Try," said Cardo.

"'She comes from out the fold
And leads her starry flock among the fields of night.'"

"Yes, that is beautiful," said Cardo. "Indeed, I am glad you find something interesting in those dog-eared old books."

"Dog-eared? But they are indeed," she said, laughing. "But how do you know? They may be gold and leather, and spic and span from the bookseller's, for all you know."

"No, I have seen them, and have seen you reading them."

"Seen me reading them? How? Where?"

"Last night I was under the elder bushes, and saw you reading to your uncle. I watched you for a long time."

Valmai was silent.

"You are not vexed with me for that?"

She was still silent; a tumult of happy thoughts filled her mind. He had found his way to Dinas! He had thought it worth while to stand under the night sky and watch her! It was a pleasant idea, and, thinking of it, she did not speak.

"Tell me, Valmai, have I offended you?"

"Offended me? Oh, no; why should you? But indeed it was very foolish of you, whatever. If you had come in and listened to the reading it would be better, perhaps," she said laughingly.

"If I had come in, what would your uncle have said? He would have been very angry."

"Well, indeed, yes; I was forgetting that. He is very hospitable, and glad to see anybody who comes in to supper; but I don't think," she added, with a more serious air, "that he would be glad to see you. He hates the Church and everything belonging to it."

"Yes. How wearisome all this bigotry is. My father hates the chapels and all belonging to them."

"Perhaps you and I will begin to hate each other soon," said Valmai, as they reached the boulders through which the Berwen trickled.

It was absolutely necessary that Cardo should help her over the slippery stones, and with her hand in his she stepped carefully over the broad stream, subsiding into quietness as it reached the sea. At last she was safely over, and as he reluctantly dropped her hand he returned to the subject of conversation.

"Will we hate each other?"

Again there was no answer, and again Cardo looked down at Valmai as he pressed his question.

She had taken off her hat, and was walking with her golden head exposed to the cool night breezes. It drooped a little as she answered his persistent questioning.

"No, I think," she said, with her quaint Welsh accent.

"No, I think, too," said Cardo; "why should we? Let us leave the hatred and malice and all uncharitableness to our elders; for you and me, down here on the sands and by the banks of the Berwen, there need be nothing but content and—and friendship."

"Yes, indeed, it is nice to have friends. I left all mine behind me in my old home, and I did not think I should ever have another; but here we are across the shore, and here is the path to Dinas."

"Oh, but the walk has been too short. You must come back and let us have it over again."

"What! back again?" said Valmai, laughing so merrily that she woke the echoes from the cliffs.

"Yes, back across those slippery stones and across the shore, and then back again to this side. I can help you, you know."

Cardo's voice was very low and tender. It seemed ridiculous, but somehow he gained his point.

CHAPTER IV.

THE STORM.

A day or two later on, the weather changed, the wind blew up in angry soughs from the south-west, and, meeting the strong flow of the spring tide, curled the green wave-tops into those small feathers of foam, always the fore-runners of rough weather. The sea-gulls let themselves go before the wind calling to each other excitedly, the little sea-crows stayed quietly at home in the safe crannies of the cliff. Old Dan Griffiths the fisherman hauled his boat further up the strand, and everything betokened the brewing of a storm, nevertheless Valmai was out early. Her small household duties had been attended to. She had skimmed the cream in the dairy, and fed the new calf; she had scattered the grain before the flocks of fowls and pigeons in the farm-yard; had brushed her uncle's coat, and, while helping him to shuffle into it, had asked him:

"Are you going from home to-day, uncle?"

"Yes, merch i, didn't I tell you? I am going to a meeting at Pen Morien, and won't be back to-night."

"Are you going to walk?"

"Why, no! ride, of course. Where's Malen?"

"I think Shoni was just putting her into the cart."

"Oh! I forgot to tell him," said the absent-minded man. "Tell him to saddle her, and bring her here at once."

Valmai ran out, and picking her way daintily through the stubble of the farm-yard, caught sight of Shoni fastening the last buckle of Malen's cart harness.

"Wants her saddled?" he said, looking hot and flustered. "Dear, dear! there never was such a man! Wasn't I settle with him yesterday to take the two pigs to the fair to be sell? There's what it is to live in the clouds!"

and, grumbling, he unfastened the buckles, and soon led Malen saddled and bridled to the door.

"Didn't you tell me we was to sell the pigs to-day?" he said sulkily, as soon as his master was seated safely on the saddle.

Essec Powell, who had for some time been hopping about on one leg, finding it difficult to mount the spirited Malen, now looked thoughtfully at Shoni.

"Pigs," he said, "pigs? Oh, of course; yes, Shoni, quite right, you shall take them to market tomorrow."

"To-day is the fair; you had forgotten that, I suppose."

"Well, well! next week will do," and he trotted away, Shoni looking after him with undisguised contempt.

"There's a man, now," he said in English, for he was proud of his proficiency in that language. "Wass you ever see such a man? I tell you, Valmai, he would be ruined and put in gaol for debt long ago if I wasn't keep him out of it."

"Yes, I think—indeed, Shoni, I am sure of it; but where is the fair to-day?"

"At Llanython, of course; wasn't you hear of it? Why! you ought to be there, pranked out in your ribbons and finery, talking and laughing with the young men, and coming home in the evening with your pocket-handkerchief full of gingerbread and nuts," and he looked her over from top to toe.

It had never struck him before that there was any charm in her appearance, but now he seemed to realise that she was worthy to be seen at the fair.

"Yes," he said pensively, with his thumbs in the armholes of his waistcoat; "I wouldn't wonder a bit now if you wass to pick up a sweet'arr amongst the gentry, because you are beginning to speak English as good as the Vicare, and you are not quite like the girls about here, Valmai."

"Am I not?" she said laughingly.

"No," he said seriously; "and that's where you will be failing. There's not a chap about here will take a miladi like you for a wife. You must learn to kom over the farm-yard without picking up your skirts, and looking at your shoes to see if they are dirty, if you want to marry a farmer."

"Indeed, I don't wish to marry a farmer," said Valmai, "nor anyone else who doesn't want me."

Shoni again shook his head solemnly. "Yes, yes," he said, "I see how it is; s'not only the pigs, and the calves, and hens, but you too I must take to markets and fairs, or we shall never marry you," and he turned away pondering seriously over his self-imposed duties.

Valmai looked after him a little wistfully. Where should she go now? How should she spend the long day? Gwen would see to the housework, and would brook no interference with her management. Nobody wanted her, and nobody thought of her, except Shoni, and to him she seemed rather a burden; or was there one who thought of her sometimes?—who cared a little for her? With heightened colour and quick step she turned from the farm-yard down the steep path which led to the river's banks, and as she made her way through the thick hazel and willow brushwood she could not quite suppress the hope that she might meet Cardo. But no, perfect solitude reigned over the Berwen.

Down in the valley she could not feel the wind, but she heard its roar in the tree tops; the birds were silent, the sky was grey, and a little sadness fell over her spirits as she continued to thread her way under the tall bracken and brambles, onwards and upwards, until she at length reached the stile by the bridge upon which she and Cardo had eaten their gingerbread on the first evening of their acquaintance. The road which had that night been so quiet and deserted was now full of busy life, and as Valmai approached the stile and saw the many pedestrians and vehicles she shrank back a little, and, through the branches of a hazel bush, looked out on the passers-by, realising that all these hurrying footsteps, and faces full of interest, were turned towards the Fair at Llanython.

Presently she heard the rumbling of wheels, and in a cloud of dust saw the Vicar of the next parish drive by with his two pretty daughters. Just as they reached the bridge they were overtaken by a young man, who reined in his spirited, well-groomed horse and addressed the party. At once Valmai recognised the voice, and peeping through the greenery, saw it was Cardo, stalwart and strong, with his rough freize coat and buttoned gaiters, looking every inch a gentleman-farmer.

There was a bluff and hearty greeting from the clergyman as Cardo took off his hat to the two young ladies, who simpered and blushed becomingly, for Cardo Wynne was the catch of the neighbourhood; his good looks, his father's reputed wealth, and the slight air of mystery hanging over the silent "Vicare du" making quite a halo of romance around his son's personality.

"Good-bye," said Mr. Hughes; "we shall see you at the fair, I suppose?"

"Yes," said Cardo, "good-bye," and he reined in his horse for a moment so as to avoid riding in the cloud of dust raised by the Vicar's carriage wheels.

Valmai's heart thumped loudly, for Cardo was looking at the stile, he was dismounting, and now he was leaning on the bridge lost in thought, and looking down into the green depths of the valley. There was a pleased look on his face and a gleam in his black eyes, which Valmai saw, and which made her heart beat faster and her cheek flush a more rosy red, but she shrank further back into the shade of the hazel bush, and only peeped out again when she heard by the horse's hoofs that his rider was remounting; then she ventured over the stile and looked at the retreating figure, with his broad shoulders, his firm seat, and his steady hand on his bridle as he galloped out of sight. A flood of happiness filled her heart as she re-crossed the stile and began her way again down the shady path.

What mattered it that at every moment the wind rose higher, and the branches creaked and groaned above her? What mattered it that the birds were silent, and that the roar of the sea reached further than usual into the nut wood? She would go home and eat her frugal dinner of brown bread and bwdran,[1] and then she would set off to Ynysoer to spend a few hours with Nance Owen, who had nursed her as a baby before her parents had left Wales. In spite of the increasing storm she reached the beach, and turned her face towards Ynysoer, a small island or rather a promontory, which stretched out from the shore. At low tide a reef of rocks, generally known as the Rock Bridge, connected it with the mainland, but at high tide the reef was completely under water, the sea rushing in foaming breakers over it as if chafing at the restraint to its wild freedom.

Had Valmai been better acquainted with the coast, she would not have dared to cross the bridge in the face of the storm which was every moment increasing in violence. The tide was down, and the rocks were bare, and the high wind helped to hurry her over the pools and craggy points. Gathering her red cloak tightly around her she made her way safely over to the island, which was a frequent resort of hers, as here she found the warm love and welcome for which her heart craved, and which was so sorely missing in her uncle's house.

Amongst the sandy dunes and tussocks were scattered a few lonely cottages, in one of which Nance lived her uneventful life; its smoke-browned thatch looked little different from the rushes and coarse grass which surrounded it, for tufts of grass and moss grew on the roof also, and Nance's goat was frequently to be seen browsing on the house-top. At the open door stood Nance herself, looking out at the storm. Suddenly she caught sight of Valmai, who was making a difficult progress through the soft uneven sand, and a look of surprise and pleasure came over her face.

"Oh, dear heart, is it you, indeed, come to see old Nance, and on such a day? Come in, sweetheart, out of the storm."

"The storm indeed," said Valmai, in Welsh as pure as Nance's own, as the old woman drew her in to the cottage and closed the door. "Why, you know nothing about it on this side of the island, nothing of what it is in the village. The boats have all been drawn up close to the road, and the waves are dancing and prancing on the beach, I can tell you."

Nance loosened her cloak and hat, and smoothed her hair with her horny hands.

"There's glad I am to see you, merch fach-i, and if you have no grand friends to keep you company and no one to look after you, you have always got old Nance to love you."

"Yes, I know that, Nance, indeed. What do you think of my new frock?" said the girl, holding out her skirt to the admiring gaze of the old woman, who went into raptures of admiration.

"Oh, there's pretty. 'Tis fine and soft, but white, always white you are wearing—"

"Yes, I like white," said Valmai.

"And didn't I dress you in your first little clothes? Well I remember it."

"There's just what I wanted to ask you about, Nance; I love to hear the old story."

"After tea, then, merch i, for now I must go and fetch water from the well, and I must milk the goat."

"I will fetch the water," said Valmai; "you can go and milk."

And taking the red stone pitcher from the bench by the wall she went out, and, sheltered by the ridge of rocks behind which the cottage stood, made her way to the spring which dripped from a crack in the cliffs. While she waited for the pitcher to fill, she sang, in sheer lightness of heart, the old ballad which not only floated on the air of Abersethin and its neighbourhood, but which she had heard her mother sing in the far-off land of her childhood.

"By Berwen's banks my love has strayed
For many a day through sun and shade,"

and she paused to peep into the pitcher, but finding it only half full, continued:

"And as she carolled loud and clear
The little birds flew down to hear."

"By Berwen's banks the storm rose high,"

but the pitcher was full, so, resting it on her side, she carried it home, before Nance had caught her goat. When she returned with her bowl of rich milk, Valmai was busy, with skirt and sleeves tucked up, tidying and arranging the little room; the hearth had been swept and the tea-things laid on the quaint little round table, whose black shining surface and curved legs would have delighted the heart of a collector of antique furniture.

"Oh, calon fâch![2] to think your little white hands have been working for me! Now I will cut the bread and butter thin, thin—as befits a lady like you; and sorry I am that it is barley bread. I don't forget the beautiful white cakes and the white sugar you gave me at Dinas the other day! And your uncle, how is he?"

"Quite well; gone to Pen Morien, and not coming home till to-morrow; but tell me now, Nance fâch, of all that happened so long ago—when I was born."

"Not so long ago for me, dear heart, as for you. It is a whole life-time for you, but for me—" and the faded blue eyes filled with tears, and the wrinkled lips trembled a little as she recalled the past—"for me! I had lived my life before you were born. My husband was dead, my boy drowned, and my little Mari, the last and brightest, had suddenly withered and died before my eyes—a fever they say, perhaps it was indeed; but the sun has never shone so brightly, whatever, since then; the flowers are not so sweet—they remind me of my child's grave; the sea does not look the same—it reminds me of my boy!" and she rocked herself backwards and forwards for some time, while Valmai stroked with tender white fingers the hard, wrinkled hand which rested on her lap. "Well, indeed," said the old woman at last, "there's enough of my sorrows; let us get on to the happy time when your little life began, you and your twin sister. When you were washed and dressed and laid sleeping together in the same cradle, no one could tell which was which; but dir anwl! who cared for that? too much joy was in our hearts that your dear mother was safe. No one at least, except the grand English lady who was lodging there at your grandfather's house. Her husband was dead, and she was very rich, but she had no children; and when she heard your mother had twins, she begged of us to let her have one for her very own, and she was like thorns to us because we could not tell for sure which was the oldest."

"Well, go on, Nance," said Valmai, as the old woman stopped to rake the peat embers together.

"Well! then, we all thought it was a very good thing, and no doubt the Almighty had His plans about it, for how could your poor mother take two babies with her to that far-off land where your father went a missionary? Well! there was a message come to fetch the lady to the death-bed of her mother, and she only waited at Dinas long enough to see you both christened together, Valmai and Gwladys. The next day she went away, and took your little sister with her. Oh! there's crying your mother was at losing one of her little ones; but your father persuaded her it was for the best."

"And what was the English lady's name?" asked Valmai.

"Oh! my dear, ask it not; the hardest word you ever heard, and the longest; I could never twist my tongue round it. It is with me somewhere written out on paper, and her directions, and if she ever moved to another place she would write and tell us, she said; but that was not likely to be, because she went to her father's and grandfather's old home, and she has never written to anyone since, as far as I know."

"Well, indeed," said Valmai, looking thoughtfully into the glowing embers, "I should like to see my sister, whatever."

"Twt, twt," said the old woman, "there's no need for you to trouble your head about her; she has never troubled to seek you."

"Does she know about me, do you think?"

"That I can't tell, of course," said Nance, going to the door to have another look at the storm. "Ach y fi! it's like a boiling pot," she said; "you can never go home to-night, my child."

"Oh, yes, indeed I must; I would not be away from home in my uncle's absence for the world," said Valmai, joining the old woman at the door, and looking out rather anxiously at the angry sea. "Oh, when the tide goes down at nine o'clock the moon will be up, and perhaps the storm will be over."

They sat chatting over the fire until the evening shadows fell, and the moon shone fitfully between the scudding clouds.

Meanwhile Cardo had ridden in to Llanython. A fair had generally much attraction for him—the merry laughter, the sociable meetings, the sound of music on the air, and the altogether festive character of the day; but on this occasion its pleasures seemed to pall, and quickly dispatching the business which had brought him there, he returned to the inn, and, mounting his horse, rode home early in the afternoon. Why he thus hurried away he never could explain. Ever since he had leant on the bridge over the Berwen in the morning he had been haunted by a feeling of Valmai's presence. Little had he guessed that she had been so near him while he looked down through the interlacing scenery which hid the river from his sight. It was nearly four o'clock in the afternoon as he reached that part of the high road from which the beach was visible, and here he stopped a moment to look and wonder at the storm, which had so suddenly increased in violence.

"How far up the beach at Ynysoer those breakers run! And the Rock Bridge!—I wouldn't like to cross that to-night; but surely that was a woman's figure crossing it now!" A sudden fear darted through his mind, and dismounting, he climbed to the top of the turfy bank at the side of the road to gain a better view of the coast. "Yes, a woman—a girl, surely, and a graceful girl, wearing a scarlet cloak. She carried her hat in her hand—not on her head, at all events. Surely it was not Valmai in such a storm going over by such a dangerous path? Probably a fisherman's wife or daughter!" But he gazed long and steadily before he once more resumed his ride. In hot haste he rode the rest of the way to Brynderyn.

"The storm is rising," said the "Vicare du," as he joined his son at the tea-table.

"Yes," said the latter, pausing in his attack upon the roast fowl to gaze at the clouds which scudded before the wind, "I expect it will be a furious gale before midnight."

As soon as the meal was over he rose, and fixing his hat firmly on his head, said:

"I am going down to the beach to see the waves, father. If I am not back to supper you won't be frightened?"

The old man muttered something about "folly to go out in such weather," as Cardo disappeared into the stone passage. Making his way down to the beach, he found the storm raging fiercely, and, gaining the shelter of a rock, he sat down to rest and think.

The sullen south-west wind moaned and shrieked as it rushed up the long beach; it lurked in the hollows of the crags, and drove the sand and foam before it. The Berwen looked yellow and muddy as it washed over its stony bed. Above all came the roar of the breakers as they dashed against the rocky sides of the island, which lay, a black mass, in the seething water a few hundred yards from the shore.

He looked across the blinding spray of the waves and thought of his boat; but no, no boat would live in such a sea; besides, what ridiculous fear was this that haunted him?

At so great a distance as that between the road and the island it was impossible that he could have distinguished Valmai from any other girl, and what more natural than that one of the women living on the island should be crossing the Rock Bridge.

"I must be a fool to have nervous fears like a silly girl. I daresay I shall meet Valmai on the shore."

But he sought in vain for any sign of her, as she had sought him in the morning. Indeed it was not likely that any tender girl would be out in such a storm—and yet—"was it Valmai?"

The thought *would* come, the fear would haunt him. He was surprised to find himself overtaken by a woman.

"Dir, dir, what a storm," she remarked as she passed, hurried on her way by the driving wind.

One or two of Cardo's long steps brought him up with her.

"Don't you come from Ynysoer?" he said. "I think I know your face."

"Yes, gwae fi![3] that I had got safe back again, but my mother is ill," she shouted, as the wind carried her words away, "and I must stay with her till tomorrow, no one could go back over the Rock Bridge to-night; though, indeed, I met a young girl crossing—"

"Had she a red cloak?" asked Cardo.

"Yes. She was Essec Powell's niece, and if she tries to come back to-night I wouldn't give much for her life."

"Here we part—good-bye," said Cardo.

"Nos da, Ser," said the woman, but her voice was drowned by the roar of the wind.

"It was Valmai! I knew it was! Why did I not take my boat at once? Now it is too late; and yet," he thought, "she cannot come till the tide is low. I may get there in time. Surely she would not attempt to cross the bridge yet?"

For the rest of the evening Cardo paced restlessly over the beach, buffeted by the strong wind, wetted by the spray, but still watching narrowly the bridge of rocks, which connected the island with the mainland. He knew for a certainty that Valmai was there, and he watched with intense interest the darkening island, over which the storm gathered with increasing fury. His plan was to wait until the tide went down, and then to cross the bridge himself, so as to help Valmai, or to prevent her attempting to return.

After several hours' waiting in the shelter of the cliff, he saw by his watch, which he was able to decipher by occasional gleams of moonlight, that it was near upon nine o'clock. The moon was hidden at intervals by heavy storm-clouds, which were hurrying before the wind; but when her light shone out fitfully, it disclosed a scene of wild confusion; the horizon was as black as ink, the seething sea beneath was white as snow, and the sound of the wind and waves was deafening.

Over the Rock Bridge the sea rushed like a mill race one moment leaving it bare and black, the next covering it again with strong rushing billows of foam.

"She will not dare to return to-night," he thought, as he watched a tossing, foaming tower of spray, which rose in the centre of the bridge, where two streams of the seething waters met, and rose high in the air together.

The moon had again hidden her face, and in the darkness Cardo was seized with a trembling fear. With bent and bare head (for he had long before lost his hat) he made a blind rush over the bridge. For the first few yards he got on safely, as each end was sheltered by high rocks, which stood as sentinels looking across at each other.

"So far, so good," thought Cardo, standing still a moment for breath; "and now to cross this mill race!"

But he was too late. Already he saw that Valmai had begun her way across.

On the island side the bridge was more sheltered from the storm, and the girl was not only in a measure protected from the wind, but was also hidden from the moonlight, and it was not until she had left the shadow of the rocks and entered upon the open and unprotected reef that Cardo in a sudden absence of clouds saw in the moonlight the delicate figure wrapped in its scarlet cloak. For a moment she hesitated as she felt the full force of the wind, and in her hesitation decided upon the wrong course: she would run, she would reach the opposite rocks, and be safe before the next gust of wind came.

"Good God!" said Cardo, "she is lost!" as he saw her approach with flying hair and fluttering garments towards the centre of the bridge, which was for a moment left bare, and in that moment Cardo realised how completely this stranger girl, who had seemed to drop from the clouds into his quiet, uneventful life, had taken possession of his heart. All this flashed through his mind and opened his eyes to the true state of his feelings.

Instantly he was making his way towards her, with strong steps and sturdy shoulders fighting with the wind, which seemed determined to baffle his attempts to reach Valmai before the periodical recurring inrush of opposite streams should once more meet, and rise in towering strife together. Thoroughly frightened and trembling, Valmai looked in horror at the two opposing streams of water approaching her on either side, and in her terror losing her self-command, was on the point of giving herself up to the angry waters, which she felt herself too weak to withstand. At this critical moment a dark form dashed through the blinding spray—a form which she instantly recognised, and which as quickly restored courage to her sinking heart. She felt the strong arms clasped round her, but too late! for the next moment the approaching waves had met, and rising high in the air in their furious contact, had fallen with terrific force, sweeping her and her rescuer into the boiling surf. Valmai became unconscious at once, but Cardo's strong frame knew no sense of swooning nor faintness. His whole being seemed concentrated in a blind struggle to reach the land—to save Valmai, though he was fighting under terrible disadvantage.

She had relaxed her grasp, and he had now to hold her safe with one arm, thus having only one with which to struggle against the suffocating, swirling waters. In a very few minutes he realised that the fight was dead against him; in spite of all his strength and his powerful frame, he was lifted and tossed about like a straw. The only thing in his favour was the fact that the tide had turned, and was even now combining with the strong wind to carry him towards a sheltered corner on the mainland. With choking breath and blinded eyes he felt himself carried on the crest of a wave, which bore him landwards, but only to be drawn back again by its receding swell. He felt he was helpless, though, had he the use of his two arms, he knew he would be able to breast the stormy waters, and gain the land in safety; but clutched in the nervous grasp of his left arm he held what was dearer to him than life itself, and felt that to die with Valmai was better than to live without her! His strength was almost gone, and with horror he felt that his grasp of the girl was more difficult to retain, as a larger wave than usual came racing towards him with foaming, curling crest. He gave himself up for lost—he thought of his old father even now poring over his books—he thought of Valmai's young life so suddenly quenched—and with one prayer for himself and her, he felt himself carried onward, tossed, tumbled over and over, but still keeping tight hold of his precious burden.

He was suddenly struck by a stunning blow, which for a moment seemed to take away his senses—but only for a moment—for what was this calm? what was this quiet sense of rest? was he sinking out of life into some dim, unconscious state of being? had he seen the last of the clouds? the moon—the stormy waters? Had Valmai already slipped away from him? No; he still felt her within his grasp, and in a few moments he was able to realise the meaning of the change in his feelings. He had been carried like a shred of seaweed by that strong wave far up the beach on the mainland, and in its receding flow it had swirled him into a round cavity in the rocks, where as a boy he had often played and bathed and fished; he knew it well, and saw in a moment that he was saved! Clasping Valmai firmly, he ran up the beach, another combing, foaming wave coming dangerously near his hurrying footsteps; but in spite of the buffeting wind, he gained the shelter of the cliffs, and at last laid his burden tenderly down on the rocks. And now the fight for life was replaced by the terrible dread that Valmai might already be beyond recall.

The clear, cold moon looked down between the scudding clouds upon her straightened form, the wind roared above them, and the lashing fury of the waves still filled the air; but Valmai lay white and still. Cardo looked round in vain for help; no one was near, even the fishermen had safely bolted their doors, and shut out the wild stormy night. A faint hope awoke in his heart as he remembered that Valmai had swooned before she was engulfed with him in the sea, and he set to work with renewed vigour to rub her cold hands, and press the water out of her long, drenched hair; he was soon rewarded by signs of life in the rigid form—a little sigh came trembling from her lips, her hand moved, and there was a tremor in her eyelids. Cardo placed his arm under her shoulders and, lifting her into a sitting posture, rested her head upon his breast, the movement, the change of position—something awoke her from her long swoon; was it the sense of Cardo's presence? did his earnest longing call her spirit back? for she had been close upon the shadow land. She came back slowly, dimly conscious of escaping from some deadly horror, and awakening to something pleasant, something happy. She slowly opened her eyes, and observing Cardo's strong right hand, which still held and chafed her own, while his left arm upheld her drenched form, she moved a little, and murmured:

"Are you hurt?"

"No," said Cardo, trembling in every limb with the excitement which he had controlled until now, and with the delight of seeing life and movement return to her, "hurt? no! only thankful to find you safe; only anxious to get you home."

Valmai's voice was weak and low, and he had to bend his head over her to catch the words:

"You have been near death for my sake—those dreadful waves!"

"Do not think of them! I was in no danger. But I have been nearer death since I have sat here watching your slow recovery. Now, Valmai," he said, realising that every moment of exposure in her cold, drenched garments was danger to her, "be brave; give yourself up to me, and I will carry you home."

But this adjuration was needless, for as he placed her gently down while he rose to his feet he felt that she was limp and powerless as a baby; he lifted her in his arms, and felt her weight no more than if he had carried a storm-beaten bird. His own drenched condition he did not consider—did not feel, while he climbed with careful footsteps up the rugged path to Dinas, lighted only by the moon, whose beams were continually obscured by the flying clouds. Pushing his way between the furze and broom bushes, he was careful to let no stray branch catch Valmai's face or hair, and as he reached the farm-yard in the rear of the house, he was delighted to feel a strong and swift motion in her frame.

"Put me down, please," she whispered, "on the bench by the door."

Cardo did so, reluctantly loosing his grasp of the tender form.

"Now knock."

And he obeyed, rapping loudly on the back door. The sound seemed to rouse the inmates at once, for, with considerable thumping and fumbling, somebody shuffled down the stairs.

"Go now, I am safe," said Valmai, in a whisper.

And Cardo went, but not before he had stooped down and pressed an impassioned kiss upon the little listless hands. Neither spoke. Valmai felt too weak and full of awakening happiness to trust her voice, while Cardo felt the occasion was above the necessity for any words. He waited behind the elder bushes until Gwen's full-moon face appeared in the doorway, and her ejaculations of reproachful astonishment (in which the Welsh language is prolific) showed that she had seen Valmai, and fully appreciated the urgency of the situation.

"Mawredd anwl! what is the meaning of this? Where have you been? and I thinking you were in your warm bed!"

"I have been to see Nance, and coming back over the Rock Bridge the sea washed me away."

"Nance! Nance! all the time! What you want to go there so often? It's no wonder if you are drowned crossing that nasty place in such a storm, You are like a wet sea-gull. If you were a baby you wouldn't be more trouble," etc., etc.

Cardo still waited until he saw in the kitchen the blaze of freshly-piled logs on the culm fire, Gwen's voice still reaching him in snappish, reproving tones through the closed door. Then he turned away, and though he was bodily cold and saturated with the sea water, his heart was full of warmth and a newly-awakened sense of the joy and fulness of life.

[1] Oatmeal and water kept until fermentation has commenced, and then boiled into a thin porridge.

[2] Dear heart.

[3] Woe is me.

CHAPTER V.

GWYNNE ELLIS ARRIVES.

For a few days, Valmai, although she had received no serious harm from her watery adventure, still felt a little languor and indisposition, which kept her a prisoner in the house. As she lay on the old shabby sofa, her time was fully occupied by reading to her uncle, books of Welsh history or the effusions of the old bards, which interested him so much. Ever and anon, while he searched for a reference or took notes of some special passage, she would fall into a dreamy reverie, a happy smile on her lips and a light in her eyes which her uncle saw not. Yes, Cardo loved her! She knew now that he did, and the world was changed. She would make haste to get well and find him again on the shore, on the cliffs, or on the banks of the Berwen. Her uncle had heard from Gwen of her drenched condition on the night of the storm, but had already forgotten the circumstance, and only recalled it when he missed her active help in some arrangement of his heavy books.

"How did you get wet, merch i?"

"Coming over the Rock Bridge I was, uncle. I had been to see Nance, and the storm increased so much when I was there that when I returned the waves washed right over the bridge."

"Well, to be sure! Now on the next page you will find a splendid description of such a storm; go on, my girl," and Valmai continued the reading.

Meanwhile, Cardo, after a good night's rest, was no whit the worse for his battle with the storm; but he was full of fears lest Valmai's more delicate frame should suffer. He rose with the dawn and made his way over the dewy grass across the valley, and into the field where Essec Powell's cows were just awaking and clumsily rising from their night's sleep under the quiet stars. The storm had disappeared as suddenly as it had arisen, and all nature was rejoicing in the birth of a new day. Gwen was already approaching with pail and milking stool as he crossed the field through which a path led to Abersethin. She dropped a bob curtsey and proceeded to settle her pail under "Corwen" and to seat herself on her low stool.

"Your young mistress got very wet last night?" said Cardo, in an inquiring tone.

"Yes, Ser, did you see her?"

"Yes—I was crossing the bridge at the same time. Is she any the worse for her wetting?"

"Not much the matter with her," said Gwen; "'tis lying down she is, a good deal,—miladi is a bit lazy, I think," and with this scant information he had perforce to be content.

When he returned to Brynderyn to breakfast, he found his father looking somewhat discomposed as he read and re-read a letter which he had just received. He made no comment upon its contents, however, but looking up said:

"You must have found the storm very interesting, Cardo; what kept you out so late?"

He did not add that he had paced up and down for an hour in his bedroom after retiring for the night, peering out into the darkness in great anxiety for his son's safety.

"Very interesting, father; nothing less than a ducking on the Rock Bridge! The storm was raging furiously there, and a girl was crossing in the midst of it; she was in some danger, and I was able to help her to cross in safety."

"One of our congregation?" asked the old man.

"By Jove! no, father; there isn't one girl under seventy in our congregation!"

"A Methodist, then, I suppose—one of Essec Powell's lot?"

"Yes," said Cardo, beginning to redden; "but surely you wouldn't let a woman be drowned without making an effort to save her because she was a Methodist?"

"I did not say so, Cardo; but certainly I should prefer my son's risking his life for a member of the church."

Cardo made a gesture of impatience which his father saw and felt. It irritated him, and, fixing his eyes steadily on his son's face, he said:

"I don't know how it is, but of late that subject has frequently been on your tongue. I have no cause to love the Methodists, and I hope they are not now going to add to my reasons for disliking them by coming between me and my son. I simply wish you not to mention them to me, Cardo—that is not much to ask."

"I will not, father," said Cardo, pushing his plate away; "I will never mention them to you again—"

"Good!" replied his father. "I have a letter here which I would like to read to you, but not this morning, as I am very busy."

"All right, father—in the afternoon," said Cardo; and when Betto appeared to clear away the breakfast things he was lost in a profound reverie, his long legs stretched out before him and his hands buried deep in his pocket.

Betto tried in vain to recall him to outward surroundings by clattering her china and by sundry "h'ms" and coughs, but Cardo still remained buried in thought and jingling his money in his pocket. At last she *accidentally* jerked his head with her elbow.

"Hello, Betto! what is the matter?"

"My dear boy," said Betto, "did I hurt you? Where were you so late last night?"

"Oh, out in the storm. Have you seen my wet clothes? I flung them out through my bedroom window; you will find them in a heap on the garden wall."

"Wet clothes? Caton pawb! did you get in the sea then?"

"Oh, yes! tumbled over and over like a pebble on the beach," he said, rising; "but you know such duckings are nothing to me; I enjoy them!"

Betto looked after him with uplifted hands and eyes.

"Well, indeed! there never was such a boy! always in some mischief; but that's how boys are!"

Cardo went out whistling, up the long meadow to the barren corner, where the furze bushes and wild thyme and harebells still held their own against the plough and harrow; and here, sitting in deep thought, and still whistling in a low tone, he held a long consultation with himself.

"No! I will never try again!" he said at last, as he rose and took his way to another part of the farm.

In the afternoon he entered his father's study, looking, in his manly strength, and with his bright, keen eyes, out of keeping with this dusty, faded room. His very clothes were redolent of the breezy mountain-side.

Meurig Wynne still pored over apparently the self-same books which he was studying when we first saw him.

"Sit down, Cardo," he said, as his son entered; "I have a good deal to say to you. First, this letter," and he hunted about amongst his papers. "It is from an old friend of mine, Rowland Ellis of Plas Gwynant. You know I hear from him occasionally—quite often enough. It is waste of stamps, waste of energy, and waste of time to write when you have nothing special to say. But he has something to say to-day. He has a son, a poor, weak fellow I have heard, as far as outward appearance and bodily health go—a contrast to you, Cardo—but a clever fellow, a senior wrangler, and an M.A. of his college. He has just been ordained, and wants to recruit his health before he settles down to a living which is in the gift of his uncle, and which will be vacant in a short time; and as he offers very good remuneration, I don't see why he shouldn't come here. He would be a companion to you. What do you say to it?"

"As far as I am concerned, let him come by all means, if you wish it, father; it can make no difference to me."

"Indeed it will, though! You will have to show him about the neighbourhood, and lay yourself out to make his stay here as pleasant as possible, for he will pay well."

"Pay!" said Cardo, with a frown, his sense of hospitality chafing under the idea. "Pay! that spoils it all. If you take my advice in the matter, you will write to your friend, and tell him to send his son here by all means, but decline to take any remuneration."

"Cardo, you are a fool! Do you think I would take a stranger into my house, to have him always at my table, upsetting all my domestic arrangements, for nothing? You ought to know me better. Fortunately for you, with your pride and extravagant ideas, I am here to look after affairs, and hitherto, thank God, I have been quite capable of doing so! I only consulted you on the matter because I wanted to know what chance there was of your making yourself agreeable to the young man, as I cannot be bothered with him."

"Oh, well, that is settled," said Cardo. "I shall be glad of a companion, and will do my best to make him happy. I hope he'll be a jolly fellow."

"Jolly fellow? I hope he will be a steady young man, and a fit companion for you. You don't seem to think of the necessity of that!"

"I leave that to you, sir," said Cardo, with a humorous smile. "I should never dream of questioning your prudence in the matter."

The old man nervously fingered his papers.

"Well, that is settled. I will not keep you longer from your fishing or your rowing—which is it to-day, Cardo?" and he raised his black eyebrows, and spoke with a slight sneer.

Cardo laughed good-naturedly.

"Neither fishing nor boating to-day, sir. No! it's that field of swedes this afternoon," and he turned away with his hands dug deep in his pockets.

"A bad habit, Cardo! An industrious man never walks about with his hands in his pockets."

"All right, father! here goes for the swedes; and you bet I won't have my hands in my pockets there. I flatter myself I can do good work as well as any man."

His father looked after him with a curious wistfulness.

"A fine fellow!" he said to himself, as Cardo's steps receded along the passage. "Not much fault to be found with him! How can I spare him? But he must go—he must go."

Meanwhile Cardo, no longer with his hands in his pockets, stood in the swede field directing Shoni and Dye, and not only directing, but often taking his share in the weeding or hoeing. He was full of interest in the farming operations, which, in truth, were thoroughly congenial to his tastes.

"Bless the turnips and mangolds," he would often say; "at least they take you out under the blue sky, and into the fresh air." He pondered upon the proposed addition to his father's household. Suddenly an unpleasant thought seemed to strike him, for his face flushed, and he gave a long, low whistle. "Phew! I never thought of that! Why! I shall never have an hour with Valmai with this confounded wrangler at my heels! Deuce anwl! how shall I manage it? one thing only I know, no power on earth—not even an 'M.A.'—shall keep me from her."

But neither that day nor the next was Valmai to be seen. It was two or three days before she was able to throw off entirely the languor which followed her immersion in the sea; but on the evening of the third day, as the sun drew near its setting, she once more roamed down the path to the beach, a new light in her eyes and a warmer glow on her cheek.

The long shadows of evening stretched over the shore, and the sun sank low in the western sky, all flooded with crimson, and purple, and pale yellow, as she flung herself down under a towering rock, still a little languid, but full of an inrushing tide of happiness. The green waves came rolling in, their foaming crests catching the rosy pink of the sunset; the sea-gulls sailed lazily home from their day's fishing. The sheep on the hillside were folded, and the clap clap of the mill in the valley came on the breeze.

Valmai sat long gazing at the crimson pathway over the sea, both heart and soul filled to over-flowing with the beauty of the sunset hour. Not even Cardo's presence was missed by her, for she knew now that he loved her; she knew that sooner or later she should meet him, should see him coming, through the golden sunlight of the morning, or in the crimson glory of the evening, with buoyant steps and greeting hands towards her; and almost as the thought crossed her mind, a sound fell on her ear which brought the red blood mantling to her cheek. Thud, thud on the sands; it was surely his footsteps, and in another moment Cardo was beside her.

"At last, Valmai!" he said, stretching out both hands to clasp her own as she rose to meet him, "at last! Where have you been the last three years? do not say they have been days! are you well and none the worse for your wetting?" and still holding her hands in his, he made her sit again on the rock, while he stretched himself on the dry sand at her feet.

A little silence fell upon them both—a strange constraint which was new to them, and which Valmai was the first to break.

"I ought to be thanking you for saving my life, Cardo Wynne; but indeed I have no words to speak my thanks. I know I owe my life to you. What will I say?"

"Nothing," he said, leaning on his elbows and looking up into her face, "nothing; there is no need for thanks, for I could not help myself. It was the simplest thing; seeing you in danger I helped you out of it, for, Valmai," and here his voice sank low and trembled a little, "it is like this with me, and you must know it; had you been washed away by those cruel waves, there would have been no Cardo Wynne here to-night! I could not live without you! And you—Valmai, how is it with you?"

Her head drooped very low. Cardo, lying on the sands, looked up into the blushing face; but still she made no answer. Starting to his feet, he stretched out both hands to her, and said:

"Come, fanwylyd;[1] let us walk together—I cannot rest. Valmai, tell me, have I the same place in your heart that you have in mine? Place in my heart! Good heavens! There is no room there for anything else. You own it all, Valmai; you sway my very being! Have you no comfort to give me? Speak to me, dearest."

"Cardo," said Valmai, "can I give you what you have already stolen from me? I was alone and friendless when I met you that night in the moonlight, now I am happy though my heart has gone from me. What shall I say more? my English is not very good."

"But you can say, 'Cardo, I love you.' Say that again."

"Yes, I can say that, whatever."

"Say it, then, Valmai."

"Oh, well, indeed! You know quite well that I love you. Cardo, I love you." And to the sound of the plashing waves the old, old story was told again.

He had asked, while he held her face between both hands, gazing earnestly into the blue eyes, "Does this golden sky look down to-night upon any happier than we two?" and with her answer even he was satisfied.

An hour later the moon added her silver glory to the scene, and under her beams they continued long walking up and down, lingering by the surf, whispering though there was no one to hear. They parted at last under the elder bushes at Dinas.

Cardo was right. In all Wales there were not that night two happier hearts than theirs. No fears for the future, no dread of partings, no thought of life's fiery trials, which were even now casting their shadows before them.

Valmai lay long awake that night, thinking of her happiness and blushing, even in the darkness, as she remembered Cardo's burning words of love; and he went home whistling and even singing in sheer exuberance of joy. Forgotten his father's coldness; forgotten his bare, loveless home; forgotten even the wrangler who was coming to trouble him; and forgotten that nameless shadow of parting and distance, which had hovered too near ever since he had met Valmai. She loved him, so a fig for all trouble! They had pledged their troth on the edge of the waves, and they thought not of the mysterious, untried sea of life which stretched before them.

Early in the following week Cardo drove to Caer Madoc to meet the mail-coach, which entered the town with many blasts of the horn, and with much flourishing of whip, at five o'clock every evening. In the yard of the Red Dragon he waited for the arrival of his father's guest. At the appointed time the coach came rattling round the corner, and, as it drew up on the noisy cobble stones, a pale, thin face emerged from the coach window and looked inquiringly round.

"Mr. Gwynne Ellis, I suppose?" said Cardo, approaching and helping to tug open the door.

"Yes," said a high but pleasant voice, "and I suppose you are Mr. Wynne's son," and the two young men shook hands.

They were a complete contrast to each other. Cardo, tall and square—the new-comer, rather short and thin, but with a frank smile and genial manner which gave a generally pleasant impression. He wore gold spectacles, and carried a portfolio with all an artist's paraphernalia strapped together.

"Too precious to be trusted amongst the luggage, I suppose," said Cardo.

"You are right! As long as I have my painting materials safe, I can get along anywhere; but without them I am lost." And he busied himself in finding and dragging down his luggage.

In less than ten minutes the two young men had left Caer Madoc behind, and were fast lessening the distance between them and Brynderyn.

"Very kind of you to meet me; and what a splendid horse," said Gwynne Ellis. "Carries his head well, and a good stepper."

"Fond of horses?" asked Cardo.

"Oh! very," said the high-toned voice; "riding and painting are the chief delights of my life—"

"We can give you plenty of riding—'Jim,' here, is always at your service;

and as for the painting—well, I know nothing about it myself, but I think I can show you as pretty bits of scenery as you ever saw within the four sides of a gilt frame." And as they drew near the top of the moor, where they caught sight of the long stretch of coast, with its bays and cliffs and purple shadows, the new-comer was lost in admiration.

Cardo, who had been accustomed all his life to the beauties of the coast, was amused at his friend's somewhat extravagant exclamations.

"Oh, charming!" he said taking off his glasses and readjusting them on his well-shaped nose; "see those magnificent rocks—sepia and cobalt; and that cleft in the hills running down to the shore—ultra marine; and what a flood of crimson glory on the sea—carmine, rose madder—and—er—er—"

"By Jove! it will be a wonderful paint box that can imitate those colours," said Cardo, with a nod at the sunset.

"Ah, true!" said Gwynne Ellis, "one would need a spirit brush dipped in ethereal fire,

"'A broad and ample road whose dust is gold, Open, ye heavens! your living doors—'"

"That is very pretty," said Cardo, "but I am not much acquainted with English poetry—a farmer's life, you know, is too busy for that sort of thing."

"I suppose so; but a farmer's life *is* poetry itself, in its idyllic freshness and purity."

Cardo shrugged his shoulders.

"I don't know so much about that, but it is a life that suits me. I was meant for a farmer, I am sure—couldn't soar much above turnips and hay, you know. See here, now, there's a crop of hay to gladden a farmer's heart! In a week or two we shall have it tossed about in the sun, and carried down through the lanes into the haggard, and the lads and lasses will have a jolly supper in the evening, and will give us some singing that will wake the echoes from Moel Hiraethog yonder. Then the lanes are at their best, with the long wisps of sweet hay caught on the wild rose bushes."

"Aha! my friend, I see I am right," said Ellis, "and a farmer is a poet, whether he knows it or not."

Cardo laughed heartily, as they alighted at the front door.

"Tell my father that—do. Cardo Wynne a poet! that is something new, indeed!"

Here Mr. Wynne, followed by Betto, joined the group. The former, though in his usual undemonstrative manner, made the new-comer welcome, and Betto in her excitement was so lavish with her bob curtseys, that Cardo came in for a few, until he recalled her to her senses by gravely taking off his hat to her, at which she winked and nudged him with her elbow, as she flew about in the exuberance of her hospitality.

Seated at the tea-table, the three men soon became quite at their ease.

"We are plain people," said Mr. Wynne; "I hope you will not find us too primitive in our ways."

"Nothing can be too simple for me, sir," said the visitor, in his high-pitched voice, and speaking a little through his nose. "What can be more idyllic than to drive through the glowing sunset, and find such a meal as this waiting for me—broiled fish, cream, honey?"

Meurig Wynne reflected with satisfaction that none of these luxuries were expensive.

"I hope you will get strong here," he said; "the air is pure and bracing, and you can roam about where you please. If you prefer riding, you can always have 'Captain' or 'Jim.' I want to sell 'Jim,' but if I don't get 40 pounds for him, I shall keep him till September fair."

Gwynne Ellis put down his knife and fork, and sat gazing silently at the fair scene which lay stretched before him.

"What's the matter? said Cardo.

"Oh! exquisite charming! That view alone is worth coming down for! See those purple shadows! see that golden light on the gorse bushes!"

"Well," said Mr. Wynne, rising, "I must return to my study, and leave you young men to finish your meal together."

Cardo, though amused at, and somewhat despising his friend's sentimental enthusiasm, yet on the whole did not dislike him.

"Oh! I believe the fellow is all right," he thought, when they had parted for the night; "in fact, I rather like him; and, by Jove! I had forgotten all about his being a wrangler! There's no conceit about him anyway; if there had been, I should have had to pitch him out of the dogcart—upset him into the sea or something—but I think he is all right." And he went satisfied to his bed, and slept the sleep of the just, or, at all events—of the busy farmer!

[1] Beloved.

CHAPTER VI.

CORWEN AND VALMAI.

Gwynne Ellis soon found himself quite at home at Brynderyn, and enjoyed the freedom and variety of his life in its picturesque neighbourhood.

To Cardo, who had hitherto been so much alone, his presence was a very pleasant change, and though Ellis was a complete contrast to himself in every way, he liked him, and felt the advantage of companionship; more especially in the evenings, when, his father shut up in his study, and the old parlour but dimly lighted, he had always found the time hang rather heavily. He was wont to relieve the tedium of the evening hour by strolling into the kitchen, sitting in the rush chair, always looked upon as the young master's, and freely entering into the games or gossip of the farm-servants. He was much amused at the enthusiasm and romance of his new-found friend, who, coming from a populous and uninteresting border country, was charmed by the unconventional ways of the Welsh coast. He threw a glamour of poetry and romance over the most commonplace incidents; and Cardo, to tease him, would often assume a stolid and unimpressionable manner that he was far from feeling.

On the whole, they pulled well together, and the acquaintance, begun accidentally, bid fair to become a lifelong friendship.

Immediately after breakfast every morning, Gwynne Ellis, armed with brushes, palettes, and divers other encumbrances, would ramble away over shore or cliff, bringing with him in the evening the most beautiful scenes and views of the neighbourhood, which his deft brush had transferred to the pages of his portfolio. He was a true artist, and, moreover, possessed one admirable trait, generally lacking in inferior artists, namely, humility! And as he held up for Cardo's inspection an exquisite sketch of sea and sky and tawny beach, he waited anxiously for his criticisms, having found out that though his friend was no artist himself, his remarks were always regulated by good taste and common sense.

"*That* Nance's cottage?" Cardo was saying to-night as he sat in the rush chair by the fire in the farm kitchen—Ellis on a bench beside him, the little round table supporting the portfolio before them, "that cosy, picturesque-looking cottage Nance's! those opal tints over sea and sky—that blue smoke curling from the chimney, and that crescent moon rising behind the hill! Come, Ellis, you have given us a dose this time!"

"Dose of what?" said Ellis, putting on his gold-rimmed glasses.

"Why! of romance—of poetry—of imagination of course!"

"Give you my word, my dear fellow, that's how it appears to me. You are blind, dead to the beauties which surround you. Now, what would that scene appear like to you?"

Cardo laughed. "Why, exactly what it appeared to you, Ellis, only I like to tease you. I see all these beauties, old chap, though I lack the power to pourtray them as you do."

"I believe you, Cardo, though I doubt if you realise the blessing you enjoy in living amongst such picturesque scenes. To me, coming from a flat, uninteresting country, it seems a privilege to thank God for on your knees."

"Perhaps I feel it as much as you do, Ellis, though I couldn't put it into words, all I know is, I had rather live here on five shillings a week than I would on five pounds elsewhere."

"You are a matter-of-fact fellow. Five shillings a week indeed! and five pounds—worse! If you were not so much bigger and stronger than me I'd knock you down, Cardo. Come, let us have a stroll in the moonlight."

And they went out, the one to rhapsodise and to quote poetry; the other to shock his friend with his plain, unvarnished remarks, while his eyes and thoughts crossed the valley, and followed the moonlight which lightened up the old grey house looking down from the opposite hill.

"Where was Valmai?" He had caught a glimpse of her in the afternoon as he returned from Abersethin, the path to which led him through Essec Powell's fields. Caught a glimpse of her only, for as ill luck would have it, as he crossed one corner of the field she was reaching the gate at the further corner. Other maidens wore white frocks and straw hats, but his heart told him that this was no other than Valmai. He could hear her singing as she went, a long wreath of ox-eyed daisies trailing behind her, the gate open and she was gone; but surely here were signs of her recent presence, for round the horns of Corwen, the queen of the herd of cows, was wreathed the rest of the daisy chain. She was a beautiful white heifer, with curly forehead and velvet ears. As Cardo approached and patted her neck, she looked softly at him out of her liquid brown eyes shaded with long black lashes.

"She is a beauty!" said Cardo, looking at her with the critical eye of a farmer, "and worthy to be Valmai's pet. What a picture for Ellis to paint!

Valmai and Corwen. By Jove, I'll try to manage it."

Gwynne Ellis was delighted when Cardo broached the subject as they roamed over the cliff in the moonlight.

"Can you paint animals and—er—er—human beings as well as you can scenery, Ellis?"

"Not quite, perhaps, but still pretty well. You liked that sketch of 'The priest and the girl at the confessional,' didn't you?"

"Yes—very much. Well, now, what do you say to a pretty white cow and her mistress?"

"Oh! 'a pretty girl milking her cow'—a charming subject. Show it me, Cardo—not Betto, now—you don't mean Betto? though, 'pon my word, I have seen her look very picturesque on the milking stool."

"No, no, no! Caton pawb! man, I'll show you a prettier picture than that. She's a lovely creature! with brown velvet eyes, her forehead all covered with little round curls."

"What! a friz?"

"Well, if you like to call it so. Lovely ears and a little soft nose, the whole surmounted by a pair of short brown horns."

"Good heavens! the woman?"

"Why, no! the cow, of course!"

"Oh, I see; the friz and the brown eyes belong to a cow then,—but what of her mistress? My dear fellow, don't waste all your poetry on the cow."

"As I haven't much to spare, you think. Well, her mistress is—Valmai!" and Cardo lifted his hat as he spoke.

Gwynne Ellis took two or three long puffs at his pipe, and looked curiously at Cardo, who stood looking over at the glimmering light in one of the windows at Dinas.

"Cardo Wynne, I am beginning to understand you; I have mistaken the whole situation. Here have I been thinking myself the only man in the place capable of appreciating its beauties properly—the only poetic and artistic temperament amongst you all—and I gradually awake to find myself but a humdrum, commonplace man of the world, who has dropped into a nest of sweet things: earth, sea, and sky combining to form pictures of beauty; picturesque rural life; an interesting and mysterious host; an idyllic cow; a friend who, though unable, or perhaps unwilling, to express his enthusiasm, yet thoroughly feels the poetry of life; and, better than all, I find myself in close touch with a real romantic love affair! Now, don't deny it, my dear fellow; I see it all—I read it in your eyes—I know all about it. The pretty cow's lovely mistress; and her name is—Valmai! How tender! My Welsh is rather rusty, but I know that means 'sweet as May.' Oh, Cardo Wynne, what a lucky dog you are!"

Cardo was still silent, and his friend continued, pointing to Dinas:

"And there she dwells (haven't I seen your eyes attracted there continually? Of course, there's the glimmer of her lamp!) high on the breezy cliff, with the pure sea wind blowing around her, the light and joy of her father's home, and soon to fly across the valley and lighten up another home."

"Oh, stop, stop, for mercy's sake!" said Cardo. "Your Pegasus is flying away with you to-night, Ellis. Your imagination is weaving a picture which is far beside the truth. You have not guessed badly. I do love Valmai, Corwen's mistress, and I wish to God the rest of the picture were true."

"Pooh! my dear fellow, 'the course of true love,' you know, etc., etc. It will all come right in time, of course; these things always do. I'll manage it all for you. I delight in a love affair, especially one that's got a little entangled, you know."

"Here it is, then," said Cardo. "Valmai has neither father nor mother, and lives up there with an old uncle, who takes no more notice of her than he does of his cows or his sheep, but who would be quite capable of shutting her up and feeding her on bread and water if he knew that she ever exchanged greetings with a Churchman, for he is a Methodist preacher and her guardian to boot."

A long-drawn whistle was Gwynne Ellis's only answer, but he rubbed his hands gleefully.

"Then," continued Cardo, "on this side of the valley there is my father, shut up with his books, taking no interest in anything much except his church and his farm, but with a bigoted, bitter hatred of all dissenters, especially Methodists, and most especially of the Methodist preacher. Why, Ellis, they convene public meetings on purpose to pray for each other, and I believe if my father knew that I loved Essec Powell's niece he would *break his heart*. Therefore, I cannot tell him—it is impossible; but it is equally impossible for me, as long as I have any being, to cease to love Valmai. Now, there! what way do you see out of that maze?"

"Many ways," said Ellis, rubbing his hands with delight. "My dear fellow, you have pitched upon the right person. I'll help you out of your difficulties, but you must let me see her."

"All right!—to-morrow!" said Cardo, as they neared Brynderyn.

When their voices reached the Vicar's ears, he paused in his reading, and a look of pleasure softened his white face, but only for an instant, for as the young men passed the window a dark and mournful look chased away the momentary softness.

"Soon!" he said, "soon I will tell him he ought to be prepared—I *will* tell him!"

It was no easy matter next day to find Valmai, though Cardo and Gwynne
Ellis sought for her over shore and cliff and by the brawling Berwen. They were returning disconsolate through the turnip fields at noon, when Cardo caught sight of a red spot in the middle of a corn-field.

"There she is, Ellis," he said, turning round; "have we time to go back?"

"What! that little scarlet poppy in the corn?"

"Yes; it is Valmai's red hood; she wears it sometimes, and sometimes a broad-brimmed white hat."

Ellis looked at his watch.

"Too late to go back now; it is close upon one o'clock."

"Deucedly provoking!" said Cardo; "we will try again after dinner."

But after dinner they seemed to be no more successful, although they found their way into the very field where they had seen the red hood.

"Let us follow the path," said Ellis stoutly; "it seems to lead straight by the back of the house, and that old ivy-covered barn looks tempting, and suggestive of a beautiful sketch."

Cardo hesitated.

"Come along, Cardo; not all the Methodist preachers in the world can frighten me back when I am on the track of a pretty picture."

In the old ivy-covered barn they found Valmai. The big door was open, and in the dim, blue light of the shady interior, Shoni and she were busily engaged with Corwen, who had been ailing since the previous evening. Ellis was instantly struck by the picturesque beauty of the group before him. Corwen, standing with drooping head, and rather enjoying her extra petting; Shoni, with his brawny limbs and red hair, patting her soft, white flanks, and trying, with cheerful chirrups, to make her believe she was quite well again. Valmai stood at her head, with one arm thrown round her favourite's neck, while she kissed the curly, white forehead, and cooed words of endearment into the soft, velvet ears.

"Darling beauty! Corwen fâch!"

Here Gwynne Ellis, irresistibly attracted by the scene before him, boldly entered the barn.

The girl looked up surprised as he approached, hat in hand.

"A thousand apologies," he said, "for this intrusion; but my friend and I were roaming about in search of something to paint, and my good fortune led me here; and again I can only beg a hundred pardons."

"One is enough," said Shoni sulkily. "What you want?"

The painting paraphernalia strapped on Gwynne Ellis's back had not made a favourable impression upon Shoni. He took him for one of the "walking tramps" who infested the neighbourhood, and made an easy living out of the hospitable Welsh farmers.

Valmai saw Shoni's mistake, and rebuked him in Welsh.

"There is nothing to pardon," she said, turning to Mr. Ellis, "and if there is anything here that you would like to paint, I am sure my uncle would be quite willing. Will I go and ask him?"

"Thank you very much; but if you go, the picture will be spoiled!"

But Valmai, taking no notice of the implied compliment, began her way to the big door.

"This lovely white cow! do you think your uncle would allow me to paint her?"

"Oh! yes, I am sure, indeed!" said Valmai, turning round; "but not to-day, she has been ill—to-morrow she will be out in the field, and then I will make a daisy chain for her, and she will look lovely in a picture." And she passed out into the sunshine.

Gwynne Ellis heard a long-drawn "Oh!" of pleased surprise as she discovered Cardo hovering about the door, and he considerately entered into conversation with Shoni, endeavouring to express himself in his mother-tongue, but with that hesitation and indistinctness common to the dwellers in the counties bordering upon England, and to the "would-be genteel" of too many other parts of Wales, who, perfectly unconscious of the beauty of their own language, and ignorant of its literature, affect English manners and customs, and often pretend that English is more familiar to them than Welsh, a fatuous course of conduct which brings upon them only the sarcasm of the lower classes, and the contempt of the more educated.

"What you is clabbering about, man?" said Shoni indignantly. "Keep to the English if that is your language, 'coss me is spoke English as well as Welsh."

"Yes, I see you do," said Ellis, "and I am thankful to meet with a man so learned. To know two languages means to look at everything from two points of view—from two sides, I mean. A man who knows two languages knows half as much again of everything as a man who can only speak one."

Shoni scratched his head; he was mollified by the stranger's evident appreciation of his learning, but thought it necessary to keep his wits about him.

"With these foreigns, you know, you never know wherr they arr—these English, you know," he was wont to say, "nor wherr they arr leading you to."

"What wass you walk about the country for?" was his next remark.

"Ah, that's it now! You are a sensible man; you come to the point at once. Well, I am very fond of making pictures."

"Sell them?"

"Oh no, just for my own pleasure; every man has his—"

"Crack!" said Shoni.

"Yes, crack, if you like," said Ellis, laughing, and opening his portfolio; "here are some of my cracks."

And they drew near the doorway, leaving Corwen much dissatisfied at the cessation of attentions.

Cardo and Valmai had disappeared. Shoni was fast losing his head to this fellow with the high nose and high voice, who evidently knew a sensible man when he saw him.

"There is Nance Owen's cottage," said the artist, "at the back of the island; do you recognise it?"

Shoni was lost in admiration, but did not think it wise to show it, so he stood silent for some time, with his hands under his coat tails and his red-bearded chin first turned to one side and then to the other, as he looked with critical eyes at the pictures.

"It's the very spit of the place," he said at last; "let's see another."

And Ellis picked out his masterpiece.

"That's Ogo Wylofen," he said.

"Ach y fi!" said Shoni, with a shudder, "wherr you bin when you painted that?"

"At the mouth of the cave in a boat. It is magnificent, that rushing water, those weird wailings, and the mysterious figures of spray which pass up into the dark fissures."

But this was far above Shoni's head.

"Caton pawb, man!" he said, "not me would go in a boat to that hole for the world. It is a split in the earth, and those are ghosts or witches or something that walk in and out there; but anwl! anwl! you must be a witch yourself, I think, to put those things on paper. Oh, see that red sun, now, and the sea all red and yellow! Well, indeed!"

"Well, now," said Ellis, "I want to have a picture of Corwen."

"Yes, to-morrow, in the field, and me standing by her. I will put on my new gaiters."

"The young lady has gone to ask your master's consent."

"The master!" said Shoni, locking the barn door; "pooh! 'sno need to ask him. You kom to-morrow and make a picksher on Corwen and me. Wherr you stop?"

"At Brynderyn."

"With the Vicare du? Oh, jâr i!" said Shoni, taking off his hat to scratch his head, "there's a pity now. Essec Powell will nevare be willing for that; but nevare you mind, you kom. Here's Valmai."

Cardo was nowhere to be seen.

"I asked my uncle, sir," she said, "but I am sorry to say when he heard you were the Vicar's friend he was not willing, but he did not say no."

"Twt, twt," said Shoni, interrupting, "you wass no need to ask Essec Powell. The gentleman is kom to-morrow to make a picksher on Corwen and me."

Valmai could not resist a smile at Shoni's English, which broke the ice between her and Gwynne Ellis; and as Shoni disappeared round the corner of the barn, she gave him her hand, frankly saying:

"Good-bye, Mr. Ellis; I must go in to tea."

"Good-bye," he said, "I will venture to bring my paints to-morrow to Corwen's field. And you—you will keep your promise to come and make the daisy chain?"

"Well, indeed, I can't promise, but I will try, whatever."

"And then you will honour me by looking over my portfolio."

"And the Vicar objects to that girl," he exclaimed to himself, as he proceeded down the path to the shore. "What a sweet, sensitive mouth!

Oh, Cardo, Cardo Wynne, I can only say, as I said before, you are a lucky dog!"

He had wondered what had become of Cardo, but with his full appreciation of a secret love-affair, had had too much tact to ask Valmai, and was not much surprised to find him lying at full length on the sandy beach.

"Well, Wynne," he said, pretending to sulk a little, "you *did* leave me in the lurch."

"Leave you in the lurch! my dear fellow, do forgive me. To tell the truth I forgot all about you until Valmai went indoors to find her uncle. I waited to see if she would come out again, but she never did. I believe she was waiting until I had gone; she's dreadfully chary of her company."

"Another charm," said Ellis; "one would get tired of an angel who was always *en evidence*. She is an ideal girl. Tell me when you are going to retire, old fellow, and then I will try my luck. That sweet mouth, though the delight of a lover, is the despair of an artist."

Cardo sighed.

"Well, she came back after you were gone, then, and shook hands with me, but said her uncle did not seem delighted to hear I was the Vicar's friend."

"Of course not."

"But I made love to Shoni and gained his consent, and he is the real master there, I fancy."

"You did?" said Cardo, lost in admiration of his friend's shrewdness.

"I did," said Ellis. "To-morrow I am to go to the field and paint Corwen and Valmai has promised to come and make a daisy chain for the occasion."

"Has she indeed?" said Cardo, with great interest. "She would not promise me. I believe she loves to see me miserable."

"Well, cheer up," said Ellis, "for I shall be a precious long time at those curls of Corwen's and those expressive brown eyes. Shoni, I know, will stick to me like a leech, but you and Valmai, I expect, will meanly desert me again."

Next day Valmai was as good as her word, for, as the young men entered the field at one corner, she appeared at the gate in the other, and as she came towards them, Gwynne Ellis was struck anew by the beauty and freshness of her appearance. She wore a simple white frock, her fair, broad forehead was shaded by a white sun-bonnet, and she carried a wreath of moon daisies, which she flung over Corwen's neck who was grazing peacefully among the buttercups, ignorant of the honour awaiting her.

Valmai nodded playfully to Cardo and his friend as they drew near, and, taking Corwen's soft, white ear, drew her towards them with many endearing terms.

"Come then, my queen, dere di, come along, then, and show your beautiful brown eyes, and your pretty white curls. Here we are, Mr. Ellis; will we do?" and, holding up her white frock, she made a demure little curtsey to the two young men, while Shoni, also arriving on the scene, looked at her with amused surprise, not unmixed with reproof.

"Iss you must excuse Valmai, gentlemen," he said, tugging his red forelock; "she iss partly a foreign, and not know our manners about here."

"Oh, we'll excuse her," said Gwynne Ellis, while Cardo clasped her hand and gazed rapturously at the blushing face under the white bonnet.

"I wass want her," said Shoni, with a jerk of his thumb towards Valmai, "to put on her best frock, but no!" and he clicked his tongue against the roof of his mouth, "there's odd things woman are! 'ts 'ts!"

"Well, indeed," said Valmai, "I did not think a smart gown would suit the fields, whatever!"

"Couldn't be better, Miss Powell," said Ellis, arranging his group, and introducing Shoni as a shadowy background. With a few deft touches of his brush he had drawn the outlines of his picture, with good-natured artfulness devoting much time to finishing off Corwen and dismissing Valmai and Cardo.

"Now you two can go," he said, "but I can't do without Shoni. A little black spot at the back of that ear?"

"No, no—brown," said Shoni, delighted to be of such importance, "and the same brown smot on the nother ear, and that's the only smot upon her!"

He watched with intense interest the progress of the picture, calling the artist's attention to all Corwen's good points as though he were appraising her at a cattle sale, and an hour passed away quickly both to the artist and Shoni; but to Cardo and Valmai, what a golden hour! to stroll away together over the soft grass studded with buttercups, down to the edge of the cliffs, where they sat among the gorze bushes looking out at the rippling blue bay, silent from sheer happiness, but taking in unconsciously the whole beauty of the scene, for it was engraved upon their minds and often recalled in after years.

"There!" said Gwynne Ellis at length, closing his portfolio with a snap, "I can finish the rest at home—"

"Iss, iss," said Shoni, "iss not so much otts about Valmai."

"And to-morrow I will finish your gaiters, Shoni."

"Very well, sir; pliss you remember, seven buttons on both of the two legs."

CHAPTER VII.

THE VICAR'S STORY.

The spring had gone; summer had taken her place and was spreading all her wealth of beauty over the scene. The sea lay shimmering in the golden sunshine, the little fishing-boats flitted about the bay like white-winged butterflies. On the yellow sands the waves splashed lazily; up on the cliffs the sea crows cawed noisily, and the sea-gulls sailed high in the air, and day after day Gwynne Ellis sought and found some new scene of beauty to transfer to his portfolio. Every day he trudged away in the morning and returned late in the evening, fast gaining strength and health, and bidding fair soon to rival Cardo in his burly breadth of chest.

And where was Cardo through all this summer weather? The duties of his farm were never very onerous, as, under Ebben's practical management and his father's careful eye all the work was carried on regularly, and he well knew that with every year, and with their inexpensive menage, his father's riches were increasing, and that there was no real reason why he should work at all; but he was one of those to whom idleness was intolerable. True! he could lie on the sands with his hat over his face for an hour sometimes, listening to the plashing waves and the call of the sea-birds; he could sail in his boat on the bay for many a sunny afternoon, the sails flapping idly in the breeze, while he with folded hands leant against the mast, lost in thought, his eyes narrowly scanning the cliffs and rocks around for some sign of Valmai, and sometimes rewarded by a glimpse of her red hood or a wave of her handkerchief; but for the lounging laziness which shirks work, and shrinks from any active exertion, he had nothing but contempt. Dye always averred "that the work never went so well as when the young master helped at it."

"Twt, twt, he is like the rest of the world these days," said Ebben, "works when he likes, and is idle when he likes. When I was young—" etc. etc.

When the haymaking began he was everywhere in request, and entered with much energy into the work of the harvest. Early and late he was out with the mowers, and, at a push, with his strong shoulders and brawny arms could use the scythe as well as any of the men. The Vicar paid occasional visits to the hayfields, and Betto was busy from morning to night filling the baskets with the lunch of porridge and milk, or the afternoon tea for the haymakers, or preparing the more substantial dinner and supper.

"What's Dinas thinking of?" said Ebben, drying his heated face; "not begun to mow yet?"

"Begin to-morrow," answered Dye. "Essec Powell forgot it was hay harvest, until Valmai pulled him out by the coat, and made him look over the gate."

"Hast seen the picture," said Ebben, "Mr. Ellis has made of her and Corwen? Splendid!"

"No," said Dye; "has he? What will the Vicare say? Jâr-i! there'll be black looks!"

But Gwynne Ellis had been wiser than to show his sketch to the Vicar; he was learning like Cardo that if there was to be peace at Brynderyn, neither Essec Powell nor his flock nor his family must be mentioned.

The last full wain of sweet scented hay had been carted into the haggard, amidst the usual congratulatory comments of the haymakers, who had afterwards trooped into the farm-yard, where, under the pale evening sky, with the sunset glow behind them, and the moon rising full before them, they seated themselves at the long supper table prepared by Betto and Shan in the open yard.

First the bowls were filled with the steaming cawl, and then the wooden platters were heaped with the pink slices of home-cured bacon, and mashed up cabbages. Last of all came the hunches of solid rice pudding, washed down by "blues" [1] of home-brewed ale; and the talk and the laughter waxed louder and merrier, as they proceeded with their meal.

Gwynne Ellis sat perched on the wall under the elder tree sketching the group, and evidently affording them much amusement. The Vicar looked at them through his study window, but Cardo, who had worked hard all day in the field, was absent.

Down in the shady path by the Berwen, he and Valmai walked and sang together. Of course she could sing, with the clear, sweet voice and the correct ear common to most Welshwomen, and Cardo sharing also in the national gift, their voices frequently blended together in song, and the sylvan valley often echoed to the tones of their voices, more especially in the old ballad, which tradition said had been composed by a luckless shepherd who had lived in this valley,

"By Berwen's banks my love hath strayed," etc.

The June roses bent down towards them, the trailing honeysuckle swept her cheek, and as the sunset faded and the clear moon rose in the sky their voices were low and tender.

"I have seen so little of you lately, Valmai."

"So little!" said the girl, in feigned astonishment. "Indeed you are a greedy man. How oftentimes has Gwen called me and I have been absent, and even my uncle asked me yesterday, 'Where dost spend thy time, child; on the shore?' and I said, 'Yes, uncle, and by the Berwen.'"

"How strange it is," said Cardo, "that no one seems to come here but you and me, and how fortunate."

"Well, indeed," returned the girl, "there was scarcely any path here till I came, the ferns and nut trees had quite shut it up."

"Yes," said Cardo, "I always thought it was a thicket, though I often roamed the other side of the stream. And now the dear little dell is haunted by a sweet fairy, who weaves her spells and draws me here. Oh, Valmai, what a summer it is!"

"Yes," she said, bending her head over a moon-daisy, from which she drew the petals one by one. "Loves me not," she said, as she held the last up for Cardo's inspection with a mischievous smile.

"It's a false daisy, love," he said, drawing her nearer to him, "for if my heart is not wholly and entirely yours, then such a thing as *love* never existed. Look once more into my eyes, cariad anwl,[2] and tell me you too feel the same."

"Oh, Cardo, what for will I say the same thing many times?"

"Because I love to hear you."

The girl leant her cheek confidingly on his breast, but when he endeavoured to draw her closer and press a kiss upon the sweet mouth, she slipped away from his arms, and, shaking her finger at him playfully, said, "No, no, one kiss is enough in a week, whatever—indeed, indeed, you shan't have more," and she eluded his grasp by slipping into the hazel copse, and looking laughingly at him through its branches. "Oh, the cross man," she said, "and the dissatisfied. Smile, then, or I won't come out again."

"Come, Valmai, darling, you tantalise me, and I begin to think you are after all a fairy or a wood nymph, or something intangible of that kind."

"Intangible, what is that?" she said, returning to his side with a little pucker on her brow. "Oh, if you begin to call me names, I must come back; but you must be good," as Cardo grasped her hand, "do you hear, and not ask for kisses and things."

"Well, I won't ask for kisses and things," said Cardo, laughing, "until—next time."

And thus, while Essec Powell was lost in dreams of the old bards and druids, and the Vicar counted his well-garnered hayricks, these two walked and sang in the mazes of the greenwood, the soft evening sky above them, the sweet sea-breezes around them, and talked the old foolish delicious words of love and happiness.

What wonder was it that, as alone under the stars, they returned to the haunts of men, the links of the love that bound them to each other grew stronger and stronger; and that to Valmai, as they parted on the shore, all of earthly delight seemed bound up in Cardo; and to him, as he watched the lithe, graceful figure climbing up the rugged path to the cliffs, all the charm and beauty of life seemed to go with her.

After supper, at which the Vicar had been more silent than usual, he rose, and for a moment stood still, and, looking at his son, seemed about to speak, but appearing to change his mind, after a curt good-night, he walked away through the long stone passage with his usual firm step. He was so regular and fixed in his habits that even this little hesitation in his manner surprised Cardo, but he had not much time for conjecture, as his father's voice was heard at the study door.

"Caradoc," he called, "I want to speak to you."

Cardo cast an involuntary glance of astonishment at Gwynne Ellis as he rose from the table and put his pipe back on its bracket.

"I think I shall go to bed," said Ellis, leaning back with a yawn and a stretch. "I have been on my legs all day, and a jolly day it has been!"

The Vicar was standing at the study door holding it a little ajar; he opened it wide for his son's entrance, and closed it carefully before he seated himself in his usual place by the writing-table.

"Shall I light your candles, father?"

"Yes—one will do."

And, while Cardo busied himself with the candle and matches, and drew down the blinds, his father fumbled amongst his papers and coughed awkwardly.

"Sit down, Cardo. I have something to say to you which I have been wanting to say for some time, and which I hope will give you pleasure."

Cardo said nothing, his attention being rivetted upon his father's countenance; the marble face seemed whiter than usual, the deep shadows round the eyes darker and—was it fancy?—or were the lips whiter?

"What is it, father?" said Cardo, at last pitying the old man's evident nervousness; "no bad news, I hope?"

"Bad news!" said the Vicar, with a forced smile, which disclosed a row of large and rather yellow teeth. "Didn't I say I hoped it would please you?"

"Yes, I forgot, sir."

"Well, it is this: you live a very quiet, monotonous life here, and though it has many advantages, perhaps to a young man it would also appear to have many drawbacks. You have lately had Mr. Gwynne Ellis's company, which I am glad to see you have thoroughly appreciated. I should have been annoyed, had it been otherwise, considering that it was not without some change of my usual domestic ways that I was able to arrange this little matter for you. I own I should not like you to imbibe all his ideas, which I consider very loose and unconstitutional; but on the whole, I have liked the young man, and shall be sorry when he leaves, more particularly as he pays well."

Cardo winced. "I am very happy working on the farm, and if I have appeared discontented, my looks have belied me."

"No, no," said his father, tapping with his finger on the open page before him. "No! you seem to have a fund of animal spirits; but I am quite aware that your life is uneventful and dull, and I think a young man of your er—er—" (he was going to say "prospects," but thought that would not be politic), "well, a young man of your position should see a little of the world."

"My position is that of a farmer, sir, and few farmers can afford to travel about and see the world."

"Certainly not, certainly not; and for heaven's sake don't run away with the idea that I can afford it any better than other poor vicars or farmers; but knowing that you have a 100 pounds a year of your own, Cardo, which, by the by, you never spend much of, and which I am glad to hear you are already beginning to save up, I thought it well to suggest to you a little holiday, a little break in your occupation."

"Once for all, sir, I have no wish to travel, so do not trouble your head about me; I am perfectly contented and happy."

There was a moment's silence, except for the Vicar's tapping fingers, and when he next spoke there was a little shake in his voice and a little droop in his straight back.

"Well," he said at length, "if that is the case, I need not expect you to accede to my proposals. When a young man is contented and happy, it is not to be expected he will alter his mode of life to please an old man."

"And that man his father! Indeed it is," said Cardo, standing up and taking his favourite attitude, with his elbow on the mantelpiece. "Why do you keep me at arm's length? Why do you not tell me plainly what I can do for you, father? There is nothing I would not do, nothing I would not sacrifice, that is—" and he made a mental reservation concerning Valmai.

"That is—nothing except what I am about to ask you, I suppose?" said the old man.

The words were not amiable. They might have angered another man; but Cardo detected a tremor in the voice and an anxious look in the eyes which softened their asperity.

"What do you want me to do, sir?"

"In plain words, I want you to go to Australia."

"Australia!" gasped Cardo. "In heaven's name, what for, sir?"

"I have often told you that some day I would wish you to go to Australia, Cardo. If you cannot afford your own expenses, I will help you In fact—er—er—I will place funds at your disposal which shall enable you to travel like a gentleman, and to reap every advantage which is supposed to accrue from travel and seeing the world."

Cardo way speechless from astonishment, not so much at the idea of banishment to the Antipodes—for his father had sometimes, though at long intervals, hinted at this idea—but at the unusual coolness with which he had alluded to such a lavish expenditure of money; and as he looked at his father with an earnest, inquiring gaze, the old man seemed to shrink under the scrutiny.

At last, turning away from the table, and placing both hands on his knees, he continued in an altered tone:

"Sit down again, Cardo, and I will tell you the story of my life, and then you shall tell me whether you will go to Australia or not."

His son sat down again and listened eagerly. He had always longed to hear something of his father's early life; he had always rebelled against the cold barrier of mystery which seemed to enshroud him and separate him from his only son.

"Well, to begin at the beginning," said the Vicar, fixing his eyes on one spot on the carpet, "there was a time when I was young—perhaps you can hardly realise that," he said suddenly, looking up; "but strange as it may seem to you, it is a fact. I once was young, and though never so gay and light-hearted as you still I was happy in my own way, and fool enough to expect that life had for me a store of joys and pleasures, just as you do now. I was doomed, of course, to bitter disappointment, just as you will be. Well, I had one trouble, and that was the fear that I might be appointed to a curacy which would take me away from my old home, and I was greatly relieved when I was appointed to this living through the influence of an old friend of my father's. When I entered upon my new duties, I found the old church filled with a hearty and friendly congregation; but soon afterwards that Methodist Chapel was built on the moor, and that rascal Essec Powell became its minister, and from that day to this he has been a thorn in the flesh to me. My father died about a year after I was ordained, and I found the old house rather lonely with only Betto, who was then young, to look after my domestic affairs. My farm I found a great solace. About this time I met your mother, Agnes Powell. Her uncle and aunt had lately come to live in the neighbourhood, accompanied by their daughter Ellen and their niece—your mother. The two girls were said to be wealthy, and seemed to be as much attached to each other as though they had been sisters. I don't remember much about Ellen Vaughan's appearance, in fact I scarcely noticed her, for I had fallen passionately in love with Agnes Powell. Are you listening, Caradoc?"

"Yes, indeed, sir," he said breathlessly, "I have thirsted for this knowledge so long."

"You have! well, then, listen. I loved your mother with a frantic mad devotion, though I killed her."

Cardo started.

"Yes, I killed her; not by a cruel blow, or murderous attack, but quite as surely and as cruelly. I told you I had not your gay and lively disposition. I might have added that I was sensitive and suspicious to an intense degree, and from my first acquaintance with your mother until the day I married her, I was always restless and uneasy, hating and fearing every man who approached her."

He reached a glass of water which stood on the table, and, having drunk some, looked again at his son.

"You see, Caradoc, if I have withheld this information from you long, I am telling you everything now. Just about this time my brother Lewis, who had for some years been settled in Scotland to learn farming, came home to Brynderyn, although I, being the elder son, was the owner of the place. Lewis had a small annuity settled upon him. As I was on the eve of being married, he was much interested in my affairs, and spoke of his admiration of Agnes in such glowing terms, that I felt, and, I fear, showed some resentment. However, as he was well acquainted with my suspicious nature, he was not offended, but laughed me out of my doubts for the time—for the time," he repeated, again fixing his eyes on the spot on the carpet. "Bear in mind, Cardo, through every word of this history, that the suspicion and mistrust of my nature amounted almost to insanity. I see it now, and, thank God, have conquered it in some measure. Well, we were married. Lewis was my groomsman, and Ellen Vaughan was the bridesmaid. It was a very quiet wedding, as Mrs. Vaughan was in very bad health—in fact, she died soon after our marriage, and Agnes seemed to feel the loss of her aunt so acutely that I was jealous and angry, and she saw that I was so, and endeavoured to hide her tears, poor child! poor child! I don't think her uncle ever liked me, or approved of our marriage. Happily he had no control over Agnes's fortune, or I believe she would never have had a penny of it; but I think he might have trusted me there, for I have nursed it—yes and doubled it," he mumbled, as though forgetting he was speaking to anyone but the carpet. "Well, let me see—where was I?"

"But my mother, sir?" interrupted Cardo; "tell me something about her—was she pretty?"

"Yes, she was beautiful, very lovely, with a foreign Spanish look in her eyes—you have the same, I think, Cardo. There was a tradition of Spanish blood in the family."

"And had she a Spanish temper, sir? quick and hasty, I mean."

"No, no, quite the contrary; a sweet and amiable temper, but certainly with a good deal of pride, which resented a suspicion like a blow," and the old man sighed heavily. "My brother Lewis made his home at Brynderyn, while he was looking about for some suitable opening for his farming operations, and here in the midst of my newly-found happiness, with hope and love shedding their beams around me, I allowed the first insidious entrance of the serpent of distrust and jealousy of my wife into my heart. My brother Lewis was very unlike me in appearance and disposition, being of a frank and genial manner, and trustful to a fault. I think you inherit that trait from him; be careful of it, Caradoc, or you will be cheated by every man you meet. Not that I would have you follow my example—God forbid! but there is a happy mean, a safe path between these two traits of character."

The Vicar was beginning to enjoy the recital of his long past troubles, and the thought flashed through his mind that he would have lightened his burden had he sooner confided in his son. The conduct which seemed so black and stained, when brooded over alone in his study, did not seem quite so heinous when put into plain words and spread out in the light.

"Well," he continued, "in spite of my jealous temper, the first few months of our wedded life were very happy, and it was not until I had begun to notice that a very intimate friendship existed between my young wife and my brother, that my suspicions were aroused with regard to them; but once alive to this idea, every moment of my life was poisoned by it. I kept a close but secret watch upon their actions, and soon saw what I considered a certain proof that the love they felt for each other was more than, and different to, that which the relationship of brother and sister-in-law warranted. Betto noticed it, too, for she has ever been faithful and true to me. She came to me one day, and seriously advised me to get rid of my brother Lewis, refusing to give any reason for her advice; but I required no explanation. You say nothing, Caradoc, but sit there with a blacker look on your face than I have ever seen before."

"I am listening, father, and waiting for some excuse for your jealous suspicions."

"I have very little to give but you shall have the story in its naked truth. I was devotedly attached to my brother; from childhood we had been all in all to each other, and the difference in our dispositions seemed only to cement more closely the bond of union between us; but now my love seemed turned to hatred, and I only waited to make my fears a certainty to turn him out of my house. Although I was anxious to hide my suspicions for a time, I could not refrain from sneering taunts about men who spent a life of idleness while others worked. Lewis opened his blue eyes in astonishment, and his frank, open countenance wore a hurt and puzzled look; but he did not go. He bore my insults, and yet haunted the house, and lingered round the west parlour, now shut up, but where your mother always sat. I found it impossible to hide entirely from Agnes my doubts of her love, and I soon saw that my involuntarily altered manner had made a corresponding change in hers. The proud spirit within her was roused, and instead of endeavouring to soothe my suspicions, and show me my mistake, she went on her way apparently unheeding, holding her head high, and letting me form my own opinion of her actions. I ought to have told you that her uncle had been so annoyed at her marriage with me that he had forbidden her to enter his doors again; and of this I was not sorry, though it roused my anger so much that I added my injunctions to the effect that if she wished to please me she would break off all acquaintance with her cousin, Ellen Vaughan. This, however, she would not promise to do, and it was the first beginning of the rift, which afterwards widened into a chasm between us. Her cousin also was too much attached to her to be easily alienated from her, and the two girls met more frequently than either her uncle or I were aware of. There was another girl, too—I forget her name—but she was a sister of Essec Powell's. Agnes and she had been schoolmates and bosom friends, and they were delighted to meet here by accident, and I soon found that my wife continually resorted to Essec Powell's house to pour out her sorrows into the bosom of her friend; but this I could not allow. To visit the house of my bitterest enemy—to make a friend of his sister, was a glaring impropriety in a clergyman's wife, and I cannot even now feel any compunction at having put a stop to their intercourse—if, indeed, I succeeded in doing so. A cold cloud seemed to have fallen between me and your mother; and as for my brother, we scarcely spoke to each other at meals, and avoided each other at all other times. Still Lewis stayed on, with that puzzled look on his face, and still Agnes went through her daily duties with a proud look and a constrained manner.

"Poor Betto looked anxiously from one to the other of us, and I kept my still and silent watch. My heart was breaking with distrust of my wife, and hatred of my brother; but I never spoke of my failing trust in them both. I brooded upon it night and day, and my life became a hell upon earth.

"One day in the early spring, about a month before you were born, Caradoc, I had been to a funeral at the old church; and hearing of the serious illness of a parishioner who lived on the high road to Abersethin, I followed the path on the left side of the Berwen, and as I neared the bridge which crosses the valley on the top, I suddenly came upon Agnes, who was sitting on a boulder by the side of the brook, and as I approached I saw her dry her eyes hurriedly. She rose from her seat, and her colour came and went as she looked at me. I longed to take her in my arms and press her to my heart, for she looked pale and sorrowful."

An exclamation from Cardo interrupted him.

"It pains you, Caradoc—it pains me—it pained me then—it will pain me as long as I have any being. I may be forgiven hereafter, but it cannot cease to pain me.

"'Agnes,' I said, 'are you not straying very far from home?'

"'I came for a walk,' she answered; 'it is a lovely day!'

"'I did not know you could walk so far,' I said. 'Last evening when I asked you to come down to the shore with me, you said it was too far!'

"'Yesterday, Meurig, I was feeling very ill; to-day I am better.'

"Her lip quivered a little, and she looked round uneasily, I thought.

"I said, 'I am going to see old Shôn Gweydd, or I would walk back with you; but perhaps you don't mind going alone.'

"'Oh, no, not at all,' she said, as she began her way back by the Berwen.

"I went my way with a heavy heart, and as I entered Shôn Gweydd's house (it was a little way down the road) I looked back at the bridge, and saw a girl cross the stile and go down into the valley. It was Ellen Vaughan, and no doubt Agnes had been waiting for her; but when in returning I met my brother Lewis coming over the same stile into the high road, my whole soul was filled with anger, and I passed the brother whom I had loved so tenderly with a short, cold remark about the weather, and I reached Brynderyn consumed with jealousy and bitter hatred.

"The same evening, Agnes was sitting at her work at the bay window of the west parlour, while I was busily writing in the old farm parlour which we now use. Lewis entered with the strained and saddened look which he had worn in my presence latterly; he reached a book from the bookshelf, and sauntered in through the stone passage into the west parlour. In a moment I had risen and followed him, and, walking carefully on the carpet which covered it, then, reached the door of the sitting-room without being heard, and through the chink of the half-open door I saw my brother stoop down and whisper something confidentially in my wife's ear.

"I entered the room immediately afterwards, and Lewis made some casual remark about the sunset, while Agnes went on quietly sewing. How to endure my agony of mind I knew not, for I now felt convinced that my doubts were warranted; but I was determined to control my feelings and restrain any expression of anger until after the birth of her child, which was fast approaching, as I still loved her too much to endanger her health, and I knew that if once the floodgates of my anger were opened the storm of passion would be beyond my control.

"On the following Sunday Agnes came to church for the last time, and after the service I went into the vestry to take off my gown; and as I followed the stream of worshippers leaving the porch, I saw her joined by Lewis, who walked with her towards the lych gate, and before I reached them I distinctly saw him place a note in her hand. She quickly put it in her pocket, and, with a friendly and satisfied nod, he turned round to speak to a neighbouring farmer.

"The blood surged through my veins"—and the old man rose from his chair and stood before his son, who sat with his elbow on the table. Unconsciously the Vicar seemed to take the position of a prisoner before his judge; his hands were clenched nervously, and as he spoke he drew his handkerchief over his damp face.

"Yes," he said, "my blood surged through my veins, but even then I did not speak a word of complaint or anger. Had I done so, I might have been spared the years of anguish and remorse which have been my share since then.

"I walked home silently by my wife's side, forcing myself to make some casual remark. She answered as coldly. And thus passed away our only chance of explanation and reconciliation. You are silent, Caradoc; you do not like to speak the condemnation and the contempt which you feel for your father."

"Father," said Cardo, "I feel nothing but pity for you and pity for my poor mother. As for my uncle—"

"Wait, wait, Cardo; let me finish my story. That was the last time your mother came to church. In a short time afterwards you were born, and during the intervening time I struggled harder than ever, not to forgive, but to drop my wife entirely out of my life. I tried to ignore her presence, to forget that she had ever been dear to me; but I give you my word, Cardo, I *never* spoke a harsh or accusing word to her. I simply dropped her as far as possible out of my life; and she, though growing paler and thinner each day, still held her head up proudly; and while I seemed to ignore her presence—though, God knows, not a look nor a movement escaped me—Lewis was incessant in his tender attention to her.

"I had loved my brother passionately, fondly, and the feeling of bitter hatred which now took possession of me tore my very heart-strings, for, in spite of my suspicious and jealous nature, I loved these two—my wife and my brother—with an intensity few would have believed me capable of. Have I made this plain to you, Cardo? At last one evening, just at this time of the year, and at this hour of the day, Betto brought you to me in her arms. She had tears on her face, and as she looked down at her little white bundle, I noticed that a tear fell on your little hand. I did not like it, Cardo; though I thought I was perfectly indifferent to my child, I shrank from the sight of the tear on your hand, and hoped it did not prognosticate evil for you.

"Agnes was too ill to see me until the next day, when Betto said she was calling for me. I rose and went at once; but on the stairs, coming down to meet me, was a girl, whose face I recognised at once as that of Essec Powell's sister. I felt great indignation at the sight, as Agnes knew my intense dislike to the Methodist preacher, and, drawing back for her to pass, I said, 'I did not expect to meet a stranger in my own house at such a time, and I must beg that it may not happen again.'

"The girl passed on, with an angry flush upon her face. Betto gently drew me into an adjoining bedroom, and, with a troubled face, implored me not to give way to angry feelings. 'Be gentle to her,' she said; 'poor thing, she's as frail as an eggshell. Wait till she is well, master, and then—I pray God may bring some light out of this darkness.'

"I only nodded, and went gently into the sickroom. Agnes was lying propped up by pillows, her face almost as white as they. Her eyes were closed, as she had not heard my careful footsteps. I looked at her intently, while all sorts of thoughts and longings passed through my mind. At last the intensity of my gaze seemed to awaken her, for she opened her eyes, and for a moment there was a tremor on her lips.

"'Meurig,' she said, and she put out her hand, which I took in mine. Even while I held her hand I noticed on her bed a bunch of sweet violets which I had seen Lewis gather in the morning.—'Meurig, why have you been cold to me?' she asked, while her hand still lay in mine. 'If I have ever done anything to displease you, will you not forgive me, and kiss your little child?' and she looked down at your little head lying on her arm beside her. Oh, Caradoc, God alone knows the tumult of feelings which overwhelmed me. I cannot describe them! I stooped and kissed your little black head, and more, I stooped and kissed her pale forehead.

"'I forgive you,' I said.

"'Is that all?' she said.

"And as I hesitated, the old haughty flush rose to her forehead, and turning her head on her pillow, she said, 'I am tired now, and want to sleep.'

"So I turned away and closed the door gently, and I never saw her alive again, for that night she died suddenly. Swiftly the Angel of Death came, *at her call*. I believe it, Caradoc, for Dr. Hughes who was sent for hurriedly, declared he knew of no reason why she should not have lived.

"'I think she would have recovered, Wynne,' he said, 'had she wished to; but where there is no wish to live sometimes the powers of life fail, and the patient dies. Why she did not wish to live *I* do not know—perhaps *you* do,' and my old friend turned from me with a coldness in his manner, which has remained there ever since."

The Vicar sank into his chair again, as if the memory of his early trials had fatigued him, and Cardo, rising and approaching him, drew his hand gently over his black hair besprinkled with white. His son's tenderness seemed to reach the old man's heart.

Burying his face in his hands he gulped down a sob before he continued:

"Wait a minute, Cardo, you will not pity me when you have heard all my story. With the earliest dawn I rushed out of the house, which seemed to stifle me. I longed for the cool morning breezes, and God forgive me, if I thought too with longing of the cool sandy reaches that lay under the rippling waters of the bay! On the brow of the hill I met Essec Powell, who was out early to see a sick cow, and there, while my heart was sore to agony, and my brain was tortured to distraction, that man reproached me and insolently dared to call me to account for 'my inhuman conduct to my wife!'

"'Ach y fi! What are you? he said, with his strong Welsh accent, 'are you man or devil?' and he tore open the wounds which were already galling me unbearably. 'You bring a young girl from a happy home, where she was indulged and petted, and in a year's time you have broken her spirit, and you will break her heart. Because her brute of an uncle forbids his own daughter to go near her—my sister, her old schoolfellow, goes to see her in her trouble, and you turn her out of your house. I have longed for the opportunity of telling you what I thought of you, and of what all the world thinks of you.'

"I was a strong man, and he was a weak and shrivelled creature; I could have tossed him over the rocks into the sea below. It required a very strong effort to control my fury, but I did do so, and I turned away without answering him, except by a cold, haughty look. I hated him, Caradoc, and I have hated him ever since. He had not then heard of

Agnes's death, but the news flew fast through the neighbourhood, and I knew I was everywhere looked upon as her murderer!

"As I returned to my miserable home, I saw a man on horseback come out at the back gate. It was one of Colonel Vaughan's servants. I wondered what brought him there so early, but went in at the front gate to avoid meeting him. The house was very silent with its drawn blinds.

"When Betto came in with pale, tearful face, I asked her what had brought Colonel Vaughan's servant there so early.

"'A very strange thing, sir,' she said. 'He came to ask if Miss Vaughan was here? Colonel Vaughan was in great distress—if you call tearing about and swearing being in great distress—that was what Sam said, sir—because Miss Vaughan is nowhere to be found. Dir anwl! a strange thing, indeed, sir!'

"I was too miserable to pay much attention to her gossip, and began my breakfast alone, for Lewis had not appeared, and I dreaded to see him. I had thought it strange that in the turmoil of the night before, with the hurried footsteps and the arrival of the doctor's gig, my brother had not been disturbed, and he was apparently still sleeping. I shall never forget that long, long day. I thought my misery was beyond human endurance; little did I think that ere night it would be increased tenfold.

"I had refused to leave this room, though Betto had done her best to persuade me to eat the dinner which she had prepared She was always quick to read my thoughts and understand my feelings.

"'You would be quite as much alone in the parlour, sir, as you are here;' she said, 'for I can see nothing of Mr. Lewis. Indeed, I have been into his room, and I see he has not slept there last night,' and she flung her apron over her head, and swayed backwards and forwards crying 'Oh, anwl! beth na i!'[3] and she slowly and tremblingly drew a note out of her pocket and handed it to me. 'Perhaps that will tell you something, sir.'

"'Where did you find this?' I said,

"I found it on her bed after she died. Mr. Lewis had sent it by Madlen the nurse.'

"I tore the note open—I never dreamt it was dishonourable, neither do I now—and read the words which began the awakening that was to come with such force and bitterness. They were these:

"'MY DEAR AGNES,—My warmest congratulations upon the birth of your little one, and my deepest thanks for all your kindness to me and dear Nellie. Without your help we should never have been united. Good-bye, and may God grant us all a happy meeting at some future time.

"'Your ever grateful and devoted friends,

"'LEWIS WYNNE and ELLEN VAUGHAN.'

"I stared at the letter in a maze of troubled thought, the feeling uppermost in my mind being 'too late! too late! gone for ever, my beloved wife! and alienated from me for ever my little less loved brother!'

"'And this, sir,' said Betto, drawing another letter from her pocket, 'I found on Mr. Lewis's table. I think it is directed to you.'

"I hastily tore that open also, and read words that I cannot even now bring myself to repeat. They were too bitter in their tender upbraiding, in their innocent ignorance of my suspicions. They spoke of a love whose existence I had not guessed; of his devotion to Ellen Vaughan, my wife's cousin; of his deep gratitude to Agnes for her unfailing kindness to him and to his beloved Ellen; of his deep distress at my evident dislike of him.

"'What has come between us, Meurig?' he said. 'What has become of the faithful love of so many years? Is it possible you have grudged me the shelter of your roof and the food that I have eaten? I can scarcely believe it, and yet I fear it is true. Enclosed I leave you a cheque which will pay for anything I may have cost you; further than that I can only thank you for your, I fear, unwilling hospitality, and pray that some day we may meet, when this mysterious cloud, which I have deplored so much, may have cleared away.

"'When you read this, Ellen and I will have been married at St. Jorwerth's Church at Caer Madoc, and shall, I hope, have sailed for Australia, where you know I have long wished to go.'

"'Betto,' I said, 'is she lying dead and still upstairs?'

"'Yes, master, poor angel! still enough and white enough in her coffin! Why, sir, why?'

"'Because I wonder she does not come down and reproach us, for we have been wronging her from beginning to end, Betto! These letters prove to me that my brother—my beloved, innocent brother—was deeply in love with her cousin, Ellen Vaughan, and she, in the tenderness of her heart, helped to bring about their union, and was the means of delivering the letters which they wrote to each other. They were married this morning at Caer Madoc Church, and have probably already sailed for Australia.'

"Betto left me, sobbing bitterly. I think she has never forgiven herself; neither can I forgive myself, Cardo. As the years went on, my sorrow only deepened, and an intense longing arose in my heart for the friendship of the brother who had been so much to me for so many years. I wrote to him, Caradoc—a humble, penitent letter, beseeching his forgiveness even as a man begs for his life. He has never answered my letter. I know he is alive and thriving, as he writes sometimes to Dr. Hughes; but to me he has never sent a message or even acknowledged my letter, and I thirst for his forgiveness—I cannot die without it.

"I have long cherished the thought that when you came to man's estate I would send you to him. I would send the best of earthly treasure that I possess—my only son—to plead for me, to explain for me, and to bring back his love and forgiveness. Now, Cardo, will you go?"

"I will, father," said Cardo, rising and placing his hand in his father's.

"And can you think over what I have told you and still retain a little love and pity for your old father?"

"Father, I feel nothing but the deepest sorrow and pity for you both—father and mother. I don't know which is to be pitied most. Thank you for telling me all this, it explains so much that has puzzled me—it accounts for your sadness and gloom—and—and your apparent coldness. I will go to Australia, and, please God, I will bring back my uncle's love and forgiveness to you."

"God bless you, my boy, and good-night."

There was a warm hand-clasp, and Cardo left his father sitting by the flickering candle, which had burnt down to its socket.

[1] A blue mug containing a little over half a pint.

[2] Dear sweetheart.

[3] "Oh, dear! what shall I do?"

CHAPTER VIII.

THE OLD REGISTER.

The summer had passed, with all its charms of June roses and soft July showers, with its sweet, long days of sunshine, and its soft, west winds brine-laden, its flights of happy birds, and its full promise in orchard and corn-field.

Cardo and Valmai still haunted the woods by the Berwen, and walked along its banks, or sat listening to its trickling music as it hastened down to the sea; but there was a sadder look on both their faces. Cardo had new lines about his mouth, and Valmai had a wistful look in her blue eyes; both had an unaccountable premonition of something sorrowful to come.

"Oh, I am afraid of something," the girl had said one day, as she sat beside her lover, throwing pebbles into the brook, "something worse even than this terrible parting, which must come next month. What is it, Cardo? What is hanging over us? Something that darkens the sunlight and dims the moonlight to me? Are we parting for ever, do you think?"

"Nonsense, dearest," said Cardo cheerfully, though the little pucker between his eyes seemed to speak of the same anxiety and fear. "Isn't the separation which we must bear enough to account for all sorts of fears and depressing thoughts? It is that only which dims the sunshine to me, and makes me feel as if I were losing all the light and happiness out of my life; but let us cast our fears to the wind, Valmai, for a year will see all our troubles over; in a year's time I shall have returned, bringing, I hope, reconciliation and love to my dear old father—peace for his last days, Valmai. It is worth trying for, is it not?"

"Yes, yes; no doubt your presence will be more effectual than a letter."

"He thinks, too," said Cardo, "that a little travel by land and sea will brighten my life which he imagines must be so monotonous on this lonely west coast. He doesn't know of the happy hours we spend here on the banks of the Berwen, but when I return with loving greetings from his brother, and, who knows, perhaps bringing that brother with me in person, then, Valmai, while his heart is softened and tender, I will tell him of our love, I will ask his consent to our marriage, and if he refuses, then we must take our own way and be married without his consent. There is the thatch house just above the mill already waiting for us—it is my own, you know; and although old Sianco and his wife don't make much of it, think how lovely you and I would make it. Think of me sitting in the thatched porch behind those roses smoking, and you looking out through those pretty little lattice windows under the eaves."

Valmai sighed and blushed. "Oh, what dreams, Cardo; I cannot reach so far. My thoughts stop short at the long winter, when that glistening sea will be tossing and frothing under the fierce north-west wind. Oh, I know how it looks in the winter; and then to think that all that lies between me and you. What a trouble has come upon us when all seemed so bright and glorious."

"Yes, I have brought sorrow and unrest into your peaceful life. Will you give me up; will you break the bonds that are between us; and once more be free and happy?"

"Cardo," was all her answer, in a pained tone, as she placed her hand in his, "what are you talking about?"

"Nonsense, love, foolish nonsense. I know too well that nothing on earth or heaven can break the bonds that bind us to each other. And this terrible parting. I could bear it far more easily if you were mine, my very own, my wife, Valmai. Then I should feel that nothing could really part us. Can it not be? Can we not be married here quietly in the old church, with none but the sea-breezes and the brawling Berwen for company?"

"And the old white owl to marry us, I suppose. Oh, Cardo, another dream. No, no; wait until you return from that dreadful Australia, and then—"

"And then," said Cardo, "you will not say no."

"No," said the girl, looking frankly into his eager face, "I will not say no. But I must go; I am late. Shoni begins to ask me suspiciously, 'Wherr you going again, Valmai?' I am sure we could not go on much longer meeting here without his interference."

"How dreadful to have Shoni's red hair and gaitered legs dogging our footsteps in this fairy dell."

"To whom does this sweet valley belong, Cardo? To you?"

"To my father. If it ever comes into my possession, it will be so guarded that no stray foot shall desecrate its paths."

Cardo was not without hope of being able to overcome Valmai's reluctance to be married before he left the country, and as he and Gwynne Ellis returned one day from a sail he broached the subject to his friend.

"To-morrow will be the first of September," he said, as he watched the bulging sail and the fluttering pennon against the blue sky.

"Yes," answered Ellis, "I am sorry my holiday is coming to a close."

"I don't see why you should leave, although I am obliged to go."

"Oh, it will be quite time for me; everything jolly comes to an end some time or other."

"True," said Cardo, with a sigh.

"Well, you heave a sigh, and you look as grave and solemn as any of Essec Powell's congregation, and, upon my word, I don't see what you've got to look so glum about. Here you are, engaged to the prettiest girl in Wales; just going out for a year's travel and enjoyment before you settle down as a married man in that idyllic thatched cottage up the valley—a year to see the world in—and a devoted father (for he is that, Cardo, in spite of his cold ways) waiting to greet you when you come back. And Valmai Powell following every step you take with her loving and longing thoughts. No, no, Cardo; you have nothing to pull such a long face about. On the contrary, as I have said before, you are a lucky dog." (Cardo grunted.) "Besides, you are not obliged to go. It seems to me rather a quixotic affair altogether, and yet, by Jove! there is something in it that appeals to the poetic side of my nature. You will earn your father's undying gratitude, and in the first gush of his happiness you will gain his consent to your marriage with Valmai. Not a bad—rather a clever little programme."

"Oh, it is all very well for you to talk like that, Ellis; but nothing you say can lessen the bitterness of parting from Valmai. It is my own wish to go, and nothing shall prevent me; but I could bear the separation with much more fortitude if only—"

And he stopped and looked landwards, where the indistinct grey blur was beginning to take the pattern of fields and cliffs and beach.

"If what?" said Ellis, shifting the sail a little.

"If only I were married to Valmai."

"Phew! what next?" said Ellis, "married! Cardo Wynne, you are bringing things to a climax. My dear fellow, it would be far harder to part from a wife of a week than from a sweetheart of a year. That's my idea of wedded bliss, you see."

"Nonsense; it would not!" said Cardo. "It would give me a sense of security—a feeling that, come fair or come foul, nothing could really come between me and Valmai; and besides, I should not want her to be the wife of a week—I should be satisfied to be married even on the morning of my departure. Come, Ellis, be my friend in this matter. You promised when I first told you of my love for Valmai that you would help us out of our difficulties. You are an ordained priest; can you not marry us in the old church on the morning of the 14th? You know the *Burrawalla* sails on the 15th, and I go down to Fordsea the day before, but not till noon. Can you not marry us in the morning?"

"Has Valmai consented?" asked Ellis, sinking down in the prow of the boat and looking seriously at his companion.

"I—I—have not pressed the question, but if she agrees, will you do it?"

"Do it? My dear fellow, you talk as if it were a very simple affair. Do it, indeed! Where are the banns?"

"I would buy a license."

"And the ring?"

"At Caer Madoc." And Cardo began to look in deadly earnest.

"And what about the witnesses?"

"I have even thought of that. Are not your two friends, Wilson and Chester, coming to Abersethin next week?"

"So they are," said Ellis, "to stay until I leave. The very thing. They will be delighted with such a romantic little affair. But, Cardo, how about my duty to your father, who has been a very kind friend to me?"

"Well," said Cardo, "shall you be doing me an unkindness or the reverse when you make Valmai my wife? Is she not all that a woman can be? has she not every virtue and grace—"

"Oh, stop, my dear fellow! don't trouble to go through the inventory. I'll allow you at once she is perfect in mind, body, and soul—and the man to whom I marry her will owe me an eternal debt of gratitude!"

"True, indeed!" said Cardo, beginning energetically to lower the sails, and guide the boat safely to shore.

He said no more, until, after a tramp over the beach, both buried in their own thoughts, they drew near the path to Brynderyn.

"You will help me, then, at the old church on the morning of the fourteenth?"

"I will," said Ellis.

Before that morning arrived, Cardo had won from Valmai a frightened and half-reluctant consent.

She was no longer a child, but seemed to have matured suddenly into a woman of calm and reflective character, as well as of deep and tender feeling.

To be married thus hurriedly and secretly! How different to the beautiful event which she had sometimes pictured for herself! Where was the long, white veil? Where were the white-robed bridesmaids? Where were the smiling friends to look on and to bless? There would be none of these indeed, but then—there would be Cardo! to encourage and sustain her— to call her wife! and to entrust his happiness to her. Yes, she would marry him; she would be true to him—neither life nor death should shake her constancy—no power should draw from her lips the sweet secret of their marriage, for Cardo had said, "It must be a secret between us, love, until I return and tell my father myself—can you promise that, Valmai?" and with simple earnestness she had placed her hand in his, saying, "I promise, Cardo." And well might he put his trust in her, for, having given that word of promise, no one who knew her (they were very few) could doubt that she would keep it both in the letter and in the spirit.

The morning of the fourteenth dawned bright and clear, but as Cardo threw up his window and looked over the shining waters of the bay he saw that on the horizon gray streaky clouds were rising, and spreading fan-like upwards from one point, denoting to his long-accustomed eye that a storm was brewing.

"Well! it is September," he thought, "and we must expect gales."

He dressed hurriedly though carefully, and was soon walking with springy step across the beach, and up the valley to the old church. He cast a nervous glance towards Dinas, wondering whether Valmai would remember her promise—fearing lest she might have overslept herself— that Essec Powell or Shoni might have discovered her intentions and prevented their fulfilment; perhaps even she might be shut up in one of the rooms in that gaunt, grey house! Nothing was too unreasonable or unlikely for his fears, and as he approached the church he was firmly convinced that something had happened to frustrate his hopes; nobody was in sight, the Berwen brawled on its way, the birds sang the ivy on the old church tower glistened in the sunshine, and the sea-gulls sailed overhead as usual.

It had been decided the night before that Gwynne Ellis should leave the house alone at his usual early hour, and that his friends should come by the high road from Abersethin, and down by the river-path to the church. They were not to stand outside, but to enter the church at once, to avoid any possible observation; but in spite of this prior arrangement Cardo wondered why no one appeared.

"Can Gwynne Ellis be late? or those confounded fellows from Abersethin have forgotten all about it, probably? It's the way of the world!"

As he crossed the stepping-stones to the church he felt sure there would be no wedding, and that he would have to depart at midday still a bachelor, leaving Valmai to all sorts of dangers and trials!

When he entered the porch, however, and pushed open the door of the church, in the cool green light inside, he found his three friends waiting for him.

"I wonder why she doesn't come," he said, turning back to look up the winding path through the wood; "it's quite time."

"Yes, it is quite time," said Ellis. "I will go and put on my surplice. You three can sit in that ricketty front pew, or range yourselves at the altar rail, in fact—there she is coming down the path, you won't be kept long in suspense."

And as the three young men stood waiting with their eyes fixed upon the doorway, Valmai appeared, looking very pale and nervous. Gwynne Ellis had already walked up the church, and was standing inside the broken altar rails. Valmai had never felt so lonely and deserted. Alone amongst these strangers, father! mother! old friends all crowded into her mind; but the memory of them only seemed to accentuate their absence at this important time of her life! She almost failed as she walked up with faltering step, but a glance at Cardo's sympathetic, beaming face restored her courage, and as she took her place by his side she regained her composure. Before the simple, impressive service was over she was quite herself again, and when Cardo took her hand in his in a warm clasp, she returned the pressure with a loving smile of confidence and trust, and received the congratulations of Gwynne Ellis and his two friends with a smiling though blushing face.

The two strangers, never having seen her before, were much struck by her beauty; and indeed she had never looked more lovely. She wore one of her simple white frocks, and the white hat which had been her best during the summer, adorned only with a wreath of freshly gathered jessamine, a bunch of which was also fastened at her neck. With the addition of a pair of white gloves which Cardo had procured for her, she looked every inch a bride. She wore no ornament save the wedding ring which now glistened on her finger.

"Let us do everything in order," said Ellis. "Take your wife down to the vestry."

Cardo drew her hand through his arm, and at the word "wife," pressed it gently to his side, looking smilingly down at the blushing face beside him. When they reached the vestry, whose outer wall in the old tower was lying crumbling on the grass outside, while the two young men chatted freely with the bride and bridegroom, they were joined by Gwynne Ellis, carrying an old and time-worn book under his arm.

Cardo gasped, "I never thought of the register; it is kept in the new church! Is it absolutely necessary, Ellis? What shall we do? What have you there?"

"Why, the old register, of course! I furraged it out last night from that old iron chest inside the altar rails. There is another there, going back to the last century, I should think. I must have a look at them; they will be interesting."

"Ellis, you are a friend in need," said Cardo. "I had never thought of this part of the ceremony."

"No, be thankful you had a cool and collected head to guide you. See, here is a blank space at the bottom of one of these musty pages. It won't be at all *en règle* to insert your marriage here; but I dare not bring the new register out of the other church; moreover, there may be another wedding soon, and then yours would be discovered."

"What a genius you are!" said Cardo, while Gwynne Ellis wrote out in bold, black characters, under the faded old writing on the rest of the page, the certificate of Cardo and Valmai'a marriage.

"There, you have tied a knot with your tongue that you can't untie with your teeth! Here is your marriage certificate, Mrs. Wynne. I need not tell you to keep it safely."

Suddenly there was a rustling sound above them, which startled them all, and Cardo grasped Valmai hastily, to the great amusement of the young men.

It was the white owl, who had solemnly watched the proceedings in the vestry, and now thought it time to take her flight through the broken wall. "There Cardo," said Valmai, "I said the white owl would be at our wedding, and the sea breeze, and the Berwen; I heard them both while you were writing your name."

"Well now," said Gwynne Ellis, "Wilson, Chester, and I will leave you both, as I know what a short time you will have together."

And with many congratulations and good wishes, the three young men left the old church, leaving Cardo and Valmai to their last words before parting.

There was a ricketty, worm-eaten bench in the vestry, and here they sat down together. Cardo trying to keep up a cheerful demeanour, as he saw her face sadden and her eyes fill with tears.

"How lovely you look, my darling," he said. "How did you manage to escape Shoni's shrewd eyes in such finery?"

"I put my scarlet cloak on and drew the hood over my head, and it tumbled my hair," she said, with a little wan smile. Already the glamour of the wedding was giving way to the sorrow of parting. "I had my hat under my cloak. Oh, anwl! I am getting quite a deceitful girl!"

Cardo winced; was he sullying the pure soul? But there was no time for retrospection, the minutes were fleeting rapidly by, he had to return to his breakfast with his father, who would expect his last hours to be spent with him.

"When do you start from Brynderyn?" she asked, her voice growing lower and more sorrowful.

"At two o'clock, love, punctually; the cart has already gone with my luggage. Valmai, how can I part from you—how can I leave you, my beloved, my wife?"

"Oh, Cardo, Cardo!" was all her answer. She buried her face in her hands, and the tears trickled through her fingers.

Cardo drew them away tenderly.

"There is a tear on your ring, dear," he said, kissing it, "that must not be; let that at all events be the emblem of meeting and happiness and joy. Think, Valmai, only a year, and I shall come and claim you for my own! Confess, dearest, that it is a little solace that we are united before we are parted, that, whatever happens, you are my wife and I am your husband."

"Yes, indeed; indeed, it is my only solace, and I am going to be brave and hopeful. My ring I must not wear on my finger; but see, I have brought a white satin ribbon to tie it round my neck; it shall always be there until you take it off, and place it on my finger again."

"And you will keep our secret until I return, darling?"

"Yes," said Valmai impressively, "*until you come back, Cardo, and give me leave to reveal it.*"

"We must part, fanwylyd; my father must not miss me."

"No, no—go, I will not keep you back."

There was a long, passionate embrace, during which the white owl flapped in again to her nest.

"Good-bye and good-bye, darling, and farewell until we meet again."

"Leave me here, Cardo. Good-bye, dearest husband!"

And so they parted, and, in the memory of both, for many a long year the sound of the Berwen held a place, and the flap of the white owl's wings brought back to Valmai memories of pain and happiness, mixed together in a strange tumult. Slowly she made her way up the path to Dinas, the scarlet cloak was taken out from the bush under which it had been hidden, and, enveloped in its folds, she entered the house. Going up to her own room, she took off the sacred wedding dress, and, folding it carefully, laid it away with its bunch of jessamine, while she donned another much like it, but of a warmer material, for she loved white, and seldom appeared in a coloured dress.

With Cardo the hours slipped by quickly. His father had many last directions to give him, and Betto had endless explanations to make.

"You will find your gloves in your pocket, Mr. Cardo, and your clean handkerchiefs are in the leather portmanteau; but only six are by themselves in the little black bag."

Gwynne Ellis had accompanied his friends to their lodgings at Abersethin, and after breakfast returned to Brynderyn; they had all been charmed with the bride's appearance.

"By Jove! Ellis," Chester had said, "I think I envy that Wynne in spite of the parting. I have never seen such a lovely bride!"

"Any more pearls of the sort to be found in this out-of-the-way place?" asked Wilson.

"No, I have seen none," said Ellis; "and I doubt if you will find one anywhere," for he was an enthusiastic admirer of Valmai.

"I have quite enjoyed the part we have taken in this romantic little affair —eh, Wilson?"

"Ra—ther!" he replied.

"But don't forget it is to be a dead secret," said Ellis, as he left the door.

"Oh! honour bright!"

At two o'clock punctually Cardo and his father seated themselves in the light gig, which was the only carriage the Vicar affected, and when Betto had bid him a tearful good-bye, with all the farm-servants bobbing in the background, Gwynne Ellis, grasping his hand with a warm pressure, said:

"Good-bye, Wynne, and God bless you! I shall look forward with great pleasure to meeting you again when you return from Australia. I shall stay here a week or two at your father's invitation."

"Yes," said the Vicar, in a wonderfully softened tone, "it would be too trying to have the house emptied at one blow."

As they drove along the high road together and crossed the little bridge over the Berwen Valley, the Vicar, pointing with his whip, drew Cardo's attention to the stile beside the bridge.

"This is the stile which I saw Ellen Vaughan crossing the day I met your mother waiting for her. I met my brother afterwards, and oh! how blinded I was! But there, a man who is carried away by his passions is like a runaway horse, which, they say, becomes blind in the eagerness of his flight."

It was needless to call Cardo's attention to the stile. His first meeting with Valmai was so intimately connected with it; and as he crossed the bridge, he called to mind how they had shared their gingerbread under the light of the moon.

"Perhaps you never noticed there was a stile there?" said the Vicar.

"Yes," said Cardo, turning round to take a last look at it and the bridge, and—was it fancy, or did he see something waving in the wind?

For a moment he laid his hand on the reins with the idea of running back to see, but "Jim" was fresh, and, resenting the check, swerved uncomfortably aside.

"Let him go," said the Vicar. "What do you want?"

"Nothing, sir. For a moment I thought I would go back and take a last look at the valley; but never mind, let us go on. How black it looks in front!"

"A storm rising, I think," said his father.

"Yes. There will be a gale from the north-west; we shall catch it on the *Burrawalla*, I expect. Well, I have often wished to see a storm at sea."

His father did not answer, but looked gloomily on at the gathering darkness in front. He was full of fears for his son's safety, but it was not his nature to speak openly of any tender feelings. His late confession, although it had comforted and soothed him, was yet a mystery to himself, and he thought of it with a kind of awkward surprise and something like resentment. He was, however, unusually talkative and even gentle as they drove on together. When at last he had seen Cardo fairly off in the coach, with his luggage piled on the top, he turned homewards with a heavy foreboding at his heart.

Should he ever see his son again? Had he sent him from his native land to be lost to him for ever? And how willingly he had given in to his father's wishes! But, certainly there was nothing to attract him to his home—nothing but his love for a surly old father!

"A fine fellow!" he soliloquised, with a side jerk of his head. "A fine fellow! a son to be proud of!"

And when Gwynne Ellis joined him at tea, they vied with each other in their praises of Cardo's character.

If Cardo had followed his impulse and returned to look over the stile, he would have found on the mossy hedge inside a little white heap of misery. For Valmai, who had watched for an hour to catch a last glimpse of him, had been frightened when she saw the "Vicare du" looking towards the stile, and evidently drawing Cardo's attention to it; she had shrunk back until they had passed, and then standing on the hedge, had waved a last good-bye, and immediately afterwards slipped down in an abandonment of grief. She remained for some time sobbing and moaning on the grass, until at last her passion of tears subsided. Almost suddenly growing calmer, she stood up, and, not attempting to dry her eyes, let the tears roll slowly down her cheeks. She clasped her hands, and tried to steady her voice as, looking up at the flying clouds above her, she spoke words of encouragement to herself. "Valmai," she said, "you must learn to bear your sorrow in silence; you are no longer a girl—you are a wife! and you must be a brave and good woman!"

For a moment she continued to look steadily up at the clouds and beyond them into the depths of blue sky which showed here and there between the storm rifts, then she quietly put on her hat and returned down the well-known path to the river, and with steady, set face and firm step made her way homeward.

When her uncle appeared at the tea-table, he carried two large books under his arm, and when the meal was over the lamp was lighted and the red curtains drawn. Up here on the cliffs the wind was already blowing furiously; it roared in the chimneys, and found its way in through every chink in the badly-fitting windows.

"Now, let me see—chap. xii.—Valmai, have you found it? St. Antwn's sermon to the fishes," and he settled himself in his usual position, with legs crossed, head thrown back, listening with evident pleasure, while Valmai read and read, her thoughts defying control, and for ever following Cardo on his journey.

"Oh, how the wind is shrieking, uncle; it is like a human creature in pain!"

"Wind?" said the old man, looking with dreamy eyes at the girl so full of hopes and fears—"storm? Well, it does blow a little, but it's nothing. Go on, Valmai, you are not reading so good as usual," and once more she applied herself to the page, and endeavoured to keep her thoughts from roaming.

CHAPTER IX.

REUBEN STREET.

All night the storm increased in violence, blowing straight from the north-west with an incessant fury which tossed and tore the waters of the bay. Against the black cliffs the foaming waves hurled themselves like fierce animals leaping up to reach their prey, but the adamant rocks, which had defied their rage for centuries, still stood firm, and flung them back panting and foaming into the swirling depths below, to rise again with ever-increasing strength, until the showers of spray reached up even to the grassy slopes on which the sheep huddled together.

Valmai had lain with wide-open eyes through the long hours of the night, listening with a shrinking fear to every fresh gust which threatened to sweep the old house away. No raging storm or shrieking wind had ever before done more than rouse her for a moment from the sound sleep of youth, to turn on her pillow and fall asleep again; but to-night she could not rest, she was unnerved by the strain and excitement of the day, and felt like some wandering, shivering creature whose every nerve was exposed to the anger of the elements. When at last it was time to rise and prepare her uncle's breakfast, she felt beaten and weary, and looked so pale and hollow-eyed, that Shoni, who was fighting his way in at the back door as she appeared, exclaimed in astonishment.

"What's the matter with you, Valmai? You bin out in the storm all night?"

"Almost as bad, indeed, Shoni; there's a dreadful wind it is."

"Oh, 'tis not come to the worst yet," said Shoni.

The doors continued to bang and the windows to rattle all through that day and the greater part of the next, and it was not till the evening of the third day that Valmai ventured to put on her cloak and pay a visit to Nance's cottage. The tide was low as she crossed the Rock Bridge, and there was no danger, therefore, from the waves. On her return she recalled the events of the last storm, when Cardo's strong arm had saved her from death.

Her eyes filled with tears and her lips quivered a little as she remembered that night; but she set herself bravely to struggle with her sorrow, and to look forward with hope and joy to the future.

When she entered the little parlour, which her neat fingers had transformed into a nest of cosy comfort, she found her uncle standing at the table, looking dazed and helpless.

"Oh, Valmai!" he said, "here's a letter from John, my brother, and indeed

I don't know what am I to do."

"What is the matter, uncle? Is he ill?"

"Yes, he is very ill. He has broke his leg, and he got no one to look after his house; and he is asking will you go down to take care of him. Will you go, Valmai? He got lot of money. I will drive you down to Caer Madoc to the coach. That will take you to the station to meet the train, and you will be in Fordsea by four o'clock to-morrow."

Fordsea! What visions crowded round the name. Cardo had been there so lately, and now where was he? Out on that stormy sea, every moment increasing the distance between them.

"I will go if you like, uncle, and nurse him until he gets well."

"There's a good gel, indeed; and you will kom back to me again, 'cos I am used to you now, and you are reading very nice to me, and saving a great deal of my old eyes. He got a servant," he added, "but she is only an ole ooman, coming in in the morning and going home in the evening."

"Oh, yes, I will manage very well," said Valmai.

She grasped at the idea of change of scene and life, hoping it would help her to regain her peace of mind. So the next day saw her on her way to Caer Madoc, driven by her uncle in the rickety old gig which had carried him on his preaching expeditions for years. Along the high road Malen bore them at a steady trot, and when Valmai took her place in the coach, and bid her uncle good-bye, she called to mind that only two days ago Cardo had been its occupant, and her heart was full of wistful longings. Yes, she felt she was a foolish girl, but she was always intending to grow into a sensible and useful *wife*; and, with this virtuous intention in her mind, she tried to banish all vain regrets, and a serious, composed little look came over her mouth.

Arrived at Fordsea, she sought for her uncle's house, it was in Reuben Street, she knew, and not far from the docks. Reaching the roadway, she caught sight of the foaming white waves in the harbour, and wondered how far the *Burrawalla* had already got on her way towards the Antipodes.

"Captain Powell of *The Thisbe*?" said a lounging sailor who was passing, with his hands in his pockets and his cap very much at the back of his head. "Yes, miss, Aye knows him well. It's not far from here, and Ay'll be passing his door. Will Aye carry your bag?"

And, not waiting for an answer, he hoisted it on his shoulder, and signed to her to follow him. He was right; she had not far to go before she reached the little, uneven row of houses called Reuben Street, at one of which an old woman, with bucket and cloth, was preparing to wash the doorstep.

"Here's the young leddy come," said the sailor, pushing the portmanteau into the passage.

"Will I pay you something?" said Valmai, nervously fingering her purse.

"Aw naw, nawthin' at all," said the sailor, hurrying away, with a flush on his face that showed her her hesitation had not been unwarranted.

In fact, Jim Harris considered himself a "friend of the family," and had gone to the station with the express intention of meeting the "young leddy." Having for years sailed under Captain Powell, he still haunted his house whenever he was on dry land. Every morning he went in to shave him, and in the evening he mixed his toddy for him and made him comfortable for the night, expecting and receiving no more than the friendship and grateful thanks of the old man who had, not so long ago, been his captain. Having deposited the portmanteau, Valmai had scarcely time to thank him before he had slouched away with a polite touch of his cap.

"My uncle lives here? Captain Powell."

"Yes, miss, and thank the Lord you've come, for Ay've bin ewt on the road looking for you twenty taimes to-day, though Ay towld him you couldn't come afore the train. There he is, knocking again. You go up to him, miss, that's all he wants. Ay'll bring your bag up, honey. There's your room, raight a-top of the stayurs; and there's your uncle's door on the first landing. Ye'll hear him grumbling." And, following these instructions, Valmai knocked at the first door she came to.

"Come in, and be tarnished to you," said an extraordinarily gruff voice; and, almost before she had time to enter the room, a heavy book came flying at her. Fortunately, it missed its aim, and she stood for a moment irresolute at the door, while her uncle, without looking at her, continued to rail at his much-enduring domestic, whom he was accustomed to manage by swearing at and flattering in turns. His voice was a guttural rumbling, which seemed to come from some cavernous bronchial depths.

"Ain't the little gel come yet?"

"Uncle, here I am," said Valmai, approaching the bed with a frightened look, though she tried to put on a placid smile.

The shaggy head turned on its pillow.

"Hello and so you are; in spite of that old witch saying for the last hour that you couldn't 'acome yet. Come here, my beauty, and shake hands with your old uncle. Ay've got one hand, you see, to shake with you."

"Yes, uncle, and to throw books at me when I come in."

There was a low, gurgling laugh, which deepened the colour in the old man's face so much that Valmai, fearing he was going to have a fit, hastened to say something quiet and calming.

"I came as soon as I could, uncle. We were so sorry to hear of your accident. How did it happen?"

"The Lord knows, my dear, Ay don't, for Ay've walked up that street four or five times every day the last faive years, and never done such a thing afore. But there—" and he began to gurgle again, to Valmai's horror, "there must always be a beginning to everything, so Ay slipped on a d—d stone, somehow or other, and, being no light weight, broke my leg, and sprained my wrist into the bargain. Take off your things, may dear. Are you up for nursing an old man till he's well again?"

"Indeed, I'll do my best, whatever," said Valmai, taking off her hat and cloak. "Uncle Essec said I was to stay until you were quite well."

"That's raight. Ay knew you'd come, my gel, though that old devil wanted me to think that perhaps you wouldn't. 'She'll come,' ay sez, 'and if she's like her father she'll come almost afore she's asked.' So ready, he was; and so kind. And how's old Essec? Got his nose buried in them mouldy books same as ever?"

"Just the same," said Valmai. "Shall I take my things to my own room?"

"Yes, may dear. It's the little room a-top of this. Where's that old hag now? She ought to be here to show you your room," and reaching a heavy stick, which stood by his bedside, he knocked impatiently on the bare boarded floor, calling Mrs. Finch! Mrs. Finch! so loudly at the same time, that Valmai seriously feared he would burst a blood vessel.

"Deaf as a post," he said, gasping.

"Leave it to me, uncle; don't tire yourself. She has shown me my room, and there she is taking my bag up. Now, see how quickly I'll be back, and bring you a nice cup of tea, and one for myself in the bargain, for I am famishing," and she left the room with a cheerful nod towards the old man.

"Bless her purty face!" said the rumbling voice when the door was closed. "Ay don't want her cup o' tea! Never could bear the slosh, but Ay'm blest if Ay won't drink it to the dregs to please her."

In a very short time Valmai returned, carrying a tray laid out neatly with tea-things for two; and, drawing a little round table towards the bed, placed the tray upon it, while Mrs. Finch brought in some slices of cold ham.

"There, you see," said Valmai, "I'm making myself quite at home. I asked Mrs. Finch for that ham."

"Of course you did, may dear! Didn't Ay tell you, you old addlepate," he said, turning to poor Mrs. Finch, whose only desire seemed to be to find a place for the ham and get out of the room—"didn't Ay tell you the lil gel would come?"

"Iss you did—many taimes to-day," said Mrs. Finch, while the old man fumbled about for another book to throw after her.

Valmai laughed, but chided gently;

"Oh, poor old thing, uncle! She flew about like lightning to get the tea ready. Now, here's a lovely cup of tea!"

"Ah! It do smell beautiful!" And he allowed himself to be raised up on his pillow, while he drank the tea down at a gulp.

"Bravo! uncle," said Valmai; "ready for another?"

"Another! Oh, dash it, no; one's enough, may dear. 'Twas very naice and refreshing. Now you have your tea, and let me look at you."

And as Valmai partook of her tea and bread and butter and ham, even his hospitable feelings were satisfied.

"Now I'm going to ring for Mrs. Finch to take these things away, uncle; no more books, mind!"

"No, no," he said, laughing; "she's had four to-day, and a pair of slippers, and that'll do for one day. After all, she's a good ole sole! though why sole more than whiting or mackerel Ay never could make ewt. She knows me and my ways, may dear, and Ay pay her well. Eight shillings a week regular! and she only comes at ten and leaves at faive. Oh! bless you, *she* knows when she's well off, or she wouldn't put up with the books and slippers. Ay know 'em!" he added, with a shrewd wink, which set Valmai laughing again. When Mrs. Finch came in for the tray he was quite amiable. "Well, ole gel," he said, "this is the night for your wages, isn't it?"

"Iss, sir," said the woman, with a sniff and a bob curtsey.

"There's my purse. Count it out to her, may dear. Eight shillings, every penny, and there's a shilling overhead for good luck, Mrs. Finch, becos the lil gel has come to manage the ship for us. Now remember, she's capting now and you're the mate."

"Iss, sir, and thank you," said Mrs. Finch, disappearing with practised celerity through the doorway.

And so Valmai took her place at once as "captain" of her uncle's house, and, in spite of his gruff ways and his tremendous voice, she felt more at home with him than with Essec Powell, for here her presence was valued, and she felt sure that she had a place in the old man's warm heart.

She slept heavily through the next night, and in the morning awoke refreshed, and with a feeling of brightness and cheerfulness which she had not expected to feel so soon. Her new life would give her plenty to do, to fill up every hour and to drive out all useless regrets and repinings.

Deep in her heart lay the one unsatisfied longing. Nothing could alter that; nothing could heal the wound that Cardo's departure had made except the anticipation of his return. Yes, that day would come! and until then she would bear her sorrow with a brave heart and smiling face. The weather continued rough and stormy, and, looking out from her bedroom window, the grey skies and windswept streets made no cheerful impression upon her. The people, the hurrying footsteps, and the curious Pembrokeshire accent, gave her the impression of having travelled to a foreign country, all was so different to the peaceful seclusion of the Berwen banks. It was a "horrid dull town," she thought and with the consciousness of the angry white harbour which she had caught sight of on her arrival, her heart sank within her; but she bravely determined to put a good face on her sorrow. On the second morning after her arrival she was sitting on the window-seat in her uncle's room, and reading to him out of the newspaper, when the bang of the front door and a quick step on the stair announced the doctor's arrival.

"Well, captain," he said, "and how is the leg getting on?"

He was a bright, breezy-looking man, who gave one the impression of being a great deal in the open air, and mixing much with the "sailoring." Indeed, he was rather nautical in his dress and appearance.

"You have a nurse, I see," he added, looking at Valmai with a shrewd, pleasant glance.

"Yes," said the captain, "nurse and housekeeper in one. She is may niece, poor Robert's daughter, you know."

"Ah! to be sure," said the doctor, shaking hands with her. "He went out as a missionary, didn't he?"

"Yes, to Patagonia, more fool he," said the captain. "Leaving his country for the sake of them niggers, as if there wasn't plenty of sinners in Wales for him to preach to. But there, he was a good man, and Ay'm a bad 'un," and he laughed, as though very well satisfied with this state of affairs.

"Have you heard the news?" said the doctor, while he examined the splints of the broken leg.

"No, what is it?" rumbled the captain.

"Why, the *Burrawalla* has put back for repairs, Just seen her tugged in— good deal damaged; they say, a collision with the steam-ship, *Ariadne*.

"By gosh! that's bad. That's the first accident that's ever happened to Captain Owen, and he's been sailing the last thirty years to my knowledge. Well, Ay'm tarnished, but Ay'm sorry."

"Always stops with you?" inquired the doctor.

"Yes, has all his life. There's the little back parlour and the bedroom behind it always kept for him."

"Well, you are going on very nicely. Now for the wrist."

The captain winced a little and swore a good deal while his wrist was under manipulation. It evidently pained him more than the broken leg.

"What the blazes are your about, doctor? Leave it alone—do."

"Come, come, now that's all over. You must mind and keep it very quiet. No shying of books and things, remember. Well, good-bye; come and see you again to-morrow. I daresay you'll see Captain Owen by and by. Good-bye, my dear," turning to Valmai, "take care of your uncle." And like a gust of wind he ran down the stairs, banged the front door, and was gone.

Valmai had dropped her paper and listened breathlessly to his communications, and she was sitting, pale and silent, as a tumult of exciting thoughts rushed into her mind.

"The *Burrawalla* come back! damaged! a collision! And Cardo, where was he? Was it possible that the dull grey town contained her lover?"

"Well, to be sure, here's a pretty kettle of fish," said her uncle, using strong compulsion to adapt his words to the squeamishness of a "lil gel." "Here's the *Burrawalla*, Valmai, put back for repairs, may friend Captain Owen's ship, you know. Sech a thing has never happened afore. You'll have to put his rooms ready, may dear, and laight a fayer by 'm by, for he's sure to be here to-night. You'll look after him, won't you?"

"Yes, uncle, I'll do my best, whatever. I had better go and get his sheets aired at once." And she left the room, glad to hide her pale face and trembling hands from her uncle.

Once outside the bedroom door, she crossed her hands on her bosom, as though to stop the tumultuous beating of her heart. What was going to happen? Should she hear Cardo's name from Captain Owen? Could she find her way to the docks? and as a gleam of sunlight shone in through the little window in the linen cupboard, she thought what a bright and happy place Fordsea was after all.

She hurried through her domestic preparations, and then, after a consultation with her uncle, made an expedition into the market, ordering supplies for the following days. When she returned, the front door was open, and, entering the passage, she heard loud voices in her uncle's room, and gently pushing the door open, saw a rough-bearded, blue-eyed man standing by the bedside.

"Well, that's all settled, then; you'll let the young man have my rooms? 'Twill only be for two or three days. And this is your niece? Well, upon my word, I begin to repent of my bargain. Hard lines for me! to be tied to the docks night and day to watch those repairs, while my young friend comes here to be taken care of and fussed about by my old friend and such a pretty girl."

Valmai felt disappointed; she had hoped to learn something from their guest of Cardo and his whereabouts.

"I am sorry," she said, as he took his departure, "that you can't stay here."

The gallant captain taking her hand, looked admiringly at the blushing face.

"By Jove, and so am I; but dooty is dooty, my dear, especially your dooty to your ship. Good-bye, come and see you again soon." And once more Valmai was left to conflicting emotions.

The day passed quickly, while she divided her attention between her uncle's wants and her preparations for the guest who was to arrive about six o'clock. Mrs. Finch would prepare the tea and roast the fowl which was to accompany it, and Valmai added little dainty touches of flowers and lights for the table.

"We won't light the candles till he knocks at the door; and when he has once sat down to his meal, I can manage about taking it out; but I am very nervous. I wonder what he will be like."

Her uncle knocked and called incessantly, giving fresh directions and asking innumerable questions, in his anxiety that his friend's friend should be made comfortable under his roof. At last everything was ready, a bright fire burning in the grate threw its glow through the open door of the adjoining bedroom, and flickered on the prettily-arranged dressing-table. All looked cosy and home-like, and when everything was completed, Valmai retired to put on a fresh frock of white serge.

"His name is Gwynn," said her uncle at last, while she listened breathlessly to the opening of the front door, and the entrance of the stranger.

"This is Captain Powell's house?" said a voice which set Valmai's pulses throbbing, and all the blood in her body rushed to her face and head. For a moment she felt dizzy, and she all but dropped the tray which she was holding for her uncle.

"Don't you be afraid, may dear," said the captain consolingly. "Captain Owen tells me he's a ra-al gentleman, and they are always easily pleased. He won't look at you, may dear; but, by Jingo, if he does, Ay'm not ashamed of you. Now, you go down, and make a nice curtsey, may dear, not like Mrs. Finch makes it, you know, but as, Ay bet, you have larnt it at the dancing school; a scrape behind with one foot, you know, and hold your frock with two hands, and then say, 'My uncle hopes you will make yourself quite at home, sir.'"

"Oh, uncle!" said Valmai, in despair, "he's not come out yet from his bedroom. Won't I wait till he is seated down at his tea, and till Mrs. Finch has gone?"

"Well, confound the ole 'ooman," said the captain, knocking violently on the floor, "where is she now? Why don't she come and tell me how he's getting on? Roast fowl nicely browned, may dear? Egg sauce?"

"Yes, and sausages, uncle. There, he is come out now, and Mrs. Finch is taking the fowl in; he is saying something to her and laughing. Now he is quite quiet," said the girl.

"Of course; he's attending to business." And for the next quarter of an hour, Valmai had the greatest difficulty in restraining her uncle's impatience.

"Let him have time to finish, uncle!"

"Yes, yes; of course, may dear, we'll give him time."

"I can now hear Mrs. Finch say, Is there anything else, sir? So she is going. Yes, there, she has shut the front door. Oh, dear, dear! Now if he rings, I *must* go in."

"Oh, dear, dear," said the captain, in an irritable voice, "what is there to oh, dear, dear, about? You go down and do as Ay tell you, and you can just say, as the ladies do, you know, 'I hope your tea is to your laiking, sir.' Go now, at once." And as she went, with hesitating footsteps, he threw an encouraging "Good gel" after her.

CHAPTER X.

THE WEB OF FATE.

Arrived on the door-mat of the little parlour, where Cardo Wynne was coming to an end of a repast, which showed by its small remnants that it had been thoroughly appreciated, Valmai fell into a tremor of uncertainty. Was it Cardo? Yes, she could not be mistaken in the voice; but how would he take her sudden appearance? Would he be glad? Would he be sorry? And the result of her mental conflict was a very meek, almost inaudible knock.

"Come in," shouted Cardo from within. Another pause, during which Cardo said, "Why the deuce don't you come in?"

The door was slowly opened, and there appeared Valmai, blushing and trembling as if she had been caught in some delinquency.

For a moment Cardo was speechless with astonishment, but not for long, for, in answer to Valmai's apologetic, "Oh! Cardo, it's me; it's only me, whatever!" she was folded in his arms, and pressed so close to his heart that her breath came and went in a gasp half of fright and half of delight.

"Gracious heavens! What does it mean?" he said, holding her at arms' length. "My own little wild sea-bird! My little white dove! My darling, my wife! Where have you flown from? How are you here?"

They were interrupted by a thundering knock on the floor above them. Cardo started. "What is that?" he said.

Valmai laughed as she somewhat regained her composure.

"It is Uncle John," she said. "Wait while I run up to him, and then I will come back and explain everything."

"Uncle John!" said Cardo in bewilderment, as he saw through the doorway the graceful white figure flit up the narrow stairs. "Uncle John! Can that be Captain Powell? Of course, old Essec's brother, no doubt. I have heard they are Pembrokeshire people."

"Well, how is he getting on?" said the old man, as Valmai entered blushing.

"Oh, all right, uncle! there isn't much of the fowl left, so I'm sure he enjoyed it."

"That's raight, may gel, that's raight. Now make him as comfortable as you can. May jar of tobacco is down there somewhere, and there's a bottle of whisky in the corner cupboard. Ay hear Jim Harris coming to the door; now don't disturb me any more, and tell Mr. Gwyn Ay'll be happy to see him tomorrow. Now, mind, no larks."

"No what?" said Valmai, with puckered eyebrows.

"Larks, larks! Don't you know what 'larks' are, child? Ay bet you do, with that pretty face of yours."

Valmai still looked puzzled.

"Well, 'high jinks,' then; flirtation, then; will that suit your ladyship?"

"Oh, flirtation! Very well, uncle, good-night." And after a kiss and another "good gel," Valmai passed Jim at the doorway, and went slowly downstairs.

Cardo stood at the bottom awaiting her with wide open arms.

"Come, come, Valmai; how slow you are, fanwylyd. I am waiting for you. What made you step so slowly down the stairs?" he said, as he drew her towards him; "you should have flown, dearest."

"I was thinking," said Valmai.

"And of what?"

"Thinking whether I had told uncle an untruth. He said, 'no flirtations,' 'larks;' he called it; and I said, 'Very well, uncle,' and I was wondering whether husband and wife could flirt."

Cardo laughed heartily.

"Come and sit by me, Valmai," he said, "and let us see. Come and explain to me how, in the name of all that is wonderful and delightful, I find you here, with your head nestled on my shoulder, instead of being separated from me by wind and wave, as, in the natural course of events, you should have been?"

"Well, you see, Cardo, when you passed the stile on Thursday (oh, that sad Thursday!)"—Cardo shared in the shiver which shook her—"I was there, to catch a last glimpse of you; but I was afraid to show myself because of the 'Vicare du,' so I shrank down behind the hedge till you had passed, and then I stood up and waved my handkerchief, and then you were gone; and I fell down on the moss, and cried dreadfully. Oh, Cardo, I did feel a big rent in my heart. I never thought it was going to be mended so soon; and I roamed about all day, and tried hard to keep my sorrow out of my thoughts, but I couldn't; it was like a heavy weight here." And she crossed her hands on her bosom. "All that day, and all the next, I went about from place to place, but *not* to the Berwen, I could not walk there without you; and the next morning, when I came back from Ynysoer, where I had been to see Nance, I found my uncle reading a letter. It was from Jim Harris, the sailor, who does everything for Uncle

John, to say he had broken his leg, and would I come and nurse him? And indeed, I was very glad, whatever, to have something to do; so I came at once. Uncle Essec drove me to Caer Madoc, and I thought what a dull, grey town Fordsea was, until this morning when the doctor came and said the *Burrawalla* had come back for repairs; and then the sun seemed to shine out, and when I went out marketing, I could not think how I had made such a mistake about Fordsea. It is the brightest, dearest place!"

"It is Paradise," said Cardo.

"There's Jim Harris going! I must go and lock the door."

"Everything is all raight, miss, and Ay wish you good-night," said Jim, as he went out. He went through the same formula every night.

"Now for my part of the story," said Cardo, when she returned.

"First let me take the tea-things away, Cardo."

"No, no, bother the tea-things; let them be for a while, Valmai. I forbid your carrying them away at present, and, you know, you have promised to obey."

"Yes, indeed, and to love you, and no one ever did love anybody as much as I love you. Oh, I am sure of it. No, indeed, Cardo. Not more, whatever, but you know, you know," and her head drooped low, so that he had to raise her chin to look into her face.

"I know what? I know you are my wife, and no earthly power can separate us now. Where is your ring, dearest? It should be on this little finger."

"No, it is here," and Valmai pressed her hand on her neck; "you know I was to wear it here instead of on my finger until next year."

"Until I came back, darling; and until I took it off myself and placed it on your finger. Come, wifie, where is it?"

Valmai allowed herself to be persuaded, and Cardo, undoing the white satin ribbon, drew off the ring, and placed it on her finger. She looked at it thoughtfully.

"Am I, then, really your wife, Cardo?"

"Really and truly, Valmai; signed, sealed, and delivered," he said; "and let me see the man who dares to come between us!" and his black eyes flashed with a look of angry defiance which Valmai had not seen there before.

"Oh, anwl! I hope your eyes will never look like that at me," she said.

"But they will," said Cardo, laughing, "if you are the culprit who tries to divide us. You don't know how fierce I can be."

"Please, sir, can I take the tea-things now?"

"On condition that you come back at once. No, let me carry them out for you, dearest; you shall not begin by waiting upon me."

"Oh, but I must, Cardo, for old Mrs. Finch goes home when she has brought the tea in always."

And she laughed merrily at Cardo's clumsy efforts at clearing away. As she opened the door into the passage a tremendous roaring and snorting filled the air.

"What on earth is that?" said Cardo.

"It is my uncle snoring, and if you dropped that tray (which I am afraid you will) the clatter wouldn't awake him."

"Good old man! let him rest, then. You are not going to wash up those things?"

"No, Mrs. Finch will do that in the morning. And now, Cardo, I must do what my uncle told me to do," she said, as they returned into the cosy parlour, glowing with the light of the blazing fire; and, holding up her dress with her two fingers, she made a prim little curtsey, and said:

"I hope your tea has been to your liking, sir? And now for the rest of my duty. Here is his jar of tobacco, and here is the kettle on the hob, and here is the bottle of whisky, and here are the slippers which I had prepared for you."

"Little did I think, Valmai, it was you who had made everything look so cosy and sweet for me—these flowers on the table and all those pretty fal-lals on my dressing-table. Little did I think it was my little wife who had prepared them all for me. But as I entered the front door a strange feeling of happiness and brightness came over me."

"And I knew the first tone of your voice, Cardo. Oh, I would know it anywhere—among a thousand."

There were innumerable questions for the one to ask and the other to answer as they sat in the glowing firelight. First, there was the description of the repairs required by Captain Owen's ship—"Blessed repairs, Valmai!"—and the extraordinary special Providence which had caused the ss. *Ariadne* to collide at midships with the *Burrawalla*, and, moreover, so to damage her that Cardo's berth and those of the three other inmates of his cabin would alone be disturbed by the necessary repairs.

"Captain Owen thinks we shall be ready to sail in three days, so it is not worth while writing to my father," said Cardo. "The thick fog which looked so dismal as I drove into Caer Madoc with him—how little I guessed it would culminate in the darkness which brought about the collision, and so unite me with my beloved wife. Valmai, if Providence ever arranged a marriage, it was yours and mine, dearest."

"But, Cardo—"

"'But me no buts,' my lovely white sea-bird. Nothing can alter the fact that you are my own little wife."

"Yes, I know," said Valmai, "but if you love me as much as you say you do, grant me one request, Cardo."

"A hundred, dearest; what is it?"

"Well, we have had to be deceitful and secret—more so than I have ever been in my life. We could not help it; but now, here, let us be open. Give me leave to tell my uncle the truth."

"Valmai! he will write at once to his brother, and the news will reach my father, and it will break his heart to find I have deceived him. No, let me be the first to tell him. I shall have no hesitation in doing so when I return this time next year."

"But, Cardo, dear old Uncle John is quite a different sort of man to my Uncle Essec or to your father. I know he would never, never divulge our secret; he is kindness itself, and would, I know, feel for us. And it would be such a comfort to me to know that we had been open and above-board where it was possible to be so. Cardo, say yes."

"Yes, yes, yes, dearest, I know, I feel you are right, so tell him the whole truth. Oh, how proud I should be to tell the whole world were it possible, and how proud I *shall* be when I return, to publish abroad my happiness. But until then, Valmai, you will keep to your promise of perfect secrecy? for I would not for all the world that my father should hear of my marriage from any lips but my own. You promise, dearest?"

"Cardo, I promise," and Valmai looked pensively into the fire. "A year is a long time," she said, "but it will come to an end some time."

"Don't call it a year. I don't see why I should not be back in eight or nine months."

The kettle sang and the bright fire gleamed, the old captain snored upstairs, and thus began for Valmai and Cardo that fortnight of blissful happiness, which bore for both of them afterwards such bitter fruits; for upon overhauling the *Burrawalla* it was discovered that she had sustained more injury than was at first suspected, and the two or three days' delay predicted by Captain Owen were lengthened out to a full fortnight, much to the captain's chagrin and the unspeakable happiness of Cardo and Valmai.

Next day at eleven A.M. Captain Powell was lying in state, not with the trappings of mourning around him, but decked out in a brilliant scarlet dressing-gown, a yellow silk handkerchief bound round his head for a night-cap. Jim Harris had just shaved him, and as he left the room had said:

"There, capting, the Prince of Wales couldn't look no better."

Valmai flitted about, putting the finishing touches to her uncle's gorgeous toilet.

"Do Ay look all raight, may dear?"

"Oh, splendid, uncle, only I would like you better in your plain white night shirt and my little gray shawl pinned over you."

"Oh, go 'long! with your shawls and your pins! You wait another month and Ay'll be kicking may heels about on the quay free from all these old women's shawls and dressing-gowns and things. Now, you go and call the young man up."

And Valmai went and soon returned, bringing Cardo with her.

"Well, Mr. Gwyn, and how are you? Very glad to see you, sir, under may roof. Hope you slept well, and that the lil gel has given you a good breakfast."

"Oh, first rate, sir," said Cardo, shaking hands and taking the chair which Valmai placed for him beside the bed.

"Well, now, here's a quandary, the *Burrawalla* is in! but it's an ill wind that blows nobody any good, and since you must be delayed, Ay'm very glad it has landed you here."

"The delay is of no consequence to me; and it's a wind I shall bless all my life."

"Well, Ay don't know what Captain Owen would say to that nor the owners nayther. They wouldn't join in your blessings, I expect."

Cardo felt he had made a mistake, and looked at Valmai for inspiration.

"Mr. Wynne was rather hurried away, uncle, so he was not sorry to come back."

Cardo nodded his thanks to Valmai, and the captain and he were soon chatting unconstrainedly, and when at last Cardo accepted a cigar from a silver case which the captain drew from under his pillow, his conquest of the old man's heart was complete.

"If Ay *am* cooped up here in bed," he said, "Ay'm not going to be denied may smoke, nor yet may glass of toddy, though the doctor trayed hard to stop it. 'Shall Ay mix it a little weaker, sir?' sez Jim Harris. None of your tarnished nonsense, Ay sez, you mix it as usual. Ay've stuck to my toddy (just one glass or two at naight) for the last thirty years, and it's not going to turn round on me, and do me harm now. Eh, Mr. Gwyn?"

Cardo lighted his cigar with an apology to Valmai.

"Oh, she's used to it," said the captain, "and if she don't like it, she can go downstairs; you'll want to see about Mr. Gwyn's dinner, may dear."

"No, no, sir," said Cardo, "certainly not. I dine every day with all the other passengers on board the *Burrawalla*. I shall come back to my tea, and I hope your niece will always sit down to her tea and breakfast with me."

"Oh, well, if you laike. She's quaite fit to sit down with any nobleman in the land."

Later on in the day, Valmai, sitting on the window-seat reading out to her uncle from the daily paper, suddenly laid it aside.

"Rather a dull paper to-day, uncle!"

"Yes, rather, may dear; but you are not reading as well as usual;" and she wasn't, for in truth she was casting about in her mind for a good opening for her confession to her uncle. "Suppose you sing me a song, may dear!"

And she tried—

"By Berwen's banks my love hath strayed
For many a day in sun and shade,
And as she carolled loud and clear
The little birds flew down to hear."

"That don't go as well as usual, too," said her uncle, unceremoniously cutting short the ballad. "Haven't you any more news to give me?"

"Shall I tell you a story, uncle?"

"Well, what's it about, may dear? Anything to pass the taime! Ay'm getting very taired of lying abed."

"Well then, listen uncle; it's a true story."

"Oh, of course," said the old man. "'Is it true, mother?' Ay used to ask when she told us a story. 'Yes, of course,' she'd say, 'if it didn't happen in this world, it happened in some other,' so, go on, may dear."

"Well," said Valmai, laughing rather nervously, "this happened in this world, whatever! Once upon a time, there was a young girl who was living on a wild sea-coast. It was very beautiful, but she was very lonely sometimes, for she had no father nor mother, nor sister nor brother."

"Poor thing," said the old man.

"Yes, certainly, she was very lonely," continued Valmai; "but one day she met a young man, bright and brave and true."

"Handsome?"

"Yes, handsome, with sparkling black eyes, and—and—oh, very handsome! and they loved each other truly, and—and—"

"Yes, yes! skip that. Ay know that. Go on."

"You can imagine that the poor lonely girl gave all her heart to her lover, as there was no one else who cared for it; and so the days were going by, and they were all in all to each other. But he had a stern, morose father, and she had a cold and selfish uncle; and these two men hated each other with a deadly hatred, just like a story book."

"Yes, Ay know," said the old man; "like Romeo and Juliet, you know."

"Perhaps, indeed," said Valmai; "but anyway, they dare not tell anyone of their love, for they knew that the old father would never agree to their being married, and the young man was very fond of his father, although he was so dark and dour. At last, suddenly, he told his son that he wanted him to go a long way off on business for him, and, wishing to please him, he agreed to go."

"More fool he!" said the captain. "Ay wouldn't 'a gone."

"But he promised, and he hoped that when he had given his father this proof of his love, he would give his consent to his marriage."

"Was he rich?"

"Yes, rather, I think."

"Well, why in the name of common sense didn't he defy his tarnished old father, and marry the girl he liked?"

"You'll see, uncle; wait a minute. The days passed on, and their parting was drawing near, and the nearer it came the more miserable they were; and at last the lover begged his sweetheart to marry him, so that he might feel, when he was far away, that she was really his wife whatever might happen. Well, they were married the very morning on which he left; married in an old, deserted church by a young clergyman, who was a good and true friend to them."

"A jolly nice man he must have bin!"

"Yes, indeed, he was."

"You are making it all up in your head, Ay know. But what did they do next?"

"Well, as soon as they were married, they kissed and said good-bye with breaking hearts."

"Oh, dash it!" said the captain, "Ay'd have managed it better than that, anyhow."

"But they didn't. The bridegroom sailed away, for the country he was going to was miles and miles and miles over the sea, and the poor bride was left at home with her sorrow. But soon afterwards she went to live with another relation, a dear old man—the best, the kindest, the tenderest, the jolliest old man in the world. In fact, he had only one fault, and that was that he sometimes used a bad word."

"Poor old chap!" said the captain. "You mustn't be too hard upon him for that, Valmai, becos Ay dare say he couldn't help it. P'r'aps you wouldn't believe it now, but there was a taime when Ay swore like a trooper; and it grew upon me so much that Ay d——d everything!—even the milk for breakfast—and Ay'm dashed if Ay could stop it, Valmai. May poor mother was alive then, and she sez to me one day with tears in her eyes, 'Tray, may boy, to leave off swearing; it is killing me,' she sez, with her sweet, gentle voice. So Ay sez to mayself, 'John,' Ay sez, 'you are a d——d fool. You're killing your mother with your foolish swears. Pull up short,' sez Ay, 'and tray and faind some other word that'll do.' So Ay fixed upon 'tarnished,' and Ay'm dashed if may mother wasn't perfectly satisfayed. It's a grand word! Puts you in mind of tar and 'tarnal and tarpauling, and lots of shippy things. 'Twas hard to get used to it at first; but 'pon may word now, may dear, it comes as nat'ral as swearing. But there! go on with the story. Where were we?"

Valmai was a little bewildered by the captain's reminiscences.

"Well, we had just come to where the girl, or rather the young wife, had gone to live with her other uncle. Here she would have been as happy as the day is long, had it not been for the continual sorrow for her lover."

The captain began to look a little suspicious, but Valmai hastened to prevent further interruptions.

"But now comes the wonderful part of the story, uncle. A dreadful storm arose, and a thick fog came on, and the ship in which the bridegroom sailed was so damaged that she had to put back for repairs. The young man found lodgings in the town, and what house do you think he came to? but the very one where the bride lived with her dear old uncle, and they made up their minds to tell him everything, and to throw themselves on his generosity. Dear uncle, what do you think of my story?"

"Dashed if Ay didn't begin to think it was me you meant by the old man. But child, child, you are not going to cheat that kind old uncle, and tell him a pack of lies, and laugh at him. You are not the bride?"

"Yes, uncle," said Valmai, with blushing face and drooping eyelids.

"And Mr. Gwyn is the bridegroom?"

"Yes. His name is Wynne, not Gwyn."

"And you knew nothing about it until he came here yesterday?"

"Nothing; but that he had sailed in the *Burrawalla*, and when I heard she had returned a wild hope came to me, and when I heard his voice in the passage I could have fainted with joy."

"And you are both united under may roof? and are man and wife?"

"Yes. Oh, uncle, don't be angry! It was not our own doing. It was Providence who sent him back to me from the storm and fog. *Don't* be angry."

"Angry, child!" said the old man, almost lifting himself up in his bed; "why Ay'm tarnished if anything so jolly ever happened in may laife before. And to think we have dodged the old father! and the old uncle! Why, that must be Essec!" and this discovery was followed by a burst of rumbling laughter, which set Valmai more at her ease.

"But never mind who he is, here you are, and here you shall be happy. Ay'll take your parts, may dears. Ay'll see that nothing comes between you any more."

"And you will keep our secret, uncle, until Cardo comes back?"

"Of course, child. We mustn't tell anyone, for fear it will get round to the old father's ears. Bay the bay, who is he?"

"Mr. Wynne, the Vicar of the parish, the 'Vicare du' they call him, from his black looks."

"The 'Vicare du!'" said the captain, "why! he is rolling in money! You've done a tidy little job for yourself, may gel, and your old Uncle John will befriend you."

Here Mrs. Finch opened the door, and, with a sniff, said, "The gentleman's come back, and he wants to know can he see Miss Powell?"

The captain fell into another fit of laughter, while Mrs. Finch stared at him in astonishment.

"Tell him to come up," he said, at last, "you gaping old gudgeon, what you standing staring there for? Send Mr. Wynne up. Tell him the lady is here, and Ay want to see him."

In a few moments Cardo bounded up, three steps at a time, but not without fears as to the effect of Valmai's revelation, for she had whispered to him as she had let him out at the front door:

"I am going up to tell him now."

"Well Ay never!" said the Captain, with pretended severity; "how dare you show your face to me after stealing may lil gel from under may very nose? Come here, you rascal, and shake hands over it! Wish you joy, may dear fellow! And the lil one, where is she? Come here, you lil fool! What are you hiding there for? Come and put your hand in your husband's. There now! that's something like it. And God bless you. So you're husband and wife, are ye?" looking critically from one to the other. "Well, ye're a jolly good-looking pair! And so ye're married, are ye?"

"With your permission, sir," said Cardo, laughing, "and with your blessing upon us. I am so thankful to feel I shall not be leaving Valmai without a friend when I sail."

"No, no, not without a friend. Ay'll stick to her. But, look here, keep it all dark from old Finch!" And he seemed bursting with the importance and pleasure of his secret. "You go down to your tea, may dears; Ay ain't going to be a selfish old uncle. No, no, go along with you, both of you, and send old Finch up to me. But look here!" he called after them, in a hoarse whisper, "mum's the word!"

The sun shone brilliantly, and the weather seemed to repent of its late burst of temper. Never had there been such a lovely September! Never had the harbour glistened so brightly in the sunshine, and never since he had broken his leg had the captain laughed so heartily or enjoyed himself so thoroughly as he did during the fortnight which followed, when Cardo read to him out of the newspaper and Valmai sang at her work about the house.

Captain Owen came in every day with news of the repairs.

"Well, Mr. Wynne," he said one morning, "I am happy to tell you we shall sail to-morrow afternoon."

Cardo's heart sank, and Valmai turned very pale.

"Your cabin is being refitted to-day, and I shall be glad if you can come on board by four o'clock to-morrow afternoon. There's every promise of fine weather. No more fogs, no more collisions, I hope."

"I'll take care to be on board in good time," Cardo said.

"Tarnished if Ay won't be awful dull without you!" said Captain Powell.

"He's been as jolly, and as much at home here as you would yourself, Owen! He's read to me and he's brought me cigars, and always with a smile on his face; and Ay hope he's bin comfortable here."

"Thoroughly, indeed," said Cardo. "I shall never forget the fortnight I have passed under your roof."

"The lil gel has done her best, Ay know," said his host.

"A year I think you said you were going out for," said Captain Owen.

"Well, I hope to be away only eight or nine months; certainly not longer than a year," said Cardo.

And while the two old sea captains bade their last good-byes and good wishes to each other, Cardo slipped out to find Valmai, who had quietly disappeared.

She was sitting on the old red sofa in the little back parlour in an abandonment of grief.

"Oh! Cardo, Cardo, it has come! Now in reality it has come!"

Cardo drew her towards him.

"Cheer up, darling," he said. "You'll be brave for my sake, won't you?"

"Yes," she said, trying to check her sobs, "this is the last time I am going to be weak and childish. To-morrow I will be strong and brave and womanly. You will see, Cardo, a bright, courageous wife to cheer her husband at parting, and to bid him look forward with hope to meeting again. Oh! I know quite well what I ought to be."

"You are perfection in my eyes, f'anwylyd—that is what makes the parting with you so cruel. Gwynne Ellis was quite right when he said that it would be much harder to part with a wife of a week than a sweetheart of a year."

CHAPTER XI.

THE "BLACK DOG."

During the next few weeks, Cardo Wynne was generally to be seen pacing the deck of the *Burrawalla*, playing with the children or chatting with some of the passengers. He walked up and down, with his hands sunk deep in his pockets, and cap tied firmly under his chin, for there was a pretty stiff breeze blowing, which developed later on in the voyage into the furious gales and storms which made that autumn so memorable for its numerous wrecks and casualties. Cardo was a great favourite on board, his frank and genial manner, the merry twinkle of his eye, and his tender politeness to the very old or the very young had won all hearts. With good-natured cheerfulness he entered into the plans and pastimes of the youthful part of the community, so that he had made a favourable impression upon all, from the cabin boy to the captain, and from the old general, who seldom left his berth, to the big black retriever, who was making his third voyage with his master to the Antipodes.

"Always a pleasant smile on his face when you speak to him," said one of the ladies to a friend one day; "but I think he has a rather sad look sometimes, when he is pacing up and down with his hands in his pockets."

"Yes," said the other, with a sentimental air, "I wonder what he is thinking of at those times! I'll make love to the captain, and see if I can find out something about him, they seem very intimate. We must try and cheer him up, dear."

"He doesn't seem to want much cheering up now," said her friend, as Cardo passed them with two other young men, who were enjoying a story told by one of them, Cardo's merry laugh being loudest and heartiest of the three. But—there was a sober, wistful look on his face sometimes which was not habitual to it, and as the days slipped on, he might often be seen, leaning over the side of the vessel with an anxious pucker on his forehead.

The parting with Valmai had, of course, been a trying ordeal. With the fervour of a first and passionate love, he recalled every word she had spoken, every passing shade of thought reflected on her face, and while these reveries occupied his mind, there was a tender look in the deep black eyes and a smile on his lips. But these pleasant memories were apparently often followed by more perplexing thoughts. One afternoon he had been standing for some time lost in a dream, while he looked with eyes that saw nothing over the heaving waters to the distant horizon, when the captain's voice at his elbow recalled him to his surroundings.

"You are looking at the very point of the wind, the very eye of the storm."

"The storm!" said Cardo, starting; "are we going to have one?"

The captain looked critically in the direction towards which they were sailing.

"Dirty weather coming, I think."

"Yes, I see," said Cardo; "I had not noticed it before, though. How inky black the sky is over there! And the sea as black, and that white streak on the line of the horizon!"

"We shall have a bit of a toss," said the captain. "Couldn't expect to get to Australia on a mill pond."

"Mill pond do you call the swells we have had the last few days?"

"Almost," replied the captain, leaving him unceremoniously, and shouting some orders to his crew.

Thus left, Cardo fell again into a deep reverie. Yes, it looked black before them! "But I have always wished to see a storm at sea, and if I only had Valmai with me, I should be joyous and exultant; but instead of that, I am alone, and have a strange foreboding of some evil to come. I can't be well, though I'm sure I don't know where I ail, for I feel alright, and I eat like a horse."

"Come, Mr. Wynne," said one of the ladies, who had marked his serious looks, "we must really call you to account! You have fallen into a brown study again. You must let us cheer you up. We can't have the very life of the party losing his spirits. Now if you had left your wife at home, as Mr. Dawson has!"

"I have done that," said Cardo, "but I am not at all likely to fall into low spirits. I have never in my life known what that means; but a man, more especially a married man, must have his moments of serious thought sometimes."

"Yes, of course," said the lady, with a considerable diminution of interest in "the handsome Mr. Wynne!" "You have left your little ones too, I suppose?"

"No," said Cardo, laughing, "I have none."

"Ah, indeed, that's a pity!" and she took the first opportunity of joining her friend, and telling her of her discovery.

Cardo continued to look out to sea. No, bad enough to leave Valmai, but "little ones"? Would that time ever come? and as he pondered, a fresh idea seemed to strike him. It was evidently a painful one, it stung him like the lash of a whip, and clenching his hands, and muttering something between his teeth, he roused himself hastily, and joined a party of young people, who were amusing themselves with the pranks of a little boy, who, delighted with the notice taken of him, strutted about and gave his orders, in imitation of the captain.

"Oh, here's Mr. Wynne," said the little urchin, and in a moment he was lifted on to Cardo's shoulder, whooping with delight, and for the next hour, the laugh was loudest and the fun most furious where Cardo and his little friend were located. Before long, however, the storm was upon them. Masts creaked and cordage rattled; the sails had been lowered, and everything made safe, and Captain Owen, standing on the bridge, looked energetic, and "fit" to fight with the storm-fiend. The ladies soon retired, and many of the gentlemen followed them below, some of the younger and hardier remaining on deck. Amongst them was Cardo, who watched the fury of the elements as the wind tore down upon them. Once, as the captain passed him, he asked, "Is there any danger?" "I see none," was the laconic reply. It satisfied Cardo, and he gave himself up to watch the grandeur of the storm. It was natural that the thought of Valmai should enter his mind, and that he should long for her presence; but it was not natural that he, a young and healthy man, in the first flush of his manhood, should feel this strange depression, this dark cloud hanging over him, whenever he thought of his young wife. It was unlike Cardo. If his life had been devoid of any special interest or excitement, it had at least been free from care. Not even his lonely childhood, or his dull, old home had dimmed the brightness and elasticity of his spirits. He had never had a cobweb in his brain, and this haunting shadow which followed every sweet memory of his wife was beginning to rouse his resentment, and while the storm raged around him, and the ship ploughed her way through the seething waters, Cardo Wynne, set himself with manful determination to face the "black dog" which had haunted him lately; and somewhat in this groove ran his thoughts.

"Valmai, sweet Valmai, I have left her; it could not be helped. I will return to her on the wings of love as soon as I have fulfilled my father's wishes." But a year—had he provided fully and properly for her happiness during that time? Money, amply sufficient, he had left in her uncle's keeping for her, as she had firmly refused to accept it herself. "I shall not want it; I have plenty for myself. I have twenty gold sovereigns in my little seal purse at home, and I shall receive my next quarter's allowance soon. No, no, Cardo, no money until we set up housekeeping," and he had acceded to her wishes; but had, unknown to her, left a cheque in her uncle's keeping. "Why did I claim from her that promise of secrecy? What if circumstances might arise which would make it impossible for her to keep it?" He knew that having given her promise to him, she would rather die than break it. He had acted the part of a selfish man, who had no thought, but of his own passionate love; the possible consequences to her had not before occurred to his mind. But now, in the stress of the storm, while the thunder rolled above him, and the lightning flashed over the swirling waters, everything seemed clear and plain. He had done wrong, and he would now face the wrong. Their happy meeting at Fordsea, as blissful as it was unexpected, might be followed by times of trouble for Valmai—times when she would desire to make known her marriage; and he had left her with an embargo upon her only means of escape out of a difficulty. Yes, the path was plain, he would write to her and release her from her promise of secrecy. Better by far that his father should be angered than that Valmai should suffer. Yes, it was plain to him now; he had left the woman he loved in the anomalous position of a married woman without a husband. What trying scenes might she not pass through! What bitter fruits might not their brief happiness bear!

The next day they had cleared the storm, its fury having been as short-lived as it was sudden. The sea was gradually quieting down, and the sun shone out bravely. The sails were unfurled and the *Burrawalla* once more went gaily on her way.

Cardo had spent all the morning in writing; he would send his letter by the first opportunity. It was full of all the tender expressions of love that might be expected under the circumstances. His pen could scarcely keep up with the flow of his thoughts. "I have done wrong in making you promise to keep our marriage a secret," he wrote, "and I repent bitterly of my thoughtlessness. Many things might happen which would make it absolutely necessary that you should disclose it. For instance, your uncle might die; what would then become of you? Certainly you would have your good old Uncle John to fall back upon, and he is a host in himself. If any circumstances should arise which would make it desirable for you to do so, remember, dearest, it is my express wish that you should make known to all the world that you are Valmai Wynne, the beloved wife of Caradoc Wynne." Page after page was written with the lavish fervour of a first love-letter, very interesting to the writer no doubt, but which we will leave to the privacy of the envelope which Cardo addressed and sealed with such care. He placed it in his desk, not expecting that the opportunity for sending it would so soon arrive. In the course of the afternoon, there was some excitement on board, for a large homeward bound ship was sighted, which had been a good deal damaged by the storm. She had been driven before the wind, and had borne the brunt of the gale before it had reached the *Burrawalla*, having sprung a leak which considerably impeded her course. She hove to within hailing distance, and received the aid which the better condition of Captain Owen's ship enabled him to confer. She was *The Dundee* (Captain Elliotson), bound for Liverpool. All letters were delivered to her keeping, and the ships went on their way, but to what different destinations. *The Dundee*, after a stormy passage, was wrecked off the coast of France. The captain and crew were saved, but the ship became a total wreck, sinking at last in deep water; and thus Cardo's letter never reached Valmai.

Its transmission, however, relieved him of much of the uneasiness which had hung over him, and his usual cheerfulness returned in a great measure.

Meanwhile, Valmai hoped and longed for the promised letter.

"Why does he not write, I wonder?" was the question continually uppermost in her thoughts.

The voyage of the *Burrawalla* was, on the whole, prosperous, although, towards the end, she was much delayed by adverse winds, so that Sydney harbour was not reached until the end of the fourth month. A further and unexpected delay arose from the illness of a passenger who occupied a berth in Cardo's cabin, and as they were nearing their destination he died of typhoid fever. Consequently the *Burrawalla* was put into quarantine, of course to the great annoyance and inconvenience of all on board.

"You are not looking well, Mr. Wynne," said the doctor one day.

"Oh, I'm alright," said Cardo, "only impatient to get on shore. I feel perfectly well. Why, my dear doctor, I have never had a day's illness in my life, as far as I can remember."

"I can believe that," said the doctor; "and what a splendid sailor you have been. But still, let me know if you are not feeling well."

It was quite true that Cardo had latterly experienced some sensations to which he had hitherto been a stranger—frequent headaches and loss of appetite; but, being of a very hardy temperament, he tried to ignore the unpleasant symptoms, and waited for the end of the quarantine with feverish impatience.

When at last they were allowed to land, he was amongst the liveliest and most energetic of the passengers.

He drove at once to the Wolfington Hotel, to which he had been recommended by Captain Owen. As he stepped out of the cab, the portico of the hotel seemed strangely at loggerheads with the rest of the building, He managed, however, to get safely inside the hall, and, after engaging a bedroom, followed his conductor up the stairs, though each step seemed to rise to meet his foot in an unaccountable manner.

"A long sea voyage doesn't suit me, that's certain," he soliloquised, as he entered the room and busied himself at once with his luggage. He took off the labels with the intention of substituting fresh ones addressed to his uncle's farm, deciding not to stay a day longer than was necessary in Sydney, but to make inquiries at once as to the best way of getting to Broadstone, Priory Valley. He still fought bravely against the feeling of lassitude and nausea which oppressed him, and went down to his lunch with a bold front, although the place seemed floating around him. But in vain did the odour of the Wallaby soup ascend to his nostrils; in vain was the roast fowl spread before him. He scarcely tasted the viands which the attentive waiter continued to press upon him; and at last, pushing his plate away, he rose from the table.

"I shall want writing materials and some labels on my return," he said, as he left the room with a somewhat unsteady step.

"On the razzle-dazzle last night, I expect," said the waiter, with a wink at his fellow.

The fresh air seemed to relieve Cardo, in some degree, of the weight which dragged him down; he was even well enough to notice that the uneven streets were more like those of an old-fashioned English town than anything he had expected to find in Australia. But this feeling of relief did not last long. In the street which led down to the quay he observed a chemist's shop, and, entering it, asked for a "draught or pick-me-up" of some kind.

"I feel awfully seedy," he said, sinking into a chair.

"Yes, you look it," said the chemist; "what's wrong?"

"I think I must give in," said Cardo, "for I believe I am sickening for typhoid fever."

The chemist looked grave.

"I advise you to go home at once, and to bed."

"Yes," replied Cardo, trying to rise to the emergency, and still manfully struggling against the disease which threatened him. "Yes, I will go home," he said again, walking out of the shop. He took the wrong turning however, going down towards the harbour, instead of returning to the hotel, and he was soon walking under a burning sun amongst the piled-up bales and packages on the edge of the quay. A heavy weight seemed to press on his head, and a red mist hung over everything as he walked blindly on. At a point which he had just reached, a heap of rough boxes obstructed his path, and at that moment a huge crank swung its iron arm over the edge of the dock, a heavy weight was hanging from it, and exactly as Cardo passed, it came with a horizontal movement against the back of his head with terrible force, throwing him forward insensible on the ground. The high pile of boxes had hidden the accident from the crowd of loungers and pedestrians who might otherwise have noticed the fall. The sudden lurch with which he was thrown forward jerked his pocket-book from the breast-pocket of his coat, and it fell to the ground a foot or two in front of him. It was instantly picked up by a loafer, who had been leaning against the pile of boxes, and who alone had witnessed the accident; he immediately stooped to help the prostrate man, and finding him pale and still, shouted for assistance, and was quickly joined by a knot of "larrikins," who dragged the unconscious man a little further from the edge of the quay.

It was not long before a small crowd had gathered round, the man who had first observed him making a safe escape in the confusion, Cardo's pocket-book carefully hidden under his tattered coat.

"Better take him up to Simkins the chemist," said a broad-shouldered sailor; and, procuring a stretcher, they carried their unconscious burden to the chemist's shop.

"Why, let me see," said Mr. Simkins; "surely this is the gentleman who called here a few minutes ago. I told him to go home, and he said he would; but I noticed he turned down towards the quay; poor fellow, bad case, I'm afraid. He said he thought he was sickening for typhoid fever, and he's about right, I think."

"What shall we do with him?" said the sailor. "See if you can find a card or letter in his pockets? Nothing," he added, as together they searched Cardo's pockets, "not a card, nor a letter, nothing but this bunch of keys, and some loose gold and silver."

There was no clue to the stranger's identity, except the marking on his clothing.

"Here's C. W. on his handkerchief—Charles Williams, perhaps; well, he ought to be attended to at once, if he ain't dead already," said another.

"Yes, a good thing the hospital is so near," said the chemist. "You had better leave his money here, and tell Dr. Belton that you have done so. My brother is his assistant. I daresay we shall hear more about him from him."

"Now, then, boys; heave up, gently, that's it," and Cardo was carried out of the shop to the hospital in an adjoining street. Here, placed on a bed in one of the long wards, doctors and nurses were soon around him; but Cardo lay white and still and unconscious.

One of the bearers had mentioned typhoid fever, and Dr. Belton looked grave and interested as he applied himself to the examination of the patient.

"My brother has been here," said his assistant; "this man had just been in to his shop, and said he believed he was sickening for typhoid, and it wasn't ten minutes before he was picked up on the quay."

"The heat of the sun, I expect, was too much for him under the circumstances," said Dr. Belton. "A plain case of sunstroke, I think."

"This money was found in his pocket," said Simkins, handing over five sovereigns and fifteen shillings in silver; "this bunch of keys, too, and his watch; but no card or letter to show who he is."

"Fine young fellow," said Dr. Belton; "splendid physique, but looks like a bad attack."

Restoratives were tried, but with no effect; Cardo still lay like a dead man.

"Very strange," said the doctor, when next day he found the patient in the same unconscious condition. "Few constitutions would be able to fight against two such serious diseases."

"Sunstroke as well as typhoid?" said Mr. Simkins.

"Yes, I have no doubt of it. Curious combination of evils."

"Poor chap!" said Simkins, "no constitution could survive that."

"Nothing is impossible," said the doctor, "very interesting case; keep up the strength, nurse."

Everything was done that was possible for poor Cardo; the nurses were unremitting in their care and attention, but nothing roused him from his trance-like stupor.

During the course of the day, the news of the finding of an unknown man on the quay reached the Wolfington Hotel, where the waiter, with another knowing wink and shake of the head, said, "On the razzle-dazzle again, I expect. Must be the same man." And he proceeded upstairs to examine the luggage, from which Cardo had removed the labels intending to redirect them to his uncles house. There was no letter or paper found to indicate the name of the owner, even the initials C. W. gave no clue.

"What was the man's name?" said the waiter to Mr. Simkins, who happened to call the following morning.

"Don't know. Charles Williams he is called at the hospital. There was no clue to his identity, but just the letters C. W. on his linen."

"Then, no doubt, his luggage is here," said the waiter. "All his things are marked C. W., and, from your description, it must be the same man."

"Well, my brother will speak to Dr. Belton about it, and he will arrange to have it taken care of; he already has his money and his watch."

And so Cardo Wynne slipped out of his place in the outside world and was soon forgotten by all except those connected with the hospital.

In three weeks the fever had run its course, and, to the astonishment of the nurses and doctors, Cardo still lived.

"Extraordinary vitality! Has he never spoken a word?"

"Never a sound or a word until he began moaning to-day."

"Good sign, this moaning. Mind, keep up his strength."

And gradually, under the constant care of Doctor Belton, who was much interested in the case, Cardo, or Charles Williams as he was now called, recovered strength of body; and, to a slight extent, restoration to consciousness; for though he lay inert and motionless, his lips moved incessantly in a low muttering or whispering, in which the nurses in vain endeavoured to find a clue to the mystery of his illness.

CHAPTER XII.

A CLIMAX.

A bitter north wind, laden with sleet and rain, blew over Abersethin Bay, tearing the surface into streaks of foam. The fishing boats were drawn up on the grassy slope which bordered the sandy beach, and weighted with heavy stones. The cottage doors were all closed, and if a stray pedestrian was anywhere to be seen, he was hurrying on his way, his hands in his pockets and his cap tied firmly under his chin. On the cliffs above, the wind swirled and rushed, blowing the grass all one way and sweeping over the stunted thorn bushes. In the corners under the hedges, the cows and horses sheltered in little groups, and the few gaunt trees which grew on that exposed coast groaned and creaked as they bent away from the storm.

At Dinas the wind blew with bitter keenness through every chink and cranny, roaring and whistling round the bare gray house, rattling the doors and windows with every angry gust. In the little parlour at the back of the house it was not heard so plainly. A bright fire burned in the grate, and the crimson curtains gave it a look of warmth and comfort which Essec Powell unconsciously enjoyed. He was sitting in his arm-chair and in his favourite position, listening with great interest to Valmai, who was reading aloud in Welsh from the "Mabinogion." The tale was of love and chivalry, and it should have interested the girl more than it did the old man who listened with such attention, but her thoughts refused to follow the thread of the story. She stopped occasionally to listen to the wind as it howled in the chimney. All through the short, dark afternoon she read with untiring patience, until at last, when the light was fading, Gwen brought in the tea and put an end to the reading for a time.

Valmai had stayed at Fordsea until her uncle had quite recovered from his accident; and the New Year was well on its way before he had wished her good-bye at the station. She left him with real sorrow, and the old feeling of loneliness and homelessness returned to her heart. He had received her with such warmth, and had so evidently taken her into his life, that the friendless girl had opened her heart wide to him; and as his rough, hairy hand rested on the window of the carriage in which she sat, she pressed her lips upon it in a loving good-bye. There were tears in the kind old eyes, as he stood waiting for the train to move.

"Won't you write, sometimes, uncle?" she asked.

"Well, Ay won't promise that, indeed, may dear; for there's nothing Ay hate more than wrayting a letter; but Ay'll come and see you as soon as you have a house of your own. And don't you forget to look out for a little cottage for me at Abersethin. Ay'm determined to end my days near you, and *you know who*."

"Oh! there's lovely it will be, uncle, to have you to run to whenever anything vexes me, but nothing ever will vex me then."

"No, no; of course, may dear, we'll all be jolly together. Good-bay, good-bay." And the train moved out of the station.

Two months afterwards we find Valmai at Dinas, and reading to her Uncle Essec as usual. She busied herself with the preparations for tea, lighting the lamp and placing the buttered toast in front of the fire until he should awake from his dreams, and descend to real life. While the tea was "brewing," she sank back into her chair and fell into a deep reverie. She was as fair as ever, the golden hair drawn back from the white, broad brows, but the eyes were full of anxious thought, and there was a little wistful sadness about the lines of the mouth. She was paler, and did not move about her duties with the same lightness and grace which belonged to her when we last saw her. She seemed in no hurry to disturb her uncle's dozing dreams, until at last Gwen came hastily in.

"Well, indeed! What are you two doing here? There's quiet you are!"

Valmai started, rousing herself and her uncle.

"Yes. Come to tea, uncle. I was thinking, Gwen."

"Oh, yes; thinking, thinking," said Gwen, with an insolent sneer. "You may think and think—you are always thinking now; and what about, I should like to know?" and, with a shrewd shake of her head, she left the room.

A crimson tide overspread Valmai's face and neck, and, fading away, left her paler than before. She stood for a moment with her hands clasped, and pressed on her bosom, looking at the door through which Gwen had just passed, and then seating herself at the table, her eyes suffused with tears, she began to pour out her uncle's tea.

"That's a fine piece, Valmai," he said, "how Clwyn went away and never came back again, till the sea washed him one day at Riana's feet."

"Yes," said the girl, in a low voice. "Won't you eat your toast, uncle?"

"Oh, yes, to be sure," said the old man, beginning on the buttered toast which she placed before him.

When tea was over, the "Mabinogion" were brought out again and Valmai continued to read till her uncle fell asleep. Then leaving him to Gwen's care, she gladly retired for the night into her own little bedroom. Here she might think as much as she liked, and well she availed herself of that privilege. Here she would sit alone for hours every day, with her head bent over some bit of work, her busy fingers pleating and stitching, while her thoughts took wing over the leaden wintry sea before her. Away and away, in search of Cardo. Where was he? Why did he not write to her? Would he ever come? Would he ever write? And with weary reiteration she sought out every imaginary reason for his long silence.

New hopes, new fears had of late dawned in her heart, at first giving rise to a full tide of happiness and joy, the joy that comes with the hope of motherhood—woman's crowning glory; but the joy and happiness had gradually given place to anxiety and fear, and latterly, since it had become impossible for her to hide her condition from those around her, she was filled with trouble and distressing forebodings, Her sensitive nature received continual wounds. Suspicious looks and taunting sneers, innuendos and broad suggestions all came to her with exceeding bitterness. She knew that every day the cloud which hung over her grew blacker and heavier. Where should she turn when her uncle should discover her secret? In the solitude of her room she paced backwards and forwards, wringing her hands.

"What will I do? what will I do? He said he would return in seven or eight months—a year at furthest. Will he come? will he ever come?"

And, gazing out over the stormy sea, she would sob in utter prostration of grief. Every day she walked to Abersethin and haunted the post-office. The old postmaster had noticed her wistful looks of disappointment, and seemed to share her anxiety for the arrival of a letter—who from, he did not know for certain, but he made a very good guess, for Valmai's secret was not so much her own only as she imagined it to be.

Her frequent meetings with Cardo, though scarcely noticed at the time, were remembered against her; and her long stay at Fordsea, with the rumour of Cardo's return there, decided the feeling of suspicion which had for some time been floating about. There had been a whisper, then mysterious nods and smiles, and cruel gossip had spread abroad the evil tidings.

Valmai bore all in patient silence. Her longing for Cardo's return amounted almost to an agony, yet the thought of explaining her position, and clearing her name before the world, never entered her head, or, if it did, was instantly expelled. No; the whole world might spurn her; she might die; but to reveal a secret which Cardo had desired her to keep, seemed to her faithful and guileless nature an unpardonable breach of honour.

Gwen, who had not been immaculate herself, was her cruellest enemy, never losing an opportunity of inflicting a sting upon her helpless victim, whose presence in the household she had always resented.

The day following Gwen's sneering remark, Valmai took her daily walk to
Abersethin post-office.

The old man beamed at her over his counter.

"Letter come at last, miss," he said.

And her heart stood still. She was white to the lips as she sat down on a convenient sack of maize.

"It is a long walk," said the postmaster, hunting about for the letter.

"Dear me, wherrs I put it?"

And he looked in a box of bloaters and a basket of eggs.

"Here it is. I 'member now; I put it safe with the cheese was to go to Dinas."

Valmai took it with trembling fingers; it had a deep black edge.

"It is not for me," she said.

"Indeed! I was not notice that. I was only see 'Powell, Dinas.' I am sorry, miss, fâch; but you must cheer up," he added, seeing the gathering tears; "it's never so dark that the Lord can't clear it up."

"No," said Valmai, rising from her seat. "Thank you; good-bye."

And, blinded by her tears, she passed out into the driving wind and sleet. Perhaps the letter bore some news of Cardo! Perhaps bad news, for it had a black edge! She drew her red cloak tightly around her and once more bravely faced the buffeting wind which swept the path before her, and with fitful gusts threatened to lift her off her feet.

When she reached Dinas, Gwen was already laying the dinner in the little parlour.

"You have been a long time," she said. "Where have you been? To the post again to-day? You never used to go to the post, Valmai."

The girl did not answer, but sat down breathless on the sofa.

"Where is uncle? I have a letter for him." And as she spoke her uncle entered.

"A letter for me? Well, indeed! What can it be?"

Essec Powell's correspondence was very limited; he hated writing, and never answered a letter which could possibly be ignored. He adjusted his spectacles, and after turning the envelope in every direction, opened it.

"Reuben Street, Fordsea," he began. "Oh, dear, dear! here's writing! Caton pawb! I could write better myself. Read it, Valmai."

And she obeyed.

"REV. ESSEC POWELL,

"DEAR SIR,—I am grieve more than words can say to tell you this sad news, and I hope you will prepare for the worst. Becos your brother, Captain John Powell, No. 8 Reuben Street, Fordsea, was drownded yesterday in the harbour, and I have loast the best frind ever I had and ever I will have. Please to tell Miss Powell the sad news, and please to tell her that Captain Powell was oleways talking great deal about her, and was missing her very much. Oh, we shall never see nobody like him again. He went out in a small boat with two frinds to the steamer Penelope, Captain Parley, and coming back the boat was capsize and the three gentlemen was upset in the water. One was saved, but Captain Powell and Mr. Jones was drownded. Please to come and see about the funeral as soon as you can.

"I remain in great sorrow,

"Yours truly,

"JAMES HARRIS."

Valmai's trembling voice failed, and letting the letter drop, she covered her face with her hands and burst into a flood of tears, as she realised that her best friend had slipped away from her. In the trouble and anxiety which had latterly clouded her life, she had often been comforted by the thought that at all events there was one warm heart and home open to her, but now all was lost, and her loneliness and friendlessness pressed heavily upon her. Sob after sob shook her whole frame.

Essec Powell picked up the letter, and read it again.

"Well, well," he said, "to think that John, my brother, should go before me! Poor fellow, bâch! To be taken so suddenly and unprepared as he was."

"Oh, no, uncle," said Valmai, between her sobs, "he was not unprepared. There never was a kinder soul, a more unselfish man, nor a more generous. Oh, you don't know how good he was to the poor, how kind and gentle to every one who suffered! Oh, God has him in His safe keeping somewhere!"

"Well, well," said Essec Powell, sitting down to his dinner, "we won't argue about it now, but some day, Valmai, I would like to explain to you the difference between that natural goodness and the saving grace which is necessary for salvation. Come to dinner, Valmai. I wonder how much did he leave? When is the funeral?" he said, addressing Gwen.

"You've got to go down and settle that," she answered. "Will I tell Shoni to put the gig ready?"

"Yes, yes. I better go. I will be back by Sunday."

"James Harris will help you in every way, uncle, and will settle everything for you."

"Oh! very well, very well. Tis a pity about the 'Mabinogion,' too; but we'll go on with them next week, Valmai."

Shoni and Gwen continued until bedtime to discuss with unction every item of information past, possible, or prospective, connected with the death of the old Captain, while Valmai lay on the old red sofa, and thought sadly of her loss.

"There's sudden," said Gwen, "but 'twill be a good thing for the master, whatever!"

Valmai lay awake far into the night recalling with tears the kindness and even tenderness of her old uncle.

On the following Saturday Essec Powell returned from the funeral, and as he stepped out of the gig at the door, his face wore an unusual expression which Valmai noticed at once. He seemed more alive to the world around him; there was a red spot on each cheek, and he did not answer his niece's low greeting, but walked into the parlour with a stamping tread very unlike his usual listless shuffle.

"Are you tired, uncle?" the girl asked gently.

"No, I am not tired; but I am hurt and offended with you, Valmai. You are a sly, ungrateful girl, and it is very hard on me, a poor, struggling preacher very badly paid, to find that my only brother has left all his worldly goods to you, who are already well provided for. What do you think yourself? Wasn't it a shame on you to turn him against his brother?"

"Oh, I never did," said Valmai; "I never thought of such a thing! Dear, dear Uncle John! I didn't want his money, I only wanted his love."

"What is the matter?" said Gwen, coming in.

"Matter enough," said her master, in angry, stammering tones. "John, my brother, has left all his money to this Judas of a girl! A hundred and fifty pounds a year, if you please! and only a paltry 100 pounds to me, and the same to Jim Harris, the sailor. Ach y fi! the greediness of people is enough to turn on me."

Between Gwen's exclamations and Essec Powell's angry harping on the same string, the evening was made miserable to Valmai, and she was glad enough to escape to her bedroom.

The next day she awoke with a throbbing headache.

"You are not going to chapel to-day, I suppose?" said Gwen.

"No, my head aches too badly. I have never missed before, but to-day I think I will rest at home."

"Yes, rest at home, certainly," said Gwen. "You ought to have stopped at home long ago; in my opinion, it would be more decent."

Her meaning was too plain, and Valmai's head drooped as she answered:

"Perhaps it would have been wiser, considering all things."

"Considering all things, indeed!" sneered Gwen. "Yes, they will turn you out of the 'Sciet, because when the calf won't go through the scibor door he has to be pushed out!" And with a toss of her head she carried the tray away.

It was a miserable day for Valmai, and not even after events of more bitterness were able to efface it from her memory.

She roamed about the house restlessly, and round the garden, which was beginning to show signs of the budding life which had slept through the storms and snows of winter. Already in a sheltered corner she detected the scent of violets, an early daffodil nodded at her, a bee hummed noisily, and a sweet spring breeze swept over the garden. What memories it awoke within her! How long ago it seemed since she and Cardo had roamed together by the Berwen! Years and years ago, surely! Her reverie was disturbed by Shoni, who, coming back early from chapel, had found his way into the garden.

"You wass quite right not to go to chapel this morning," he said. "Don't go to-night again, neither!"

"No," said Valmai, "I won't. But why, Shoni?"

"Why?" he said, "because you better not. John Jones and William Hughes, the deacons, is bin speaking to master about you, and next week is the 'Sciet,[1] and you will be turn out."

Valmai turned a shade paler; she knew the disgrace this excommunication implied; but she only turned with a sigh towards the house, Shoni marching before her with the air of a man who felt he had performed a disagreeable duty. Essec Powell had stopped to dine with a farmer living near the chapel, and did not return home until near tea-time. Then burst upon the girl the storm she had so long dreaded; her uncle's anger had already been roused by his brother's "will," and his feelings of greed and spite had been augmented by the information imparted to him by his deacons.

"How dare you?" he said. His eyes flashed with anger, and his voice trembled with the intensity of his fury.

Valmai, who was arranging something on the tea-table, sank down on a chair beside it; and Gwen, carrying a slice of toast on a fork, came in to listen. To hear her master speak in such excited tones was an event so unusual as to cause her not only astonishment but pleasure.

Shoni, too, was attracted by the loud tones, and stood blocking up the doorway.

Valmai flung her arms on the table, and leant her head upon them, sobbing quietly.

"Are you not ashamed of yourself?" thundered the old man. "Sitting at my table, sleeping under my roof, and attending my chapel—and all the time to be the vile thing that you are! Dear Uncle John, indeed! what would your dear Uncle John say of you now? You fooled him as you have fooled me. Do you think I can bear you any longer in the house with me?"

There was no answer from Valmai, and the old man, angered by her silence, clutched her by the arm and shook her violently.

"Stop there!" said Shoni, taking a step forward, and thrusting his brawny arm protectingly over the girl's bent head. "Stop there! Use as many bad words as you like, Essec Powell, but if you dare to touch her with a finger, I'll show you who is the real master here."

"She is a deceitful creature, and has brought shame and dishonour on my name!" stammered the old man. "Am I, a minister of religion, any longer to harbour in my house such a huzzy? *No*; out you go, madam! Not another night under my roof!"

"Will you send her out at this late hour?" said Shoni. "Where is she to go?"

"I don't care where she goes! She has plenty of money—money that ought to belong to me. Let her go where she likes, and let her reap the harvest that her conduct deserves. Remember, when I come back from chapel to-night I will expect the house to be cleared of you."

Valmai rose wearily from the table, and went up the stairs to her own room, where she hastily gathered a few things together into a light basket, her heavier things she had packed some time before in readiness for some such sudden departure as this.

Meanwhile, in the parlour below the sturdy Shoni faced his irate master.

"Man," he said, "are you not ashamed of yourself?"

"How dare you speak to me in that tone?" said the old man. "Because I owe you two or three hundred pounds you forget your position here."

"No," said Shoni, "I don't forget, and I'll remind you sooner than you think if you don't behave yourself! Man! you haven't learnt the ABC of religion, though you are a 'preacher.' Christ never taught you that way of treating a fallen woman. Shame upon you! And your own brother's child! But I'll see she's taken care of, poor thing! And the villain who has brought this misery upon her shall feel the weight of this fist if ever he returns to this country; but he won't; he has got safe away, and she has to bear the shame, poor thing! Wait till I tell the 'Vicare du' what I think of his precious son."

"The 'Vicare du'?" said the old man, turning white with rage. "Do you mean to say that his son has been the cause of this disgrace? I'll thrash her within an inch of her life!" and he made a rush towards the door.

"Sit down," said Shoni, taking him by the arm and pushing him back into his easy-chair, "sit down, and calm yourself, before you stand up and preach and pray for other people. Tis for yourself you ought to pray."

"True, Shoni, true. I am a miserable sinner like the rest, but don't let me see that girl again."

"Put her out of your thoughts," said Shoni; "I'll see to her." And as Valmai came silently down the stairs, he opened the front door for her, and quietly took her basket from her.

"Well, howyr bâch!" said Gwen, looking after them, "there's attentions! We'd better all walk in the wrong path!" and she banged the door spitefully, and returned to the parlour to arrange her master's tea.

"And, now, where are you going to, my dear?" said Shoni kindly. "Will you come to Abersethin? Jane, my sister, will give you lodgings; she is keeping a shop there."

"No, no, Shoni," said the girl, "you are kind, indeed, and I will never forget your kindness; but I will go to Nance, on the island; she will take me in, I know."

"Will she?" said Shoni. "Then you could not go to a better place. 'Tis such lonesome place, the pipple will forget you there."

"Oh, I hope so," said Valmai; "that is all I desire."

"The tide will be down. We can get there easy, only 'tis very cold for you."

"No, I like the fresh night-wind."

"Well, my dear," said Shoni, "I daresay your uncle will be shamed of himself to-morrow, and will be wanting you to kom back. I will bring the gig for you; 'tis a long walk."

"No, never, Shoni; I will never go back there again, so don't bring the gig for me; but if you will kindly send my big box to the Rock Bridge, I will send somebody across for it."

"'S' no need for you to do that. I will take it down to the shore on the whilbare and row it over in Simon Lewis's boat. I will kom before dawn tomorrow, then no one will know where you are. I'll put it out on the rocks before Nance's house and carry it up to her door."

"Thank you, thank you, Shoni; but wouldn't tonight be better?"

"Oh, no; Sunday to-night," said Shoni, in quite another tone.

He waited until he saw Nance's door opened in response to Valmai's timid knock, and then made his way back over the Rock Bridge at once before the tide turned.

When Nance opened her door and saw the figure of a woman standing there, she was at first surprised, for the dress struck her at once as not being that of a peasant.

"Nance, fâch! it is I!" said Valmai. "You will let me in?"

"Let you in! yes, indeed. Haven't I been longing to see you all day! Come in, my child, from this bitter wind; come in and get warm. I see you have brought your basket, that means you are going to stay the night. Right glad I am. You will have the little bed in the corner. Keep your red cloak on, dear little heart, because the wind is blowing in cold here at nights, and you have been used to warm rooms. I am well used to cold, and sickness, and discomfort."

"But, Nance—" and then the terrible revelation had to be made, the truth had to be told, and then the loving arms were clasped round the sorrowful girl, and words of comfort and hope were whispered into her ear. No reproaches, no cruel taunts here; nothing but the warmth of human sympathy, and the loving forgiveness of a tender pure woman.

In the early dawn, while Valmai still slept, Shoni's "yo-hoy!" was heard from the rocks, through which he was guiding his boat. Nance opened her door, and, in the gray of the morning, the "big box" was brought in and safely deposited in the tiny bedroom, which it nearly filled.

"Good-bye," said Shoni. "Take care of her, and if she wants anything get it for her, and remember I will pay you." And he rowed away, and was busily ploughing when Gwen went out to milk the cows in the morning.

"Where is she gone?" she asked. "That shameful girl."

"Gone away," said Shoni shortly, and Gwen knew it was useless trying to get anything more out of him.

Thus Valmai slipped quietly out of her old life, though for some time she was the subject of much gossip in the neighbourhood.

It was not long before Shoni found an opportunity of speaking to the Vicar, and as he saw the effect of his tidings upon the cold, hard man, a feeling of pity stirred within him.

"Is this all news to you?" he said. "Didn't you know that your son was haunting the footsteps of this innocent girl, to bring her to ruin?"

"Had I known," said the Vicar, in a stern voice, "that my son held any communication with the Methodist preacher's family, however innocent it might be, I would have closed my doors against him."

"Where is he?" asked Shoni, clenching his fist.

"I don't know," said the Vicar, turning away.

Shoni called after him, "When he comes back he'll feel the weight of this fist, if it's twenty years to come."

[1] Society meeting.

CHAPTER XIII.

"THE BABIES' CORNER."

A glorious summer was once more brooding over sea and land, when one morning, in Nance's cottage, a feeble wail was heard; a sound which brought a flood of happiness to Valmai, for nothing could wholly crush the joyous welcome of a mother's heart. For a little while the past months of sorrow and weariness were forgotten. The bitter disappointment caused by Cardo's silence, lying deep below the surface, was of so mysterious a nature that she scarcely found words to express it even to herself. That he was false, that he had forgotten her, never entered her mind. Some dire misfortune had befallen him; some cruel fate detained him. Was it sickness? Was it death? There was nothing for her but to bear and to wait; and God had sent this tiny messenger of love to help and comfort her in her weary waiting. She still believed that Cardo would return; he had promised, and if he were living he would keep his promise—of this she felt certain. Secure from the sneers and scornful glances of the world, alone in Nance's cottage, her heart awoke afresh to the interests of life. Her baby boy was bright and strong, and she watched with delight his growing likeness to Cardo; the black hair, the black eyes, and the curve on the rosebud mouth, which reminded her so much of his smile. Nance wondered much at the girl's cheerfulness, and sometimes felt it her duty to remind her, by look or tone, of the sorrow connected with her child's birth.

"Look at him, Nance. See these lovely little feet, and there's strong he is!"

"Yes, druan bâch,[1] he is a beautiful boy, indeed," she would answer with a sigh, drawing her wrinkled finger over the fresh soft cheek.

Valmai began to chafe at the want of brightness which surrounded her little one's life. She was proud of him, and wished to take him into the village.

"No, my child," said Nance gently, "you had better not."

"Why not?" was on Valmai's lips, but she hesitated. A deep blush crimsoned her face. "My boy has nothing to be ashamed of," she said, with a proud toss of her head.

"When is he to be christened?" was Nance's next question.

"September."

"September!" gasped the old woman, "he will be three months old; and what if anything should happen to him before then?"

"Nothing *shall* happen to him," said Valmai, folding him to her heart. "My life and my body are larger than his, and they will both have to go before any harm reaches him."

"There's a foolish thing to say," said Nance, "and I wonder at you, merch i. You ought to know by this time that we are clay in the hands of the Potter. Little heart, he ought to be christened, and have a name of his own."

"He can be 'Baby' till September, and then he will be christened."

"And why, September, child?"

Here Valmai took refuge in that silence which had been her only resource since Cardo's departure. She would be perfectly silent. She would make no answer to inquiries or taunts, but would wait patiently until he returned. September! What glowing pictures of happiness the word brought before her mind's eye. Once more to stroll with Cardo by Berwen banks! Once more to linger in the sunshine, and rest in the shade; to listen to the Berwen's prattling, to the whispering of the sea-breeze. Such happiness, she thought, was all in store for her when Cardo came home in September; and the words, "When Cardo comes home in September," rang in her ears, and filled her heart and soul. Yes, the long weary months of waiting, the sorrow and the pain, the cruel words, and the sneering glances, were all coming to an end. She had kept her promise, and had never spoken a word to implicate Cardo, or to suggest that the bond of marriage had united them. He would come home, at latest in a year, and remove every sorrow; and life would be one long shining path of happiness from youth to age.

The light returned to her eyes, and the rose to her cheek; her step was once more light and springy, as she paced the lonely shore, dressed in her favourite white serge, and carrying her little white-robed baby in her arms. She was an object of great interest to the inhabitants of the fishing village on the other side of the island, and they often found an excuse (more especially the young sailor lads) to pass by the cottage, and to stop at the open door for a drink of water or a chat with Nance. They were as loud in their condemnation of her faithless lover as in admiration of her beauty and pleasant manners.

Once more life seemed full of promise and hope for her, until one day when the bay was glistening in the sunshine, and the sea-gulls, like flecks of snow, flew about the rocks; the soft waves plashing gently between the boulders, a little cloud arose on her horizon. Her baby was fretful and feverish, and Nance had roused her fears.

"He is too fat, merch i," she said, "and if he had any childish illness it would go hard with him."

Valmai had taken fright at once.

"Can you take care of him, Nance, while I go to Abersethin and fetch Dr. Hughes?" she asked.

"Yes, but don't be frightened, cariad; I daresay he will laugh at us, and say there is nothing the matter with the child."

"Being laughed at does not hurt one," said Valmai, as she tied on her hat. "I will bring him back with me if possible."

She took a long look at the baby, who lay with flushed face on Nance's knees, and ran with all speed across the Rock-Bridge, from which the tide was just receding, up the straggling street of Abersethin, and through the shady lane, which led to the doctor's house.

There was great peering and peeping from the kitchen window, as Valmai made her progress between the heaps of straw in the farm-yard to the back door, which stood open. The doctor's wife, who had her arms up to her elbows in curds and whey, looked up from her cheese-tub as she appeared at the door.

"Dear me, Miss Powell! Well, indeed, what's the matter?"

"Oh, it's my baby, Mrs. Hughes! Can Dr. Hughes come with me at once?"

"There's a pity, now," said Mrs. Hughes; "he is gone to Brynderyn. Mr.

Wynne is not well. Grieving, they say, about his son."

Valmai blushed, and Mrs. Hughes was pleased with her success.

"When will he be back, d' you think?"

"Not till evening, I'm afraid. But there's Mr. Francis, the assistant—shall I call him? he is very clever with children. Here he is. Will you go with Miss Powell, to see—h'm—a baby which she is taking a great interest in on Ynysoer?"

"Yes, certainly," said the young assistant, colouring, for he had heard Valmai's story, and never having seen her, was now rather bewildered by her beauty, and the awkwardness of the situation.

"Oh, thank you; can you come at once?" said Valmai.

"At once," said the young man. "Is the child very ill?"

"Indeed, I hope not," said Valmai; "he is very flushed and restless."

"Whose child is it?"

"Good-bye, Mrs. Hughes. It is mine," she added, in a clear voice, as they left the kitchen door together.

"Wel, anwl, anwl! there's impidence," said one of the servants, looking after them. "It is mine! As bold as brass. Well, indeed!"

"Yes, I must say," said her mistress, with a sniff, "she might show a little more shamefacedness about it."

"There's a beauty, she is," said Will the cowman, coming in.

"Beauty, indeed!" said the girl. "A pink and white face like a doll!"

"Her beauty has not done her much good, whatever," said Mrs. Hughes, as she finished her curds and dried her arms.

Meanwhile Valmai and the doctor were walking rapidly down the lane to the shore.

"Dan, will you take us across?" said Valmai to a man who stood leaning against the corner of the Ship Inn.

"With every pleasure, miss fâch; you've been out early," he said, as he pushed out his boat, and, seeing the doctor—"if you please, miss, I hope there's nobody ill at Nance's?"

"Yes," said Valmai, hesitating, "the little one is ill."

She did not say, "my baby," as she had done at the doctor's. At the first contact with the world beyond Ynysoer, where she had been so long secluded and sheltered, a feeling of nervous shyness began to overshadow her.

"Dear, dear!" was all Dan's answer,

Once on the island, Mr. Francis found it difficult to keep up with Valmai's hurrying steps. He was full of pity for the beautiful girl beside him, so young and so friendless, and was anxious to serve her, and to cure her child if possible.

As they entered the cottage together, Nance endeavoured gently to prevent Valmai's approaching the child.

"Not you, my dear, not you; let the doctor see him."

Mr. Francis was already attending to the little sufferer.

"No," he said, looking backwards, "not you, Miss Powell; let me manage him."

Valmai turned white to the lips, and, gently putting the old woman aside, took her place at the bedside, where a pitiful sight met her eyes. Her little one lay in the terrible throes of "convulsions," and again the doctor tried to banish Valmai from the scene.

"Let me be," she said, in a quiet voice, which astonished the young man. "Let me be; I am used to trouble." And passing her arm under the little struggling frame, she supported it until the last gasp put an end to its sufferings.

Mr. Francis took the child into his own arms and laid it on the bed, turning his attention to Valmai, who had fallen fainting on the floor.

"Poor thing! poor thing!" said the tender-hearted young man. "It is a pity she cannot remain unconscious."

But he applied the usual restoratives, and she soon opened her eyes, while Nance straightened the folds of the little night-gown with loving fingers, tears coursing each other down her wrinkled face.

"Oh, dear heart! how will she bear it?"

Mr. Francis was silently bathing the girl's forehead.

"You are better now?" he asked.

"Yes," she said; "thank you. You have been very kind, but do not trouble to stay longer; I am quite well," and she slowly rose from the settle.

"I will go now," said the young man. "You would like to be alone, but I will call in the afternoon. You will want someone to—to—make arrangements for you."

"Arrangements? To have my little one buried? Yes, yes, of course. I shall be thankful, indeed."

"Here, or at Penderin?"

"Oh, here—in the 'rock' churchyard."

"I will go at once," and he went out, gently closing the door upon the two women in their sorrow.

In the afternoon he came again, and, being a man of very warm feelings, dreaded the scene of a woman's tears and sobs, though he longed to soothe and comfort the girl who so much interested him. But there were no tears or wailings awaiting him.

Valmai sat in the low rush chair in stony despair, her hands clasped on her lap, her face white as her dress, her blue eyes dry, and with a mute, inquiring gaze in them, as though she looked around for an explanation of this fresh misery.

He did not tell her more than was necessary of his interview with the Vicar. The child was supposed to be illegitimate as well as unbaptised, and could not, therefore, be allowed to sleep his last sleep in the company of the baptised saints.

Old Shôn, the sexton, was already digging the little grave in a corner of the churchyard relegated to such unconsidered and unwelcomed beings as this. However, it was a sunny corner, sheltered from the sea-wind, and the docks and nettles grew luxuriantly there.

Such dry-eyed, quiet grief amongst the emotional Welsh was new to the doctor, and he knew that if tears did not come to her relief her health would suffer, so he gently tried to make her talk of her little one.

"I saw you had tried a hot bath, or I would have recommended it," he said.

"Yes, Nance had."

"I truly sympathise with you; he was a fine child."

"Yes, he is a beautiful child," said Valmai.

"I am sorry to wound your feelings, but what day would you wish him to be buried?"

"Oh, any day; it makes no difference now."

"To-day is Friday. Shall we say Monday, then?"

"Yes, Monday will do. At what time?" said Valmai.

"At four o'clock."

Nance was crying silently.

"Mrs. Hughes wants to know if you will come and stay with her till after Monday. I have my gig at Abersethin, and can row you over now."

Valmai smiled, and the sadness of that smile remained in Mr. Francis' memory.

"No," she said, shaking her head slowly, "I will not leave my baby until he is buried, but thank her for me, and thank you, oh, so much. I did not know there was so much kindness left in the world."

As she spoke the tears gathered in her eyes, and, throwing her arms over the feet of the little dead child, she rested her head upon them, and broke into long, deep sobs.

Mr. Francis, more content, went quietly out of the house, and did not see Valmai again until on Monday he met the funeral in the churchyard. Valmai, to the horror of Nance and her friends, wore her usual white dress. She had a bunch of white jessamine in her hand, and, as the little coffin disappeared from sight, she showered the flowers upon it. Nance was too infirm to accompany her, so that she stood alone beside the grave, although surrounded by the fisher folk of the island. She sobbed bitterly as she heard the heavy clods fall on the coffin, and when at last everything was over, and it was time to move away, she looked round as if for a friend; and Mr. Francis, unable to resist the pleading look, pushed his way towards her, and, quietly drawing her arm within his own, led her homewards down the grassy slope to the shore, over the rough, uneven sand, and in at the humble cottage door. Nance received her with open arms, into which Valmai sank with a passionate burst of tears, during which Mr. Francis went out unnoticed.

[1] Poor little fellow.

CHAPTER XIV.

UNREST.

The summer months had passed away, and September had come and gone, and yet Cardo had not arrived. Valmai had trusted with such unswerving faith that in September all her troubles would be over—that Cardo would come to clear her name, and to reinstate her in the good opinion of all her acquaintances; but as the month drew to its close, and October's mellow tints began to fall on all the country-side, her heart sank within her, and she realised that she was alone in the world, with no friend but Nance to whom to turn for advice or sympathy.

A restless feeling awoke in her heart—a longing to be away from the place where every scene reminded her of her past happiness and her present sorrow. Every day she visited the little grave in the churchyard, and soon that corner of the burying-ground, which had once been the most neglected, became the neatest and most carefully tended. For her own child's sake, all the other nameless graves had become sacred to Valmai; she weeded and trimmed them until the old sexton was proud of what he called the "babies' corner." A little white cross stood at the head of the tiny grave in which her child lay, with the words engraved upon it, "In memory of Robert Powell ──." A space was left at the end of the line for another name to be added when Cardo came home, and the words, "Born June the 30th; died August the 30th," finished the sad and simple story. Nance, too, who seemed to have revived a good deal latterly, often brought her knitting to the sunny corner, and Valmai felt she could safely leave her grassy garden to the care of her old friend.

"You are better, Nance," she said one day, when she had been sitting long on the rocks gazing out to sea, in one of those deep reveries so frequent with her now, "and if I paid Peggi 'Bullet' for living with you and attending to you, would you mind my going away? I feel I cannot rest any longer here; I must get something to do—something to fill my empty hands and my empty heart."

"No, calon fâch," said Nance the unselfish, "I will not mind at all, I am thinking myself that it is not good for you to stay here brooding over your sorrow. Peggi 'Bullet' and I have been like sisters since the time when we were girls, and harvested together, and went together to gather wool on the sheep mountains. You have made me so rich, too, my dear, that I shall be quite comfortable; but you will come and see me again before very long, if I live?"

"Oh, yes, Nance. People who have asthma often live to be very old. You know that, wherever I am, I will be continually thinking of you, and of the little green corner up there in the rock churchyard; and I will come back sometimes to see you."

"But where will you go, my dear?"

"To my sister. Ever since this trouble has come upon me I have longed for a sister's love, and now I think I will go to her I will tell her all my troubles, and ask her to help me to find employment."

"Perhaps she has never heard of you—what do I know?—and perhaps she will spurn you when she hears your story. If she does, come back to old Nance, my dear; her arms will always be open to receive you. Yes, begin the world again. Caton pawb! you are only twenty now You have your life before you; you may marry, child, in spite of all that has happened."

"*Nance!*" said Valmai, and the depth of reproach and even injury in her voice made plain to Nance that she must never suggest such a thing again.

"Don't be angry with me, my dear!"

"Angry with you! No, I am only thinking how little you know—how little you know. But where shall I find my sister? You said once you had her address, where is it?"

"Oh, anwl! I don't know. Somewhere in the loft—" and Nance looked up at the brown rafters. "I haven't seen it for twenty years, but it's sure to be there, I remember, then somebody wrote it out for me, and I tied it up with a packet of other papers. They are in an old teapot on the top of the wall under the thatch, just there, my child, over the door. You must get the ladder and go up. It is many a long year since I have climbed up there."

But Valmai's agile limbs found no great difficulty in reaching the brown boards which lay loosely across the rafters.

"Now, straight along, my dear."

"It is very dark, but I have found it," and coming down the ladder backwards, she placed the cracked and dust-begrimed teapot on the table. "Oh, how brown and faded the papers are! Nance, what is this? I do believe it is your marriage certificate!"

"Very likely, my dear, and you will find the bill for my husband's funeral, too; and a pattern of my scarlet 'mantell,' the one I nursed my children in; oh! I thought a lot of that, and here it is still, you see, folded over my shoulders."

"What is this? You had bad ink, but I think it must be the address. Let me see, here is 'Mrs. Besborough Power.'"

"I knew it was a hard, long name," said the old woman.

"'Carne,' but the last word, oh, Nance, what is it? It begins with M o, and ends with r e—r e is the end of the shire, of course. Merionithshire? No, it is M o, so must be Monmouthshire or Montgomeryshire, stay, there is a t in the middle. Mrs. Besborough Power, Carne—I will try Carne anyway," and next day she wrote to her sister addressing the letter:

Miss	Gwladys	Powell,
c/o	Mrs.	Besborough	Power,
Carne,		
Montgomeryshire.		

In a few days her letter was returned.

"Not known," said Valmai; "then we have not read the address aright. I will go myself, Nance. I will go next week." And the following days were occupied with arrangements for her departure and Nance's comfort during her absence.

On one of these latter days Mr. Francis came in.

"I am glad you have come to-day," said Valmai, holding out her hand. "I wanted to thank you before I left for all your kindness to me, and to ask you to continue to see Nance sometimes."

"Are you going to leave us, then?" said the young man, in a disappointed tone.

He had felt deeply interested in the girl who bore her desertion and sorrow with such patience, and had unconsciously been looking forward to a continuance of the friendship begun between them.

"You are not going away for long, I hope?"

"Yes, for long; possibly for ever, except for a hasty visit to Nance sometimes I shall trust her to you, Mr. Francis, and I hope you will be as kind to her as you have been to me."

"Certainly I will; but do not talk of kindness. It has been a great privilege to me, and a pleasure to know you, and I hope in the future if I can be of any service to you, you will let me know."

Valmai took out her purse nervously, she hesitated to speak of remuneration to this kind friend.

"You are not going to wound me," he said, gently laying his hand on her purse, "by offering to pay me?"

"No, no," said Valmai; "only for the future, for your care of Nance."

"There will be nothing much to do for her, I think; just a call in passing and a few cheering words, and *they* don't cost much." And he rose to go.

"Good-bye, then," said Valmai. "I shall never forget your kindness."

"Good-bye," said Mr. Francis, holding her hand for a moment. He seemed about to say something more, but changed his mind, and abruptly left the house.

The next day was Valmai's last in Nance's cottage. She rose early, and, after her simple breakfast, put on her white hat, and, kissing the old woman tenderly, said:

"I am going out for a few hours; there are one or two people I want to see—Peggi Bullet, and Shôn, the sexton. Then I am going to cross the Rock Bridge."

She did not tell Nance that her chief object was to pay a last visit to her old haunts by the Berwen. After making all arrangements with Peggi Bullet and Shôn, she took her way across the bridge. The year that had passed since Cardo had left her, with its varied experiences and trials, the bitter sense of loneliness and desertion, the pains and the delights of motherhood, the desolation and sorrow of bereavement, all had worked a change in the simple girl's character, that now surprised even herself, and she thankfully realised that her troubles had at all events generated a strength which enabled her to act for herself and attend to matters of business which had before been unapproachable mysteries to her. She shrank a little as she met the bold, admiring gaze of a knot of sailors, who stood at the door of the Ship Inn, where she explained to the buxom landlady that she wanted the car to meet her at the Rock Bridge on the following morning at ten.

"Yes, miss fâch, and Jackie will drive you safe; but, indeed, there's long time since we saw you! You never come to see us now, and there's many warm hearts on this side the Rock Bridge as on the island, I can tell you."

"Yes, indeed, I know, and I thank you all," said Valmai, as she went out again into the sunshine.

The sailors were gone now, and she was free to make her way over the golden sands so often trodden by her and Cardo.

Every boulder, every sandy nook, every wave that broke, brought its own sad memories.

She turned up the path by the Berwen, which led to the old church, carefully avoiding even a glance at the tangled path on the other side of the river, which she and Cardo had made their own.

Pale and dry-eyed, she pressed her hands on her bosom as if to still the aching throbbing within. Every step that brought her nearer to the old church increased the dull aching that weighed her down; but still she pressed on, longing, yet dreading, to see the spot on which she and Cardo had made their vows together on that sunny morning which seemed so long ago.

As she entered the porch, she disturbed the white owl, who emerged from the ivy with a flap of her great wings, and sailed across the Berwen.

The worm-eaten door of the church stood wide open. Entering the aisle with light footsteps, she approached the altar rails. The light was very dim in the chancel, as every year the ivy grew thicker over the windows. Surely in that dark corner within the rails some black object stood, something blacker and darker than the shadow itself, and she stood still for a moment, startled. Yes, there was a sound of heavy breathing and the rustling of paper. She drew nearer, even close to the altar rails, and, as her eyes became accustomed to the dim light, she saw a man, who stooped over a musty, tattered book.

The sound of her footstep attracted his attention, and as he rose from his stooping position, Valmai recognised the marble face and the black eyebrows of the "Vicar du."

He was looking at one of the leaves in the old registry book, and for a moment as he raised his eyes to the silent, white figure before the altar, he took her for a ghostly visitant; but Valmai, with a sudden inrush of recognition, clasped her hands, a faint exclamation escaped her lips, and the "Vicare du" knew it was no spirit who stood trembling before him. For a moment both were speechless—then pointing to the page before him, he asked in a husky voice, "What is the meaning of this?" and from beginning to end he read, with this strange hoarseness in his voice, the entry of his son's marriage to Valmai. Not a word escaped him, not even the date, nor the names of the witnesses. Then he turned his black eyes upon her once more, and repeated his question.

"What is the meaning of this? I have heard of your shame, of your dishonour—of the disgraceful way in which you have entrapped my poor boy. But what is this farce enacted here? How dare you enter the House of God and forge this ridiculous statement? Where is my son, whom you have lured to destruction?"

Valmai was shaken like a reed by this sudden and unexpected meeting, and the outburst of feeling exhibited by the "Vicare du" awoke in her own heart such a tumult of doubt and suspense, that she could no longer restrain the tears which for days she had kept in check; long, silent sobs heaved her bosom, she covered her face with her hands, and the tears trickled through her fingers, but she made no answer.

"Speak, girl," said the Vicar, "have you nothing to say for yourself? no excuse to make for your conduct? My son and I lived in perfect happiness together until you came to this neighbourhood; now you have led a young man on to his ruin and broken the heart of an old man—for this," he said, tapping the register with a trembling finger, "this is a lie—a forgery—a foolish piece of deceit, not worth the paper on which it is written!"

Still Valmai spoke not a word. Oh, what happiness it would have been to throw herself at the old man's feet, and to confess everything, here, where Cardo and she had plighted their troth—to have told him of her ignorance of his fate, of her distracted longing for his return. Surely, surely he would have forgiven her! She was torn with conflicting feelings. But, no! Had she borne the contempt and scorn of all her acquaintances and friends to break down now, and disclose her secret to the man of all others from whom Cardo desired to keep the knowledge of it? No, she would die rather than divulge it—and with an earnest prayer for strength she remained silent, for in silence alone she had taken refuge since her troubles had come upon her.

"Speak, girl, I implore you! Tell me, is this true?" His voice trembled, and he came a step nearer to her. "Tell me that it is true, and I will forgive you and him, for I shall then have a hope that his love for you will bring him home, though he has no love for me." And completely overcome by his feeling's he dropped on his knees by the table, and, leaning his head on his arms, broke into a torrent of tears. "Oh, Cardo, Cardo, my boy!" he cried. "Come back to me."

There was no answer from Valmai, and when he raised his head again she was gone. At the words, "Oh! Cardo, Cardo," she had fled down the aisle, out into the golden sunshine, down the rugged path to the shore, where behind a huge boulder she flung herself down on the sands, crying out in a long pent-up agony of tears, "Oh Cardo, Cardo, come back!"

The morning hours passed on, and noontide drew near.

The "Vicare du" emerged from the church porch, pale and calm as usual. He looked at his watch as he came out into the sunshine, and followed the same path over which Valmai had sped an hour before. He had replaced the old registry book in the rusty, iron chest, had closed the door methodically, and when he had disappeared through the trees the white owl had flapped back into the tower, and the dimly-lighted church which had been the scene of such stormy human feelings was once more silent and deserted.

At noontide, too, Valmai had regained her composure, and had risen from her attitude of despair with a pale face and eyes which still showed traces of their storm of tears.

Next day she bade her faithful Nance good-bye, leaving with her a promise to write as soon as she was settled in some place that she could call "home," and to return for a few days in the spring.

Arrived at Caer Madoc, she took her place in the coach in which she had journeyed a year before; and reaching the station at Blaennôs, soon arrived at Fordsea. Leaving her luggage at the station, she made her way into the well-remembered town. There was the white-flashing harbour, here was the crooked Reuben Street, and here the dear little house once occupied by her uncle, where she and Cardo had spent their happy honeymoon. Yes, she remembered it all; but she held her head up bravely, and crushed down every tender memory, hardening her heart, and setting herself to attend to the business of the hour.

In the broad High Street she easily found the shining brass plate which bore the words, "Mr. William Lloyd, Solicitor," and she entered the office with as business-like an air as she could assume.

"Can I see Mr. William Lloyd himself?"

"You see him, madam; I am he," said a middle-aged, pleasant-faced man, who met her in the doorway. "I was just going out, but if your business is not likely to keep us long—"

"I don't think so," said Valmai. "I am the niece of Captain Powell, who used to live in Reuben Street. He once told me you were his lawyer, and I have heard that in his will he has left me some money."

"Bless me! You are his niece Valmai! Of course. I have been wondering when you would turn up, and was really beginning to think I must advertise for you. I have written to your uncle at Abersethin, but have had no reply."

"He never writes if he can help it. I am very ignorant of money matters and business ways," said Valmai, as Mr. Lloyd handed her a chair, "but would like to know in plain words how much my dear uncle has left me, as I am leaving this part of the country to-morrow."

"Not going out of England, I suppose?" said the lawyer.

"No, oh no; not even out of Wales."

"Well, I have your uncle's will here, and I can read it to you at once."

"No, indeed," said Valmai, "I don't think I want to hear it read. I know from dear Uncle John's perfect faith in you that I can trust you. If you will only tell me plainly how much money I can have now, and how I am to receive it in the future, I shall be quite satisfied; and if I owe you anything you can deduct it, please."

Mr. Lloyd smiled and shook his head at this unbusiness-like proposal.

"Well," he said, "young ladies can't be expected to know much of business ways, but I should certainly like to go into the accounts with you at the first opportunity. He has left you the bulk of his property, the income of which is about 150 pounds a year; and, after deducting the legacies and my costs and all expenses, I shall have in hand about 300 pounds for you."

"Three hundred pounds," said Valmai, "what a lot of money! Could you take care of it for me, Mr. Lloyd? and let me send to you for it when I want it," she added nervously.

"Certainly, my dear young lady, and I will send you a statement of accounts as soon as possible."

After a few more business arrangements Valmai left the office, feeling she had quite acted up to her new *rôle* of an independent woman of business.

Making her way to a quiet hotel, the landlord of which she remembered had been an intimate acquaintance of her uncle's, she procured a bed there for the night, and in the morning arose with the feeling that the dear old past was dead, and that a new and unlovely life lay before her.

CHAPTER XV.

THE SISTERS.

In the spacious, handsomely-furnished drawing-room of a large country-house, two ladies sat on a quiet evening in autumn. The large bay window looked out over extensive grounds to the blue hills beyond. In the pale evening sky the crescent moon hung like a silver boat, the trees in the quiet air looked black as if drawn in ink. In the grate a large wood fire crackled, which the elder lady seemed much to enjoy as she rubbed her hands one over another on her knee, and spoke in a low, purring tone.

The younger occupant of the room was a girl about twenty years of age; she was fair and fragile-looking compared with her portly companion, who was rather florid in complexion.

"Put your work away, my dear," said the elder lady; "it is getting too dark for you to see."

"This is the last petal, auntie," said the girl, still bending her head with its wealth of golden hair over her work. At last with a satisfied "There!" she laid it on the table and turned towards the bay window, through which might be seen a fair view of the park, with its undulating knolls and clumps of trees, between which wound in flowing curves the well-kept drive leading to the high road.

"You had better ring for the lights, Gwladys," said the elder lady, as she settled herself to what she called "five minutes' snooze," a slumber which generally lasted till dinner-time.

"There is a carriage coming down the drive; what can it be, auntie?" But auntie was already in dreamland, and Gwladys stood still at the window watching with curiosity the vehicle which drew nearer and nearer.

"The fly from the Red Dragon at Monmouth! who can it be?" and her blue eyes opened wide as she saw alighting from it a girl in a quiet black travelling dress. "She's young and has golden hair like mine—a dressmaker, probably, for one of the servants, but she would scarcely come to the front door."

Before she had time to conjecture further, the door was opened by a servant man, who seemed rather flustered as the visitor entered quickly, unannounced. She had merely asked him, "Miss Gwladys Powell lives here?" and, receiving an answer in the affirmative, had walked into the hall and followed the puzzled man to the drawing-room door.

As she entered the room in the dim twilight, Gwladys stood still with astonishment, while William so far forgot himself as to stand open-mouthed with his hand on the door-handle, until Gwladys said, "The lamps, William," when he disappeared suddenly.

The visitor stood for one moment frightened and doubtful.

"I am Valmai," she said, approaching Gwladys with her hands extended.

"Valmai?" said Gwladys, taking both the offered hands. "I don't know the name—but—surely, surely, we are sisters! You are my twin-sister. Oh, I have heard the old story, and have longed for and dreamt of this meeting all my life," and in a moment the two girls were clasped to each other's hearts.

Gwladys seemed more unnerved by the meeting than Valmai, for she trembled with eagerness as she drew the new-comer nearer to the window, where the evening light shone upon the fresh pure face, so completely the image of her own, that both were impelled over and over again to renew their embraces, and to cling closely together.

When William entered with the lights, they were seated on the sofa with clasped hands, and arms thrown round each other's necks.

"Please, m'm, is the carriage to go or to stay?"

"Oh, to go—to go, of course," said Gwladys, rising to her feet.

"I have paid him," said Valmai; "but I couldn't be sure, you know, whether—whether—"

"No, darling, of course. Auntie, auntie, awake and see who has come."

Mrs. Besborough Power blinked lazily.

"Dinner?" she said.

"No, no, auntie, not for another hour, it is only seven o'clock; but do wake up and see who has come."

But the sight of the strange girl had already recalled her aunt to her senses; her beady black eyes were fixed upon her, and her high-bridged nose seemed to be aiding them in their inquiries, as she pressed her lips together, and sniffed in astonishment.

"Gwladys," she said, "is it possible that I have invited anyone to dinner, and then forgotten it?"

Gwladys had removed her sister's hat, and as she stood now before Mrs. Power, in the full light of the lamp and the fire, that poor lady was smitten by the same bewilderment which had taken possession of William at the front door. She could only ejaculate:

"Gracious goodness, Gwladys! What is the meaning of this? Who is it, child? and which are you? Are you this one or that one? For heaven's sake say something, or I shall be quite confused."

"It's Valmai, auntie, my twin-sister, though you could not remember her name, but of whom I have thought often and often. Auntie, you will welcome her for my sake? Is she not the very image of me? alike—nay, not so, but the same, the very same, only in two bodies. Oh, Valmai! Valmai! why have we been separated so long?" and, sinking into a chair, she trembled with agitation.

Mrs. Power held her hands out, though not very cordially. She was beginning to arrange her ideas.

"Welcome her! Why, of course, of course. How do you do, my dear? Very glad to see you, I am sure, though I can't think where you have dropped from. Gwladys, calm yourself; I am surprised at you. I thought you were in Figi, or Panama, or Macedonia, or some place of that kind."

"Patagonia," said Valmai, smiling. "My parents both died there, and I have come home to live in Wales again—"

"Well, to be sure," said Mrs. Power, rubbing one hand over another, her favourite action. "Come, Gwladys, don't cry—don't be silly; as your sister is here, she will stay with us a week or so. Can you, my dear?"

"Yes," said Valmai, whose clear mind quickly drew its own conclusions and formed its own plans. "Yes, indeed, I hoped you would ask me to stay a week or so; but do not think I am come to be dependent on you. No, I am well off, but I had an intense longing to see my sister; and having no ties or claims upon me, I made up my mind to find her out before I settled down into some new life."

Alas, poor human nature! The few words, "I am well off," influenced Mrs. Besborough Power at once in her reception of the friendless girl.

"Of course, my dear, stay as long as you like. Go upstairs now and take your things off, and after dinner you shall tell us all your story."

And arm-in-arm the two girls left the room, "like twin cherries on a stalk." The resemblance between them was bewildering; every line of feature, every tone of colouring was the same.

"Let us stand together before this cheval glass," said Gwladys, "and have a good look at each other. Oh, Valmai, my beloved sister, I feel as if I had known you all my life, and could never bear to part with you."

And as they stood side by side before the glass, they were themselves astonished, puzzled, and amused at the exact likeness of one to the other. The same broad forehead, in which, at the temples, the blue veins showed so plainly, the same depth of tenderness in the blue eyes, the same slender neck, and the same small hands; the only difference lay in the expression, for over Gwladys's upper lip and half-drooped eyelids hovered a shade of pride and haughtiness which was absent from Valmai's countenance.

"Oh, see," she said playfully, "there is a difference—that little pink mole on my arm. Valmai, you haven't got it."

"No," said Valmai, critically examining her wrist, with rather a dissatisfied look, "I haven't got that; but in everything else we are just alike. How lovely you are, Gwladys."

"And you, Valmai, how sweet." And again they embraced each other.

"I have no dress to change for dinner, dear. Do you dress?"

"Oh, only just a little, and I won't at all this evening. How strange we should both be in mourning, too! Mine is for Mrs. Power's sister. Who are you wearing black for?"

A hot blush suffused Valmai's face and neck as she answered slowly:

"I am not in mourning, but thought black would be nice to travel in. I generally wear white."

"How strange! so do I," said Gwladys; "white or something very light. Shall we go down, dear? Would you like a bedroom to yourself, or shall we sleep together?"

"Oh, let us sleep together!"

And with arms thrown over each other's shoulders, they descended the broad staircase, just as Mrs. Power, in answer to William's summons, was crossing the hall to the dining-room.

"Here we are, auntie, or here I am and here is she."

"Come along, then, my dears."

"Well, indeed, I never did," said William, when he entered the kitchen; "no, I never, never did see such a likeness between two young leddies. They are the same picture as each other! And missus says to me, 'William,' she says, 'this is Miss Gwladys's sister, her twin-sister,' she says, 'Miss Valmai Powell.' And I couldn't say nothing, if you believe me, with my eyes as big as saucers. Ach y fi! there's an odd thing!"

In the drawing-room after dinner there were endless questions and answers, each one seeming to find in the other's history a subject of the deepest interest. Mrs. Besborough Power, especially, with her nose in the air, sometimes looking over her spectacles, and sometimes under them, sometimes through them, did not hesitate to question Valmai on the minutest particulars of her life hitherto—questions which the latter found it rather difficult to answer without referring to the last eighteen months.

"H'm!" said Mrs. Power, for the twentieth time, "and ever since your father's death you have been living with your uncle?"

"With my uncles, first one and then the other; and the last few months with dear Nance, my old nurse."

"What! Nance Owen? Is she alive still?"

"Yes; she is, indeed."

"She must be very old now?"

"Yes, and frail; but as loving and tender as ever."

And so on, and so on, until bed-time; and the two girls were once more together in their bedroom.

The maid, who was deeply interested in the strange visitor, lingered about the toilet-table a little unnecessarily, until Gwladys, in a voice which, though not unkind, showed she was more accustomed to command than Valmai, said:

"That will do, thank you, I will do my own hair to-night. My sister and I wish to talk." And, having dismissed Maria, she drew two cosy chairs round the wood fire.

"Come along, Valmai, now we can chat to our heart's content." And soon, with feet on fender and hair unloosed, the sisters talked and talked, as if making up for the long years of silence which had divided them.

"And how happy that neither of us is married," said Gwladys. "We might never have met then, dear."

"Possibly," said Valmai.

"And what a good thing we haven't the same lover to quarrel about."

"Yes," said Valmai, rather absently. She was struggling hard with the tumult of feelings which she had hitherto restrained, endeavouring to smile and laugh as the occasion required; but now the tide of emotions, which had been pent up all day, threatened to burst its bonds.

"What is it, dear?" said Gwladys. "What makes your voice tremble so? There is something you are hiding from me?" and, flinging herself down on the hearth-rug at Valmai's feet, she clasped her arms around her knees, and leant her head on her lap, while Valmai, giving way to the torrent of tears which had overpowered her, bent her own head over her sister's until their long unbound hair was mingled together.

"Oh, Gwladys! Gwladys!" she said, between her sobs, "yes, I have hidden something from you. Something, oh, everything—the very point and meaning of my life. And I must still hide it from you. Gwladys, can you trust me? Can you believe your sister is pure and good when she tells you that the last eighteen months of her life must be hidden from you? Not because they contain anything shameful, but because circumstances compel her to silence."

The effect of these words upon Gwladys was, at first, to make her rigid and cold as stone. She drew herself away from her sister, gently but firmly, and, standing before her with blanched face and parched lips, said:

"I thought it was too good to be true; that I, who have so longed for a sister's love, should have my desire so fully satisfied seemed too good for earth, and now I see it was. There is a secret between us, a shadow, Valmai; tell me something more, for pity's sake!"

"I will tell you all I can, Gwladys, the rest I must keep to myself, even though you should spurn me and cast me from you to-morrow, for I have promised one who is dearer to me than life itself, and nothing shall make me break that promise. Gwladys, I have loved, but—but I have lost."

"I know very little of the world," said Gwladys, speaking in cold tones, "and still less of men; but the little I know of them has made me despise them. Three times I have been sought in marriage, and three times I have found something dishonourable in the men who said they loved me. Love! What do men know of love? Fortunately my heart was untouched; but you, Valmai, have been weaker. I see it all—oh! to my sorrow I see it all! You have believed and trusted, and you have been betrayed? Am I right?"

"Yes, and no; I have loved and I have trusted, but I have not been betrayed. He will come back to me, Gwladys—I know he will, some time or other—and will explain the meaning of this long silence. Meanwhile I must go on bearing and waiting."

"Look into my eyes, Valmai," said Gwladys, kneeling once more before her sister.

And Valmai looked full into the blue orbs, the counterpart of her own, with fearless, open gaze.

"Now speak," said Gwladys, taking her sister's hand, and holding it on her own fast-beating heart; "now tell me, here as we kneel together before the All-seeing God and His holy angels, do you know of any reason why we two, when we have dropped these bodies, should not stand in equal purity before the Throne of God?"

"Before God there is none! Of course, Gwladys, my heart is full of the frailties and sin belonging to our human nature; but I understand what you mean; and again I say, there is none!"

"I will believe you, darling," said her sister, throwing her arms around her, "I will believe you, dearest; I will take you into my warm heart, and I will cling to you for ever!"

"But I must go, Gwladys; I want to find some home where I can make myself useful, and where I can fill my mind and hands with work until—until—"

"Until when, dear?" said Gwladys.

Valmai rose with a troubled face and tearful eyes, and, stretching out her hands, she gazed over them into the far distance, with a dreamy look which gradually changed into a brightening smile.

"Until the happy future comes! It will come some day, Gwladys, and then you will be glad you trusted your sister."

"Then to-night, dear," said Gwladys, "we will bury the last eighteen months. I will never think of them or allude to them until you choose to enlighten me. One thing only, Valmai," she added, "forget *that man*—learn to despise him as I do; here is the fourth on my list! Let us go to bed, dear; we are both tired."

And the two sisters were soon sleeping side by side, so much alike in every feature and limb, that no one looking at them would have been able to distinguish one from the other.

"What a strange thing," said Mrs. Power, a few days afterwards, as they roamed about the grounds together, "that the Merediths should have written to me just the day before you came! My dear, I think it will be a delightful home for you. True, Mifanwy is an invalid, and you will be her companion; but then they are advised to amuse her as much as possible, and she sees a good deal of life, often going about from one place to another. Let me see! they will get my letter to-morrow, and I have no doubt they will write by return of post; but we can't spare you for a month, dear. You know you promised us that!" And the old lady purred on, walking between the twins, and much interested in her plans.

"Yes, indeed," said Valmai, "I shall be thankful for such a situation; it is just what I would have chosen for myself, whatever."

"'Whatever' and 'indeed' so often is very Welshy, my love," said Mrs. Power, with a sniff of disapproval.

"Yes, I am afraid, indeed," said the girl; "but you should have heard me two years ago. I could scarcely speak any English then!"

"Well, my dear, I hope Gwladys won't catch your Welsh accent; but the Merediths have it very strongly themselves."

"Oh! I hope they will like me," said Valmai. "I must not count my chickens before they are hatched!"

But they were hatched, and in this matter everything turned out well for Valmai.

The Merediths, who lived in an adjoining county, had for some time been looking out for a companion for their eldest and invalid daughter. They were delighted, therefore, when Mrs. Besborough Power's letter arrived telling them of Gwladys's meeting with her twin-sister, and of the latter's desire to find some situation of usefulness; and in less than a month Valmai was domiciled amongst them, and already holding a warm place in their regard.

Mifanwy opened her heart to her at once, and seemed every day to revive under the influence of her bright companionship; and her parents, delighted with the change which they began to perceive in their daughter, heaped kindnesses and attention upon Valmai, who was soon looked upon as one of the family; even Gwen and Winifred, the two younger girls, taking to her in a wonderful manner.

Yes! Valmai was outwardly happy and fortunate. She hid from every eye the sorrow which lay at the bottom of her heart like a leaden weight, and little did those around her guess that every night, in the privacy of her own room, she drew from her bosom a plain gold ring, and, laying it on the bed before her, prayed over it with clasped hands and streaming eyes.

Gwladys and she corresponded very regularly, and she frequently went to Carne for a few days' change when Mifanwy was well enough to spare her; always regretted by the whole family when she left, and warmly welcomed when she returned.

CHAPTER XVI.

DISPERSING CLOUDS.

Two months had slipped away, and still Charles Williams remained a patient in the Westlake Hospital at Sydney. At length, after a consultation of the doctors, it was proposed that he should be consigned to the workhouse infirmary.

"We can't keep him here forever," said Dr. Emerton; "and as all the beds will be wanted with this outbreak of diphtheria, I see nothing else to be done."

"Well," said Dr. Belton, "I am deeply interested in his case, and if you agree, I will take him under my own particular charge. You know I have a few rooms set apart for such cases in my house at Brookmere. I will take him there, and see what I can do for him."

"Very kind of you, I am sure," said Dr. Emerton. "You can afford that sort of thing—I can't. I should have sent him to the infirmary, where he would be under Dr. Hutchinson's care; but, of course, he will be better off in your private hospital."

And one day in the following week, Dr. Belton took home with him the invalid, whose case he had already described to his wife and children, so that when the stooping figure emerged from the carriage leaning heavily on the arm of the nurse who accompanied him, he was received with kindness and warmth, Mrs. Belton herself meeting him with outstretched hands of welcome.

"Very glad to see you, Mr. Williams. You will soon get better here, I think."

Cardo looked at her with no intelligence in his eyes. "Yes, thank you," was all he said, as he passed with his nurse into the bright, cosy room relegated to the use of the patients, who were so fortunate, or so unfortunate as to arouse more than usual interest in Dr. Belton's mind.

"Now, nurse," said the doctor, "give him a good tea, and a little of that cold quail, and after tea I will come and have a chat with him."

Later on in the evening he kept his word and found Cardo sunk in the depths of an arm-chair, watching with lack-lustre eyes, while the Dr.'s two boys tried their skill at a game of bagatelle.

"Well, Williams, and how are you now? tired, eh?" he asked.

"Yes," said Cardo, turning his eyes upon the doctor with a look of bewilderment, which reminded him of the look of dumb inquiry in the eyes of a troubled dog.

"You will like this better than the hospital I am sure. Do you love children?"

"No," was Cardo's laconic reply, at which the doctor smiled.

He tried many subjects but failed to get any further answer than "yes" or "no." Most men would have been discouraged when several weeks passed over, and still his patient showed very little signs of improvement. It is true, now he would answer more at length, but he was never heard to volunteer a remark, though he sat for hours in what looked like a "brown study," in which probably only indistinct forms and fantastic shapes passed before his mind's eye. And latterly the doctor too had frequently been observed to fall into a reverie, while his eyes were fixed on Charles Williams's motionless attitude. After much thought, he would sit beside his patient and try to interest him in something going on around him.

Indeed, Cardo's gentle ways, together with his handsome person, had endeared him to all who came in contact with him, and there was not one in the house, from the cook in the kitchen to Dr. Belton's youngest child, who would not have rejoiced to see health restored to the invalid.

One evening, when Jack, a boy of twelve, returned from school, he came bounding into the room in which Cardo sat with his eyes fixed on a newspaper, which he had not turned nor moved for an hour, Sister Vera sitting at the window with her work.

"See, Mr. Williams," said the boy, "what Meta Wright gave me, some gilded gingerbread! isn't it pretty? I have eaten a pig and a lamb—now there is a ship for you."

Cardo put down the paper, and taking the gingerbread in his thin fingers, looked at it with eyes that gradually filled with tears.

"Gingerbread?" he said, looking next at the boy, "gilded gingerbread in the moonlight!"

Sister Vera's eyes and ears were instantly on the alert, while she made a sign of silence to the boy.

Cardo continued to look at the gingerbread. Suddenly he held up his finger and seemed to listen intently.

"Hush!" he whispered, "do you hear the Berwen?" and he ate his gingerbread slowly, sighing heavily when it was finished.

This was good news for Dr. Belton, told garrulously at tea by his young son, and more circumstantially by Sister Vera; but for long afterwards there was no further sign of improvement in Cardo.

It was not until three more months had passed that another sign of reviving memory was seen in him, and again it was Jack who awoke the sleeping chord.

"Isn't it a shame?" he said, excitedly running into the room one day; "mother is cutting Ethel's hair; says she's getting headaches from the weight of it. Rot, I call it! See what a lovely curl I stole," and he handed it to Cardo, who first of all looked at it with indifference, but suddenly clutching it, curled it round his finger, and became very excited.

"Whose is it?" said Sister Vera, standing over him.

His lips trembled and with a husky voice he said.

"Valmai—" The sound of the name seemed to charm his ear, for he continued to speak it in all sorts of varying tones—sometimes in whispering tones of love—at others in loud and imploring accents. "Oh, Valmai, Valmai!" he called, and when Dr. Belton entered the room, he held out his hands towards him, and in a beseeching voice cried, "Valmai! Valmai!"

There was no rest for anyone in the hospital that night, for all night long the house echoed with the cry of "Valmai! Valmai!"

On the following morning, endeavouring to create some distraction from this ever-recurring cry, Dr. Belton drove his patient with him for some miles into the bush; the fresh air and motion seemed to quiet his brain, and he fell into the silent stupor so constantly hanging over him.

"Come, Williams," said the doctor at last, as they emerged into a well-kept road leading up to a handsome house which stood on a rising ground before them, surrounded by its broad acres of well-cultivated land. "You must brighten up now, for I am going to take you to see an old friend of mine. Why, here he is!" and they were greeted by a jovial shout as a portly, pleasant-faced man caught them up.

"Hello! doctor, glad to see you; you havent honoured us with a visit for some time."

"I have been so busy lately, and even now you see I have brought a patient with me. I thought a little change would do him good."

"Of course, of course! the more the merrier. I'll ride on and prepare Nellie for your coming," and off he galloped on his well-kept, spirited horse, looking as he felt, perfectly at home in the saddle.

"Nellie," a sweet-looking lady with a brunette's face, which retained much of the beauty of youth, although she had now attained to middle age, was as hearty as her husband in her greeting.

"So glad to see you—you are just in time for dinner; for a wonder Lewis is punctual today."

She shook hands with Cardo, and placed a chair for him at the well-filled table. He took his seat with a pleasant smile, but soon fell into his usual dreamy state, which the company at a sign from Dr. Belton took no notice of.

"I do believe, Williams," said Dr. Belton at last, "that I have never introduced you to my friends. These are Mr. and Mrs. Wynne."

Cardo looked up almost eagerly.

"Cardo Wynne?" he said.

"No," said the doctor; "Mr. Lewis Wynne. But do you know that name?"

"Yes, Cardo Wynne."

"Is that your name?" asked the shrewd doctor.

"Yes, Cardo Wynne."

"Merciful goodness!" said the host, in excited astonishment, which his wife seemed in a great measure to share, "that is the name of my brother's son, Caradoc, commonly called Cardo Wynne; that is what Dr. Hughes told us, Nellie, didn't he?"

"Yes, I have often thought of the name and wondered what he was like. How sad," she said, "and such a handsome fellow, too."

"Caradoc!" Dr. Belton called suddenly.

"Yes," said Cardo, with one of his pleasant smiles, "Cardo Wynne, Brynderyn."

"Good heavens!" said Mr. Wynne, "there can be no doubt about it; that is my brother's home."

And both he and Dr. Belton, aided by Mrs. Wynne's gentle suggestions, made every endeavour to elicit further information from Cardo, but in vain. He had fallen again into an apparently unconscious and deadened stupor.

"Sunstroke, did you say? are you sure of that, Belton?"

"Not at all," said the doctor; "in fact, I have had serious doubts of it lately, and to-day's experience decides me. I will have a thorough examination of his skull."

"I will ride in to-morrow, to hear what further discoveries you have made," said Mr. Wynne. And Dr. Belton returned home early, leaving his host and hostess deeply interested.

Calling Sister Vera to him he told her of his plans.

"I have long thought it possible that poor fellow might have had a blow of some kind on his head, and that he is still suffering from the effects of it. I shall at once administer an anaesthetic and have a thorough examination of his head. The idea of sunstroke was so confirmed by the symptoms when he was brought to the hospital that no one thought of anything else."

"How soon?" asked the nurse.

"To-morrow—three o'clock."

And the next afternoon, Cardo's head was thoroughly examined, with the result that Dr. Belton soon found at the back of the skull near the top a small but undoubted indentation.

"Of course," he said, "we must have been blind not to guess it before; but we are blind sometimes—very blind and very stupid."

Cardo was kept under the influence of a sedative that night, and next day Dr. Belton, with the promptness of action which he now regretted he had not sooner exercised, procured the help of one of the most noted specialists in Sydney, and an operation was successfully performed.

Mr. and Mrs. Wynne's visits of inquiry and sympathy were of almost daily occurrence during the next month, while Cardo in the darkened, quiet room, slowly regained his powers of mind and body. It was a very slow progress, though it did not seem to be wholly unsatisfactory to Dr. Belton. That good man, after weeks, nay months, of anxious interest, was, however, at last rewarded by the pleasant spectacle of a young and ardent temperament gradually re-awakening to the joys of life.

The mind which had been darkened for so long could not be expected to regain its elasticity and spring at once, in an hour, or a day. But it was evident to the doctor that the healing process which had begun would continue, unless retarded by some unforeseen accident. Gradually the children were admitted into his presence, and while they played with Cardo, Mrs. Belton came and chatted with Sister Vera.

A few days later on Mr. and Mrs. Wynne entered through the verandah with Dr. Belton, and although Cardo looked a little flustered and puzzled, the pleasant smile and warm clasp of the hand with which he greeted them showed there was no great depth of distrust or fear in his mind. His uncle and aunt possessed much good sense and judgment, and did not hurriedly thrust the recognition of themselves upon their nephew, but waited patiently, and let it dawn gradually upon him.

One afternoon, while Cardo, accompanied by his uncle and aunt, were walking up and down the verandah conversing on things in general, in a friendly and unconstrained manner, he suddenly stopped, and looking full into his uncle's face, said:

"Uncle Lewis, I cannot imagine how you and I have come here together; some things seem so very clear to me, and others so dim and indistinct."

"But every day they grow clearer, do they not?"

"Yes, I think so. Have I been ill?"

"Yes, my dear fellow," said his uncle, gently laying his hand on his arm, "you have been very ill, and your recovery depends entirely upon your keeping your mind calm and restful. Do not attempt to remember anything that does not come clearly into your mind; in fact, live in the present as much as you can, and the past will come back to you gradually."

At this moment Dr. Belton appeared on the verandah, having just returned from a visit to one of the Sydney hospitals. After greeting his friends, he sat down on a rustic chair, and with a stretch and a yawn brought out from his coat pocket a leather pocket-book which he flung across to Cardo.

"There, Cardo, is that yours?"

"Yes," he answered, carelessly taking the pocketbook and placing it in his pocket.

"Come, you have disposed of it quickly; look at it again."

Cardo drew it out once more, and, looking at it more carefully, said:

"I do not remember where I dropped it; but I do remember being in a hot, scorching atmosphere, and feeling a terrific blow on my head, and then —nothing more but cloud and darkness, until I awoke here to light and memory, though that sometimes fails me, for I cannot remember exactly what happened before that day of burning heat."

"Well! the blow on your head and the loss of your pocket-book I can explain, for to-day in the Eastlake Hospital, I was with a dying man, who confessed that about a year and a half ago he was standing idly on the docks, when he saw a gentleman suddenly struck on the back of his head by the swinging arm of a huge crane, used for lifting heavy weights to and from the shipping. The young man fell forward, his pocket-book— that one I have just given you—fell out of his pocket, and was pounced upon by the man who died to-day. That was you, Cardo Wynne; you were struck down insensible by the iron bar, and while you were quickly surrounded by a crowd and carried to the hospital, the man escaped with your pocket-book. He returned it to me with great penitence, having spent all your money, I am afraid; but your papers, I think, are intact, and I see you have in it a letter of credit upon the Bank of Australasia."

"Why, yes," said Cardo, "I remember coming to the harbour in a ship. What was it called? The *Burrawalla*!" and as he fingered the papers in the pocket-book, and came upon his father's signature, Meurig Wynne, he became much excited, and hunted eagerly until he found a folded paper, out of which he drew a long curl of golden hair.

"Valmai!" he said, "oh, Valmai, Valmai!" and dropping on to a seat, he covered his face with his hands, and through his fingers trickled some silent tears.

"I must forbid any more excitement for the present," said the doctor; "let us go in to dinner."

And as they gathered round the table, Cardo took his seat next to his uncle, with more cheerfulness and alacrity than usual.

The thread of memory, once awakened, never wholly slept again. Daily and almost hourly memories of the past returned to him, and as he gained bodily and mental strength, he gradually unfolded to his uncle the incidents which had preceded his coming to Australia.

When Lewis Wynne became fully aware of his brother's deep-seated affection for him, and of the penitence and remorse which had darkened his life, he was filled with an impatient anxiety to return to the land of his birth and the brother whom he had loved so much. Indeed, before his acquaintance with his nephew, he had already begun to arrange his affairs with the intention of disposing of his property in Australia, for he had prospered in all his undertakings, and was now a wealthy man.

It was delightful news therefore to Cardo when his uncle one day appeared at Dr. Belton's, with the information that he had concluded a satisfactory sale of his property.

"So we'll go back together, old boy," he said, slapping Cardo on the back in his usual jovial manner; "you can write to your father, and tell him to look out for a house for Nellie and me."

"I will write to him to-day," said Cardo; "poor old dad, poor old dad! What he must have suffered! I only hope the suspense has not killed him!"

"Well, if he is alive," said his uncle, "your good news will make up to him for all the past! We'll have some happy days in the old country yet. You must get married, Cardo, and settle down near us!"

"I am married," said Cardo, with a whole-hearted laugh at Dr. Belton's look of astonishment.

"Married!" said the doctor, "I never suspected that! I did think that long golden curl pointed to some love-affair."

"It did, indeed," said Cardo; "it is one of my sweet wife Valmai's curls!"

"Where is she now?" said Mr. Wynne, "with your father?"

"No," he said, with a more serious look, "living with her uncle. The truth is, my father knows nothing about our marriage, and I have only yesterday written to tell him the whole truth; and now that I am able to add the delightful news that you are returning with me, I think it will soften his heart, and he will forgive our secrecy."

"What objection has he to the lady?"

"She is the Methodist minister's niece."

At this remark Lewis Wynne burst into an uncontrollable fit of laughter.

"The richest thing I ever heard of. Ha, ha, ha! Meurig Wynne's son married to a Methodist preacher's niece. My dear boy, he'll never give his consent. Why, he hated them like the very devil himself, and now you expect him to agree to your marrying a Methodist."

"He'll have to," said Cardo, "and I think he will."

"Never, my boy, never," said Lewis, rubbing his hands gleefully. "I expect we shall have some exciting times down there, Nellie?"

"Yes; there will be one thing missing, and that will be dear Agnes."

"It will always be a mystery to me," said Lewis Wynne, "how I missed your father's letter, although certainly I was roaming about a good deal at the time, and afterwards never hearing my brother's name from Dr. Hughes, who wrote occasionally, I naturally thought he was still keeping up his unaccountable anger against me; and the busy life of an Australian station soon occupied my life entirely; but, hurrah! for old Cymry now. We'll go back and make it all right, Cardo."

And in less than a month from this time, a very bright and cheerful party went on board the fast sailing steamer *Wellingtonia*. Mr. and Mrs. Wynne especially were full of life and spirits.

Dr. Belton went on board with them, and when the last good-byes were said, he declared that Cardo's leaving would cause a great blank in his life, as not only had he been greatly interested in the young man as "a case," but he had also grown much attached to him as a friend.

The bell rang, the gangway was raised, and the *Wellingtonia* moved from the side of the quay; and when at last they had fairly bid good-bye to Australia, they turned to look at each other, and to realise that another leaf in the book of life had been turned over.

Cardo was full of the brightest hopes, but shaded by anxiety, for he knew now that two whole years had passed away since he bade good-bye to Valmai on the quay at Fordsea. What had been her fate since then? How had she borne his long and unexplained absence and silence? And as he paced up and down the deck he was full of troubled thought, as well as of bright hopes and anticipations.

"She must think me dead, but she will soon hear; in another week she will receive my letter, and, oh! I will make up to her in the future for all she may have suffered. Valmai, my darling! I am coming back to you, to kiss away your tears, and to shield you from every trouble in the future!"

CHAPTER XVII.

HOME AGAIN.

A cold, biting, north wind blew over Abersethin one morning in November, the sea tossed and tumbled its sand-stained waves in the bay, the wind carrying large lumps of yellow foam far up over the beach, and even to the village street, where the "Vicare du" was making a difficult progress towards the post-office, his hat tied firmly on, his hands buried deep in his pockets, and his long, black cloak flapping behind him. He walked on bravely. Every day he tramped over the sandy beach, under the cliffs, and down the village street to the post-office; this was quite a change in his habits, which drew many comments from the gossiping villagers.

"Well, well; he might have been kinder to his son when he had him with him; he'll never have the chance again," said Peggi "bakkare," peering through her tiny, foam-flecked window.

"No," said Madlen, who had come in for a loaf; "having got safe away 'tisn't likely the young man will turn up here again, and small blame to him considering everything."

"No, indeed, Madlen fâch; serve the old Vicare right; but 'tis a pity for the poor girl, whatever."

"And where is she, I wonder?"

"Well, now," said Madlen, "Mary, my sister, was coming home from Caer Madoc last week, and on the roadside there was a tent of gypshwns; it was dark and they had a fire, and there, sitting by the fire, was a girl the very picture of Valmai."

"Dir anwl! I daresay it was her, indeed; but yet, I thought she was too much of a lady to join the gypshwns. Well, well; strange things do happen."

And the story of Valmai having been seen in the tent of the gypshwns was spread abroad in the village, not that any one believed it, but it was, at all events, better than no news, and was a little spicy condiment in the daily fare of gossip.

"My papers," said the "Vicare du" laconically to the postmaster. "Is your wife better?"

"Iss thank you, sir, and here is a letter for you—from Australia, I think."

The Vicar took it without any show of feeling, though his heart had given a sudden bound at the postman's news.

"Stormy day," he said, as he passed out of the narrow doorway.

He was longing to get home, but he would not hurry his step. He stopped and looked impatiently as he heard the postman call after him.

"There is another letter from Australia, sir, but I dunno where was I to send it. Here it is, sir." And he touched his hat apologetically as he handed a second letter to him.

"Yes; my son's handwriting, I see. I will take charge of it."

He gasped for breath, though the postman saw no sign of emotion, and, as he bent his head against the wind, he read the address on the second letter.

"Mrs. Caradoc Wynne,
 c/o Rev. Meurig Wynne,
  Brynderyn,
   Abersethin,
    Cardiganshire, Wales."

"Oh, my God, I thank Thee," were the only words that escaped the Vicar's lips while he hurried home through the brewing storm, the letters clutched in his hand and pressed against his breast; but these words were repeated several times.

At last, in the quiet of his study, he opened his son's letter and hungrily devoured every word of its contents twice over. After its perusal he took up the second letter, and, with visible emotion, poured over every line of the address, turning the envelope over and over, and pondering in deep but silent thought, from which Betto's knock, announcing dinner, startled him.

As he stood for a moment to say grace, before sitting down to his meal, Betto raised her eyes to his face, and was so startled by the changed and softened look that, with round eyes of surprise, she asked:

"Mishtir bâch! what is it?"

"Mr. Cardo is coming home."

And Betto, quite overcome, plumped herself down on the sofa, throwing her apron over her head and shedding some surreptitious tears of sympathy; while the Vicar, forgetting his dinner, recounted to her the chief incidents of his son's absence—his long illness, and subsequent loss of memory—Betto following the tale with a running accompaniment of ejaculations.

"And this, Betto," said her master, slowly laying the other letter on the table before her, "look at it—but I forgot you can't read English."

"Howyer bâch! not I."

"Well, it is addressed to 'Mrs. Caradoc Wynne.' Did you know anything of this?"

Betto's face exhibited a succession of expressions, which followed each other like dissolving views, astonishment, indignation, fear of her master's displeasure, determination to champion Cardo in any course of combat, all ending in a broad grin of delight as she saw an unaccustomed curve on the Vicar's lips.

"Did I know it? No; if I had, I wouldn't have had words with so many people in the village. Oh! my boy, bâch! didn't I always say he was a gentleman!" And her varied emotions culminated in a rain of tears.

"Twt, twt!" said the Vicar, clearing his throat, "no nonsense, Betto; bring me the potatoes."

And that meal was finished with more cheerfulness than had lightened up that dark old room for many a long year.

From that day forth the Vicar seemed to gain strength and gladness with every hour. He took long walks in his parish, and showed more tender sympathy with the ailments and troubles of his ancient congregation. The wonderful change in the "Vicare du" was the subject of remark at many a cottage hearth, and in many a roadside conversation.

"Oh! it's his son's coming home that has brightened him up so much; and

John Jones, postmaster, says he took the other letter as meek as a lamb. But what has he done with it nobody knows. John Jones is saying that it has never been posted again, so he must have got it still."

"Well, well! how can he post it when nobody knows where Mrs. Caradoc Wynne is?"

"Mrs. Caradoc Wynne, indeed! Phrutt!"

* * * * * *

Early in the New Year, when the bare, brown hills had thrown off their mantle of snow, and the blue waters of the bay were glinting in the sunshine, and the starry, golden celandines looked up fearlessly from every bank and hedge, a heavily-laden carriage, drawn by a pair of strong horses, rolled along the dry, hard road from Caer Madoc towards Abersethin. Its occupants looked at every scene with interest, recalling reminiscences of former days at every turn of the road, and looking out eagerly for the chimneys of the village, which lay at the bottom of the valley.

The travellers were Cardo and Mr. and Mrs. Lewis Wynne. As the carriage left the firm, high road, and began to descend one of the stony lanes which led to the shores below, Cardo became silent and thoughtful; he had hitherto been the life of the party. Returning home in perfect health and spirits, he had given the rein to his fancy, and was full of buoyant hopes and joyful anticipations.

The Vicar, apprised of their coming, was watching at the gate—indeed, had been there more or less since breakfast, and it was now nearly noon.

Betto flew about with amazing agility, considering her size and weight, dusting a chair, smoothing her apron, shading her eyes with her hand, and peering towards the brow of the hill for some signs of their coming.

At last they arrived, and it would be useless to try to describe that happy meeting. The Vicar seemed overwhelmed with joy, not only to receive once more his beloved son, but also to clasp the hand of the brother whom he thought had been estranged from him for ever!

It was quite an hour or two before they had all calmed down.

"We sha'n't keep this fellow long with us," said Lewis Wynne, indicating Cardo with a jerk of his thumb; "he can scarcely take his eyes off that ramshackle old house up there on the cliff; naturally he is longing to see his wife. You must make no objection, Meurig."

"None. I have no wish to do so."

"Nellie and I," continued his brother, "are quite looking forward to see our niece—of course we make all allowance for the rhapsodies of a lover; but discounting all that, I really think, Meurig, he has found a pearl in that old, rough oyster-shell of a house."

"Wait a moment, Cardo," said his father, as he saw his son hunting about for his hat. "I am afraid I have a disappointment in store for you," and from his breast-pocket he drew out, and handed to Cardo, his own letter to Valmai.

Cardo's face blanched, as with trembling fingers he turned the envelope round and round.

"What is the meaning of this, father?" he asked at last an angry flush rising to his pale face, "Did I count too much upon your forgiveness when I asked you to give this to Valmai?"

"No, my dear boy, I would gladly have given it to her, and I grieve for your disappointment, but she has left this neighbourhood many, many months, and nobody knows where she has gone."

"Gone!" was all Cardo could exclaim, as he flung himself into a chair and hid his face in his hands.

"Yes. Much has happened since you left, and you may as well know it now. There is nothing to hide from your uncle and aunt?"

"No, no, tell me at once."

"Well, much had happened before she left."

Here Cardo started up excitedly.

"Why, she has gone to her Uncle John, of course. Where else should she go, dear innocent, without another friend in the world?"

The Vicar shook his head.

"She is not there, Cardo, for he died some months ago and left all his money to his niece."

But Cardo heard not the latter information. He was stunned by the news of old Captain Powell's death; he had never thought of this possibility, and was thrown into despair by the blow. Valmai wandering about the world friendless and alone! The thought was distracting, and in desperation he rushed out of the house.

"Poor fellow," said Lewis Wynne, "this is a terrible blow to him."

"Yes, yes, indeed! Perhaps he will be able to get some clue in the village."

Cardo flew over the beach and up the well-known path to Dinas. Shoni was standing in the farm-yard.

"Caton pawb! wass it you, Cardo Wynne?" he said. "Well, I was swear to make you feel the weight of my fist; but if the news is true that Valmai is marry to you, I will shake hands instead."

Cardo wrung his hand.

"Yes, yes, man, she is my wife, safe and sound—but where is she? Tell me for heaven's sake where has she gone?"

"Well, indeed, that I donno—Essec Powell donno—an' nobody know. You look here now," said Shoni, "an' if you listen to me you will see everything quite plain. After you gone away Valmai wass go down to Fordsea to take care on her uncle, John Powell. He wass broke his leg, and when he cum better Valmai cum back to Dinas."

"Well," said Cardo, "what then? Tell me in Welsh, you'll get on quicker."

But Shoni indignantly declined to give up the language which he considered he had so completely mastered.

"What then!" he continued severely, "you know very well what then. It wass three or four months before she cum back from Fordsea, and she wass look pale and thin and every day more like a spirit angel. Well, everybody see very soon what wass the matter with her, and at last somebody told Essec Powell. It was just the same time Captain Powell died, and when Essec Powell cum home from the funeral and find out his brother leave all his money to Valmai he go to chapel and somebody tell him about Valmai—"

"What about Valmai?" said Cardo.

"That she was gone, like many another, over the side of the path."

"For heaven's sake, tell me what are you driving at?"

"I am telling you if you wass quiet and let me alone. That night Essec Powell cum home from chapel in a devil of temper, and he call Valmai a thief to steal his brother's money from him, and worse names than that, an' he turn her out of the house that night, pwr thing, pwr thing!"

Cardo groaned and clenched his fists.

"Well! the wind wass blowing, and the snow wass fallin' shockin', and I could not let her carry her big bundle of clothes and she in the condition she wass—"

"Condition?" gasped Cardo, "what do you mean?"

Shoni looked at him with keen, searching eyes.

"Cardo Wynne," he said, "I wass ussed to think you an honest, straightforward man, though you wass a churchman, and are you mean to tell me now that you donno that Valmai Powell have a small child on the 30th June last year?"

"As God is my witness, Shoni, this is the first breath I have heard of such a thing; but she was my wife, why then should her uncle have turned her out?"

"But she nevare tell us that, see you, she nevare speak a word about that, and only now lately Betto have told that the Vicare wass tell her she was marry to you! and everybody is wonder why she didn't tell before, instead of bear the nasty looks and words of the women. Oh! I can tell you Gwen here look pretty flat when she hear the news she wass married, and I did laugh in the corner of my mouth, 'cos she bin so nasty to Valmai. Well! I went with her over the Rock Bridge, and we go to Nance's cottage, and she cry, and Nance cry, and there I leave them, and the next morning before the sun is thinking to get up, I take her box and the rest of her clothes over in a boat, and she and Nance kom out early to meet me—and for long time nobody knew she wass there—and there her small child wass born. Here, sit down, sir, on my wheelbarrow; this news is shake you very much, I see."

Cardo felt compelled to take the proffered seat on the wheelbarrow, so completely overcome was he by Shoni's information.

"Go on, Shoni," he said, "make haste."

"Well! she wass walk up and down the shore, and always looking out over the sea; the sailors wass often watch her. 'She may look and look,' they say, 'but he will nevare kom back!' And at last her child die."

"Oh, God," said Cardo, "Valmai to suffer all this and I not with her!"

"Where wass you, then?" said Shoni, "and why you not kom back?"

"Because I was ill in hospital. I caught typhoid fever, and I had concussion of the brain, and I lay unconscious for many long weeks, nay, months. As soon as I came to myself, Shoni, I came home, and I often wished I had the wings of the birds which flew over the ship, and would reach land before us!"

"Well, well, well," said Shoni, "I dunno what wass that illness you had, but it must be very bad by the name of it; but whatever, my advice to you is, go to Nance, perhaps she will tell you something, though she won't tell nobody else."

"Yes, yes, I am going at once. Thank you, Shoni; you have been kind to her, and I can never forget it." And he jumped up and unceremoniously left his companion staring after him.

"Diwx anwl!" said Shoni, returning to his Welsh, "he goes like a greyhound; good thing I didn't offer to go with him!"

Cardo made short work of the green slopes which led down to the valley, and shorter still of the beach below. He jumped into a boat with a scant apology to Jack Harris, the owner, who with a delighted smile of recognition, and a polite tug at his cap, took the oar and sculled him across.

"I am looking for my wife, Jack, so don't expect me to talk."

"No, indeed, sir, I have heard the strange story, and I hope you will find her, and bring the pretty young lady back with you, sir; she was disappear from here like the sea mist."

Nance was perfectly bewildered when Cardo appealed to her for information, and her delight at his return to clear her darling's name knew no bounds. She brought out her best teacups, settled the little black teapot in the embers, and gradually drew her visitor into a calmer frame of mind.

His questions were endless. Every word that Valmai had said, every dress she had worn, every flower she had planted in the little garden were subjects of interest which he was never tired of discussing.

But of deeper interest than flowers or dresses was Nance's account of the tiny angel, who came for a short time to lighten the path of the weary girl, and to add to her difficulties.

"And she gave it up so meekly, so humbly, as if she could *see* the beautiful angels who came to fetch it. It laid there on the settle in its little white nightgown, and she was sitting by it without crying, but just looking at it, sometimes kissing the little blue lips. Dr. Francis was very kind, and did everything about the funeral for her. It is buried up here in the rock churchyard, in the corner where they bury all the nameless ones, for we thought he had no father, you see, sir, and we knew it was unbaptised. She would not have it christened. She was waiting for you to come home, for she would not tell its name, saying, 'Baby will do for him till his father comes home,' and 'Baby' he was, pertws bâch."

Cardo sat listening, with his hands shading his eyes.

"And now, here's the directions, sir," she said, as Peggi Bullet returned from the well. "Here you, Peggi fâch, you are so nimble, you climb up the ladder and bring the old teapot down."

And the nimble woman of seventy soon laid before them the old cracked teapot, out of which Nance drew the same faded address which she had once shown to Valmai.

"It is horribly faint," said Cardo, a fresh tremor rising in his heart.

"Here it is now," said Nance, placing her shrivelled finger on the paper. "This is where she went from here, when all this trouble came upon her, and everybody pointed the finger of scorn at her; and when she had given up the hope that you would ever come back, sir, she turned to her sister, dear child!"

"I never knew she had a sister!"

"No, nor she didn't know much about her; but I knew, and I told her. Born the same time they were, and a grand lady, who was lodging at Essec Powell's at the time, took the sister away with her, and brought her up as her own daughter, and we have never heard of her since. 'But I will find her, Nance,' she said. 'I *will* find her! I know I will!'"

"But have you never heard from her?"

"Well, indeed, there was a letter," said Nance, "came soon after she left. Dr. Francis read it to me, and I think I put it in that teapot, but I am not sure; indeed, perhaps Peggie has thrown it away."

"And what did she say?"

"'Oh!' she said, 'I have found my sister, Nance, and you must not be unhappy about me, everybody is so kind to me. If anyone comes to ask for me, say I am here,' but she didn't say where!"

"But the address was at the top of the letter," said Cardo.

"Oh, anwl! I daresay it was. I never thought of that! There's a pity now; but try again to read that—she read it."

"Well, let me see," said Cardo, taking the faded paper to the window.

"Mrs. Besborough Power?"

"That's it!" said Nance.

"Carew?"

"No; that's not right."

"Carne?"

"Yes; that's what she called it."

"Montgomeryshire?"

"No; she wrote there and the letter was sent back."

"Then it must be Monmouthshire!"

And with this scant information, and a very heavy heart, Cardo left the cottage, and, telling Jack Harris to meet him at the other side of the island, he made his way up the path which led to the little burying-ground behind the Rock Church.

"Poor fellow!" said Peggi Bullet, looking after him, "you can't measure sorrow by the length of a man."

He stepped over the low wall which divided it from the coarse grass of the cliffs, and immediately found himself in a sunny corner. The little grassy mounds were numerous, few had headstones; but one, marked by a little white cross, had evidently received much care and attention. The grass was soft and fine as velvet. Cardo approached it with sorrowful reverence; he stooped to read the inscription.

"In memory of Robert Powell ——. Born, June 30th. Died, August 30th."

The blank space puzzled him for a moment, but, as he stood with folded arms looking down at the little mound, a sudden revelation seemed to flood his mind and enlighten him more thoroughly than all that he had hitherto heard and done. She had kept faithfully—ah, too faithfully—her promise to hide the secret of their marriage until he should come himself to reveal it. How selfish, how thoughtless he had been. Was it possible that his first letter to her, as well as his last, might have miscarried? What had she not suffered? Alone, friendless, disgraced in the eyes of the world. Motherhood, death, the bitterness of feeling herself deserted—all —all had been tasted by her for whom he would willingly have laid down his life; and he registered a solemn vow that the devotion and love of his whole life should henceforth shield her and guard her from every sorrow as far as in him lay.

He turned away from the little grave with a curious yearning in his heart. His own and Valmai's child! Strange and new feelings awoke within him as he crossed the rocky ridge running through the island, and began his way down to the other side to the scattered fishing village, where Jack Harris met him and quickly rowed him across to Abersethin.

Here his first visit was to the stone-cutter's.

Morris Jones received him with the usual exclamations.

"Howyr bâch! well, well! there's glad I am to see you, sir!" And he shook Cardo's hand vigorously. "And, oh, dear, dear; there's sorry I am you didn't come sooner, sir, before the poor young leddy went away. She was broke her heart too much to stop after her small child was buried—and a beautiful boy he was too, sir, the very picture of you."

"You cut that inscription on the little cross, Morris?"

"Iss, sir, I did; with my own hands, and I don't think you get it better done—no, not in Paddington itself."

"No—it is excellent. But the gap after 'Robert Powell'; you must add 'Wynne' to it at once."

"That's it, sir, that's it! before next Sunday it shall be done. I hope you will find the young leddy, sir."

"My wife, Morris."

"Iss, iss, sir; there's glad I was to hear that."

And, as Cardo left, and passed through the rest of the village, the same warm wish followed him from many a cottage window, and from every group of fishermen whom he passed on the way.

"He has not forgotten his pleasant manners, whatever," said the men, as he greeted them all with his usual frank and genial smile.

"No; nor he hasn't lost his good looks," said the women. "Though, indeed, his heart must be heavy now, druan bâch." [1]

"Well," said the Vicar next morning, as Cardo drove off to Caer Madoc to catch the train at the nearest station, "I mustn't grumble at losing him so soon; he is doing the right thing, poor fellow, and I hope in my heart he may find his wife and bring her home. What a happy party we shall be! The only thorn in my flesh will be Essec Powell; I don't think I can ever get over my dislike to that man."

"Oh, nonsense," said his brother, "let us all three go up there to-day, and take the bull by the horns, and make friends with him."

And after breakfast, the Vicar, though with a bad grace, buttoned up his long black coat, and took his way, accompanied by his brother and his wife, up the steep path to Dinas.

It was an early hour certainly, not yet eleven o'clock; but "calling" was unknown at Abersethin, and it was not the unseasonableness of the hour which made Shoni stare as the three visitors entered the "clos" or farmyard.

"Well, diwedd anwl!" he said, barely escaping an oath, "here's the 'Vicare du'! I know him by his coat tails, and his tallow face, and no doubt that is Lewis Wynne and his wife with him;" (for village gossip had already spread abroad the news of the arrivals at Brynderyn). "Well, indeed," he continued, "the preacher on Sunday night told us the end of the world was coming, and now I believe it!" and he put down his wheelbarrow, and stood stock still while the visitors approached.

"Borau-da!" [2] said the Vicare, in a constrained voice.

"Borau-da," was all Shoni's answer, and seeing a dogged look come into his face, Lewis Wynne took the lead in the conversation.

"How are you, Shoni? Do you remember the jolly day we had, you and I, out fishing when we ought to have been at school?"

"Yes, I do indeed, sir, and the lot of fish we caught."

"Yes, and the thrashing we got for it afterwards! But we want to see your master, Shoni."

"Essec Powell?"

"Yes—Essec Powell, is he too busy?"

Shoni hid his face behind his sleeve, while he indulged in a cackle.

"Has he company, then?"

"Oh, very good company—plenty of company! he got Taliesin—Owen Glyndwr—Iolo Morganwg and all the rest of them! and he's quite happy in their company. But once he comes down to live with us he's as rough and prickly as a birch-broom. Indeed he wass nevver used to be like this whatever; 'tis ever since his brother John die, and leave all his money to Valmai."

"You must try to call her Mrs. Caradoc Wynne now, Shoni," said the Vicar, with a smile.

"Yes, indeed, sir," said Shoni, quickly thawing; "there's nobody in Abersethin but won't be glad to see Val—Mrs. Wynne home again; it bin very dull here without her, ever since she gone away."

Meanwhile Mrs. Wynne had knocked at the door and had been confronted by Essec Powell himself, who presented such an extraordinary appearance that she had some difficulty in composing her face to a proper degree of gravity. His trousers of brown cloth, burnt at the knees into a green hue, were turned up above each ankle, exhibiting his blue woollen stockings and a tattered pair of black cloth shoes, his coat was of black cloth, very much frayed at the collar and cuffs, his white hair flew about in all directions, as the draught from the back door swirled in when the front door was opened. He had his finger in the leaves of an old book, and with a far-away look in his blue eyes, all he could say was a bewildered, "Eh!"

"The Vicar is coming to see you, Mr. Powell—"

"What Vicar? What, the 'Vicare du'?" and at this moment the Vicar appeared, and held out his hand.

Essec Powell stared in astonishment, and carefully exchanging his book from his right to his left hand, and glancing to see that his finger was on the right passage, he rather ungraciously shook hands with his visitor.

"Well," he said, "there's a thing I never thought I would do in this world."

"Oh, well, come," said Lewis Wynne's jovial voice. "You meant to do it in the next world evidently, so we may as well begin here."

"Will you come in?" and the old man awkwardly ushered them into the little back parlour, which Valmai's busy fingers had transformed from its original bareness into a cosy home-room.

"Oh, what a dear little room," said Mrs. Wynne as she entered.

The table was littered with books and papers, a gleam of sunlight shining through the crimson curtains giving a warm glow to the whole room.

"Yes," said Essec Powell, looking round with the air of a stranger, "it has nice bookshelves, and a nice light for reading; but I miss that girl shocking, shocking," he repeated; "got to look out for every passage now, and I was used to her somehow, you see; and I haven't got anybody else, and I wish in my heart she would come back again."

"That, I am afraid," said the Vicar, "can never be; perhaps both you and I, Mr. Powell, have forgotten too much that, while we are going down the stream of life, the young people are going up, and are building their own hopes and interests; and I called to-day to see whether we could not agree—you and I—to think more of the young people's happiness for the future, and less of our own ease or our own sorrows."

"It's very well for you to talk," said Essec Powell. "You are a rich man— I am poor; everything you see here belongs to Shoni, and it is very hard that Valmai should have all my brother's money, and I be left with none."

"I think it is hard," said Mr. Lewis Wynne, "and as my nephew will be a very wealthy man, I am certain that he and his wife will be willing to pay you every year the amount which you lost by your brother's will."

"You think that?" said Essec Powell; "150 pounds a year—you think they would give me that?"

"I am sure they would; in fact, I can give you my word for it."

"Well, indeed," he said, laying his book upside down carefully on the table, "that will make me a happy man. I can soon pay off Shoni, and then I can sleep at night without feeling that my servant is my master; and, more than all, I can give all my time to my book that I am writing."

"What is it?" said the Vicar, no longer able to restrain his interest in the old books which littered the table.

"Well, it is the history of our own county from as far back as I can trace it; and, oh! you wouldn't believe," he said, "how many interesting facts I have gathered together. I was not meant for a preacher, and I am getting too old and worn-out to travel about the country. I would like to give up preaching and spend all my time with my books. And with 150 pounds a year! Why, I would be a prince indeed!"

"Well, you may tell your congregation next Sunday," said Lewis Wynne, "that they had better take heed to their own ways now, for that you are going to retire from the ministry."

"And thank God for that," said Essec Powell; "it will be enough for me to look after my own wicked ways. Indeed, I feel I am not fit to teach others ever since I turned Valmai out of the house."

"I see you have here 'Mona Antiqua,'" said the Vicar. "I have a copy in very good preservation, and I am sure I might be able to give you a good many interesting facts for your book gathered from some old MSS. which I found stowed away in the old church tower."

"Can you, now? can you, indeed?"

And the two antiquarians bent with deep interest over the musty books on the table.

Two hours slipped away very pleasantly to the two old men before the visitors took their departure.

At the door Essec Powell held Lewis Wynne's hand for a moment.

"Do you think the little gel will forgive me? and do you think the young fellow will find her?"

"Yes, I think he will; and if all he says of her be true, I am sure she will forget and forgive the past. Of course, you had some excuse, in the mystery and doubt surrounding her at the time."

"Two hours you bin there," said Shoni, as they passed him in the yard. "I wass just kom in to see if you wass all asleep. Good-bye, sir."

He touched his hat respectfully to the Vicar; and as he returned to the house to dinner he muttered to himself several times:

"End of the world! I am sure of it! End of the world!"

[1] Poor fellow.

[2] Good-morning.

CHAPTER XVIII.

THE VELVET WALK.

"Are you going out so late, dear?" said Mrs. Power, as she crossed the hall, where Gwladys was reaching a wrap from some hooks on the wall.

"Yes, auntie, such a lovely evening—quite like spring; I can't resist it. I will put on the cloak Valmai left, and I shall be quite warm."

"Yes, and the very image of her," said Mrs. Power, looking after her through the glass of the front door.

It was one of those tender evenings that visit us sometimes at the beginning of the year to remind us that spring is not far distant, and to make us forget that the cold March winds are yet in store for us. Gwladys drew the red hood over her head and walked briskly in the direction of the lake, which lay buried in the fir wood behind the house.

The path which led towards it was called "The Velvet Walk," being overgrown with a carpet of moss. The sun had just set, and the pale blue sky was cloudless and serene as on a summer evening; but here, in the shadow of the trees, the darkness was falling fast.

Over the fir tree tops one golden star hung like a jewel in the sky. Gwladys walked with face upturned and eyes fixed upon its sparkling brilliancy, and so lost was she in admiration of its beauty, that she was quite unconscious of a hurrying figure who followed close upon her steps.

It was Cardo, who, as he walked along the drive towards the house, had caught sight of a gleam of scarlet between the fir trees.

"Valmai!" he said, with a bound of the heart, and a flood of love and happiness taking the place of the anxious doubts which had filled him since his return home.

He hastened past the front of the house and entered "The Velvet Walk" to find the scarlet cloak but a little way in front of him, and Valmai, as he thought, walking with gaze upturned to the brilliant evening star.

"At last, my darling!" he said, but softly, for he would surprise her. He would approach nearer and call her name, and then she would turn, and he would see the love-light in those starry eyes, of which he had dreamed at night and longed for by day. He was close upon her, but his footsteps made no sound on the velvet carpet.

"Valmai!" he said at last, and stood with wide-open arms and a rapturous smile on his lips.

But at the sound of his voice the girl darted forward a few steps before she turned round and faced the stranger. Her first look was of astonishment and fright, immediately followed by one of indignation.

"Valmai, my darling, I have frightened you," he said, but dropping his arms and the smile dying out of his face; for before the girl had opened her lips to speak, he saw the flush of indignation and the haughty look which passed over her face.

"Back!" she said, holding up her hand as if to keep him away; "not a step nearer. And what if I am Valmai? What is she to you after all these months of cruel neglect?"

Cardo stood still. Was this the meeting he had pictured to himself a thousand times? Had her troubles unhinged her mind? Was she distraught?

"What is it, Valmai, my darling, that has changed you so? What is that cold, haughty look on your face? I am Cardo, dearest—your own Cardo! come back to explain everything to you, and to clasp you in his loving arms," and again he approached as if to embrace her.

"Stand back," said Gwladys once more. "If you come a step nearer, I will call for help from the house."

"No, no," said Cardo, "do not do that. I will obey you, dearest; but tell me what is the meaning of this change in you? Oh, Valmai! has your love indeed perished? Have you forgotten the happy past, the walks by the Berwen, the fortnight at Fordsea? I have been ill, dearest—have lain unconscious for months in a hospital; but I swear that, from the moment I left you until now, every conscious thought, every fibre of my being, every chord of memory has been faithful to you, and to you alone! Come and sit on this bench. Five minutes will explain all to you, and I will not believe that my Valmai can have become the cold and heartless girl you seem to be."

But Gwladys continued standing, and looking at him with eyes in which scorn and contempt were but too plainly visible.

"Good heavens, Valmai!" said Cardo, with clenched hands, the cold sweat breaking out on his face; "do you remember it is a man's very soul you are trifling with? Do you know what a man's heart is? what his love means—such love as mine?"

"Such love as yours!" said Gwladys coldly. "Such love, indeed! that could lead an innocent girl into the path of deceit and dishonour; that could leave her then to bear desertion and the cold scorn of the world, alone and friendless; and now to return, and expect to find her unchanged and still blinded to the truth!"

"Valmai!" said Cardo, his hot Welsh blood suffusing his dark face with passion, "you could never have loved me. Do the strong bonds that united us count for nothing? Does that little green mound in the churchyard count for nothing? No! you never could have loved me; and yet—you did!"

"If I ever did," said Gwladys, "the love is dead. I feel no more interest in you now than I do in yonder ploughman."

"Girl, you are my wife," said Cardo, who was trembling with a mixture of anger and wounded love. "You are mine by every law of God and man, and I will not let you go." Then suddenly changing into a tone of excited entreaty, he said, "Come, darling, trust me once more, and I will bring back the light of love into those frozen eyes, and I will kiss back warmth into those haughty lips."

"Away!" said Gwladys.

"Do you wish, then, never to see me again?"

"Never!" she said. "My greatest wish is never to see you or hear of you again!"

Cardo sank on the garden seat, feeling himself more perfectly unmanned than he had ever been before. He had built such fair castles of hope, the ruin was so great; he had dreamt such dreams of happiness—and the awakening was so bitter!

Gwladys saw the storm of feeling which had overwhelmed him, and for a moment her voice softened.

"I am sorry for you," she said; "but I have given you my answer."

The slight tone of tenderness in her voice seemed to restore Cardo to life. He crossed the velvet path, and, laying hold of her hands, which she in vain tried to wrest from his grasp.

"You are mine!" he said, "and I challenge heaven and earth to take you from me!"

"It is base and dishonourable," said Gwladys, still struggling in his grasp, "to frighten a friendless girl and force your presence upon her."

But Cardo's grasp was suddenly relaxed. Dropping his arms at his sides, and going back a step or two, he stood aside to let her pass. His long-tried temper had over-mastered him, as with a scornful voice he spoke for the last time.

"One word before you go—dishonourable! not even *you* shall call me that twice. Some strange cloud is over you—you are not the same Valmai that walked with me beside the Berwen. You cannot kill my love, but you have turned it to-night into gall and bitterness. I will *never* intrude my presence upon you again. Go through life if you can, forgetting the past; I will never disturb the even tenor of your way. And if, in the course of time, we may cross each other's paths, do not fear that I, by word or sing, will ever show that we have met before."

"I hold you to that promise," said Gwladys haughtily. And she passed on in the deepening twilight, under the fir trees, Cardo looking after her with an aching heart.

She met Mrs. Power on the stairs.

"You have been a long time, dear; I hope you haven't taken cold."

"Oh! no, I will be down directly; it must be near dinner-time."

She walked steadily up the broad staircase, and into her own room; but once there, she threw herself on the couch, and buried her face in the cushions.

"Oh! Valmai, my sister!" she sobbed, "what have I not borne for you to-night! I have kept to my determination; but oh! I did not know it would be so hard! You shall never more be troubled with this man; you are beginning to find peace and joy in life, and you shall never again be exposed to his cruel wiles. But oh! Valmai, having seen him I forgive you; he can pretend to be passionately and truly in love with you! but he is false, like every other man! He left you in despair and disgrace; or what did he mean by 'the little mound in the churchyard'? Oh! Valmai, what have you suffered? But now I have saved you, darling, from further temptation from him. God grant my cruel deception may bear good fruit for you, my sister!"

It was late on the evening of the next day when Cardo reached Caer Madoc, and, hiring a carriage from there, was driven over the old familiar road to Abersethin. The wind blue keenly over the brown, bare hills, the grey clouds hurried from the north over the pale evening sky, one brilliant star shone out like a golden gem before him. Once he would have admired its beauty, now the sight of it only awoke more poignantly the memory of his meeting with Valmai in the "Velvet Walk," and with a frown he withdrew his gaze from it. Here was the spot where he had first seen her! here was the bridge upon which they had shared their gingerbread! and oh! cruellest of all sounds, there was the Berwen gurgling and lisping below, as though there were no breaking hearts in the world!

On the brow of the hill they saw the lights of Brynderyn.

"I will get out here," he said; "you need not drive down these rough roads; I shall enjoy the walk." And as he paid his fare, the driver wondered "what had come to Mr. Cardo Wynne, who was used to be such a jolly young man! That voyage to Owstrallia done him no good whatever!" And as he turned his carriage round, he muttered to himself, with a shake of his head, "I heard some odd story about him and that purty young niece of Essec Powell's the preacher."

Arrived at Brynderyn, Cardo found his father and uncle and aunt seated round a blazing fire in the old parlour, which had not looked so cheerful for years. They had been recalling old memories and events of the past, and when Cardo's footsteps were heard in the passage, they turned with expectant eyes towards the door. When he entered the room, pushing his fingers through his hair as was his habit, he was silent and grave.

"Well, well!" said the whole party at once, "have you found Valmai?"

"Yes, father, I have found my wife," he answered, in measured and serious tones; "but she is unforgiving, and refuses to have anything more to say to me. In fact, I have heard from her own lips that she no longer loves me! There is nothing more to be said. I have come back to my old home, to work again on the farm, to try to pick up the threads of my past life, and to make your life happier for my presence."

"Cardo, my dear boy," said the old man, rising as if in reverence for his son's grief, "is this possible? I do indeed feel for you."

"Oh, nonsense," said Lewis Wynne, "it is only a lover's quarrel; you will make it up before long. I will go to the girl, and make it all right for you."

"If you wish to do me a kindness, uncle, and you, too, dear aunt, you will never mention the subject to me or to anyone else. It is a thing of the past; let us bury it out of sight and hearing."

"We will do what you wish, my dear boy; but I am afraid, amongst these gossiping villagers, you will often hear the subject alluded to in joke or in earnest."

"Oh! I quite expect that," said Cardo, with an attempt at a laugh, but it was a sorry attempt. "I am not going to play the *rôle* of a love-sick swain, my grief will be buried too deep for a careless touch to reach it, and I hope I shall not forget I am a man. I have also the comfort of knowing that my sorrow is the consequence of my misfortunes and not of my faults."

Soon things seemed to fall into the old groove at Brynderyn, as far as Cardo and his father were concerned, except that that which had been wanting before, namely, a warm and loving understanding between them, now reigned in both their hearts, and sweetened their daily intercourse. The west parlour and all the rooms on that side of the house, which had been unused for so many years, were opened up again, and delivered over to the care of Mr. and Mrs. Lewis Wynne, who kept their own establishment there, thus avoiding the necessity of interfering with Meurig Wynne's eccentric habits, and still enabling them to meet round the cheerful hearth in the evening, or whenever they chose.

As for Cardo, he threw all his energies into the busy work of the farm— the earliest in the field in the morning, the latest to leave it at night, nothing was too small for his supervision, no work was too hard for him to undertake; and though he declared he was well, quite well, still, it was evident to those around him that he was overtaxing his strength. The flashing light had gone out of those black eyes, the spring from his gait, the softness from his voice. He paid frequent visits to Nance's cottage, always returning across the corner of the churchyard. The stone-cutter had kept his promise, and had added the surname of "Wynne" on the little cross, and Cardo read it over and over again, with a sort of pleasurable sorrow. The banks of the Berwen he avoided entirely, the thought of wandering there alone was intolerable to him. Every bird which sang, every flower that nodded at him, the whispering river, everything would ask him, "Where is Valmai?" And what answer could he give to his own aching heart which echoed the question, "Where is Valmai? Gone—worse than gone! changed, she whom I thought was the counterpart of my own unchangeable nature. No, no, anywhere but by the banks of the Berwen!" And he plodded on at his work, doing his best to regain the placid calmness, though not the bright joyousness of his life, before he met Valmai. But in vain; the summer found him languid and depressed in spirits. It was Shoni who first suggested to him the idea of a change of scene and companionship. A strange friendship had grown up between these two men. Shoni had been kind and tender to Valmai in her sorrow, and seemed to belong to the bright, happy past which was gone for ever.

"Where that Mr. Gwynne Ellis wass ussed to be with you at Brynderyn? Very good sort, indeed! Why you not go and stop with him a bit, and bring him back here with you?"

Cardo thought the matter over silently, while Shoni whittled a stake for a hay band.

"I think I will, Shoni; I feel I must go away from here for a time."

"Yes, you so rich there's no need for you to work like you do."

"No—that's the worst of it," said Cardo; "I feel my hard work is benefiting nobody."

"Iss, benefit you, cos it help to fill your mind."

"Yes, but I am tired of myself," and Cardo heaved a deep sigh. "Well, it's no use grumbling and grunting, Shoni, and if you don't see me about next week you will know where I am gone to."

"Yes—but, indeed, I am thinking Essec Powell will miss you. He think now s'no one like you in the world, 'he help me a lot, Shoni,' he say, 'with his Latin and his Greek,' and the Vicare, he says, 'it wass wonderful how many books he got on his shelfs!' and indeed I think," continued Shoni, "the two old men will live much longer now they got their noses over the same old book so often!"

"I hope so," said Cardo, "and I am glad to think that the provision we have made for him has taken the sting out of his brother's 'will.'" And he went homewards as broad-shouldered and as handsome as ever, but not whistling or humming as was his wont.

His father, who saw how utterly his son was failing in his endeavour to regain his peace of mind, fell in with his proposal of a visit to Gwynne Ellis with great willingness.

"The very thing, Cardo, and bring him back with you if you can; he was a nice fellow on the whole in spite of his radical ideas."

Once more Cardo took his way from Caer Madoc to the little wayside station which connected that secluded neighbourhood with the busy, outside world. He had written to Gwynne Ellis to inform him of his coming, and had received a warm and welcoming answer to his letter.

"Come, my dear fellow; I shall be delighted to receive you in my diggings, and bring some of the poetry and charm of your lovely neighbourhood with you if you can, for this place is flat, and dull, and gray. But, by the by, I haven't told you I am likely to be removed very soon to a good, fat living, old boy, near Monmouth—but I will tell you all about it when we meet."

Gwynne Ellis's present abode was on the borders of Gloucestershire, and here Cardo found him waiting for him at the station.

"It's only a mile, and I thought you would like a walk, so I have told the boy to fetch your luggage in the donkey cart."

"A walk will be very acceptable after sitting all day cooped up in a railway-carriage."

"Well, now, tell me all about your wife. You know I have heard nothing since that one letter you wrote after you turned up again. What adventures you have had, my dear fellow! and wasn't Valmai overjoyed to see you back again?"

"No, Ellis, and that is all I can say to you now. It is a long story, and I would rather wait until later in the evening."

"All right, old fellow, in the smoking-room to-night."

And in the smoking-room that night they sat late, Cardo opening his heart to his friend, recounting to him the tale of his unfortunate illness in Australia, his return home, and the unexpected blow of Valmai's unrelenting anger and changed feelings towards him, culminating in her utter rejection of him, and refusal to live with him.

"Astounding!" said Gwynne Ellis, "I will not believe it. It is a moral impossibility that that loving nature and candid mind, could ever so change in their characteristics, as to refuse to listen to reason, and that from the lips of one whom she loved so passionately, as she did you."

"That is my feeling," said Cardo, "but alas! I have her own words to assure me of the bitter truth. 'If I ever loved you,' she said, 'I have ceased to do so, and I feel no more love for you now, than I do for yonder ploughman.' In fact, Ellis, I could not realise while I was speaking to her that she was the same girl. It was Valmai's lovely outward form, indeed, but the spirit within her seemed changed. Are such things possible?"

Ellis puffed away in silence for some seconds before he replied:

"Anything—everything is possible now-a-days; there is such a thing as hypnotism, thought transference—obsession—what will you? And any of these things I will believe sooner, than that Valmai Wynne can have changed. Cheer up, old fellow! I was born to pilot you through your love affairs, and now here's a step towards it." And from a drawer in his escritoire he drew out an ordnance map of the county of Monmouth.

"Now, let me see, where lies this wonderful place, Carne Hall, did you call it? I thought so; here it is within two miles of my new church. In a month I shall be installed into that 'living,' and my first duty when I get there shall be to find out your wife, Cardo, and to set you right in her estimation."

"Never," said Cardo; "she has encased herself in armour of cold and haughty reserve, which not even your persuasive and cordial manners will break through."

"Time will show; I have a firm conviction, that I shall set things straight for you, so cheer up my friend, and await what the wonderful Gwynne Ellis can do for you. But you look very tired."

"Yes, I will go to bed," said Cardo.

"And to-morrow we'll have a tramp round the parish, and visit some of the old fogies in their cottage. A mongrel sort, neither Welsh nor English; not so interesting as your queer-looking old people down at Abersethin. Good-night."

CHAPTER XIX.

THE MEREDITHS

There is no part of Wales more rural and unspoilt by the inroads of what is called "civilisation" than some of the secluded valleys lying between the Radnorshire hills. Here Nature still holds her own, and spreads her pure and simple charms before us. Large tracts of moor and rushy fen are interspersed with craggy hills, rising one behind another in lovely shades of purple and blue; and far from the haunts of men, or at all events of town men, many acres of uncultivated land are still tenanted by the wild mountain pony and the picturesque gipsy. On the edge of one of these moors stood a quaint old family mansion, surrounded by extensive grounds and woods. In front lay a descending plain of varied beauty, green meadows, winding streams, and placid lakelets; behind it, the wild vales and moor stretched up to the brown and blue hills.

Colonel Meredith had lived there all his life, his ancestors before him, and here it was that Valmai had found a home as companion to the delicate eldest daughter of the family, who was delighted to find in her so congenial a friend. Her beauty had made a great impression upon the whole amiable family, as good looks often do upon people who cannot boast of the same advantages. It was a good thing that the girl had no vanity in her character, for her charms were continually brought before her in the household. Her pet name was "Beauty," and Colonel Meredith was fond of dilating upon her attractions of person wherever he went. Cecil, a boy of sixteen, was completely her slave, and considered himself the victim of a hopeless passion; while the girls vied with each other in their love and adulation of their friend, so Valmai led at least an outwardly calm and happy life. Her character had developed rapidly during the last two years, and she found herself, to her own surprise, possessed of a power of repression and a control over her emotions which she would have thought impossible a few years earlier. The memory of Cardo, the glamour of their rural courtship, the bliss of their honeymoon, his departure and her subsequent sorrows, were kept locked in the deepest recesses of her soul, and only recalled during the silent hours of the night. She had become less impatient of the stripes of sorrow; she had taken the "angel of suffering" to her heart with meek resignation, endeavouring to make of her a friend instead of an enemy, and she reaped the harvest always garnered by patience and humility. But forgotten? No, not a tender word—not a longing wish—not a bitter regret was forgotten! She seemed to lead two separate lives—one, that of the petted and admired friend of the Merediths; the other, that of the lonely, friendless girl who had lost all that made life dear to her. Gwladys's love alone comforted her, and the frequent visits which they paid to each other were a source of great happiness to both. Her invalid charge soon benefited much by her presence, and was really so far recovered that there was scarcely any further need for Valmai's companionship, but she was glad to stay on as a visitor and friend of the family. She was reading to Miss Meredith one evening in the verandah, when Gwen and Winifred came bounding up the steps from the lawn, hatless and excited.

"Oh, fancy, Beauty; we are going to have a visitor—a young man, too! a friend of Dr. Belton's in Australia; he is travelling about somewhere, and will come here to-morrow. Won't it be jolly? He writes to say he is bringing a note of introduction from Dr. Belton, who wished him to call and give us a personal account of him. I don't tell you, Mifanwy, anything about it, because you are quite above these things; but Winnie and I are looking forward to see Cecil's black looks when the stranger falls in love with Beauty, which he will do, of course!"

"When you stop to take breath I will ask a question," said the more sober Mifanwy. "What is the young man's name?"

"Oh, I don't know," said Gwen. "Papa stuffed the letter in his pocket, and he has driven off to Radnor, and won't be back till dinner to-morrow evening. Probably he will drive the young man with him from the station. Larks, isn't it? I hope he will be a good tennis player."

And she waltzed down the verandah as she went.

"What a girl!" said Mifanwy.

Valmai smiled pensively. The word "Australia" had wakened sad memories, which had to be controlled and driven back at once.

"Let us go in; it is getting late for you," she said.

And they passed through a French window into the unlighted drawing-room.

The next evening Colonel Meredith returned, and, as Gwen had foretold, brought with him the expected visitor. The girl ran excitedly into Valmai's room.

"He is awfully handsome, dear. I have just taken a peep at him through the hall window as he alighted. He'll be seated opposite to you at dinner, but *next* to *me*, and I mean to make the best of my opportunity. You'll see how charming I can be in spite of my plain face."

And off she went, singing as usual, to return in another moment and ask:

"What dress are you going to wear, Beauty? That soft white cashmere? Oh, you look sweet in that, but I bet you a button that I'll cut you out to-night."

As Valmai sat down at the dinner-table she was conscious that the stranger sat opposite to her, and, looking across at him, met the eyes of Cardo Wynne!

A sharp spasm darted through her heart, for at the moment in which she had met his gaze she had seen his look averted from her; and the long-cherished hopes of months and faith in his constancy, held to through so many discouraging circumstances, gave way at a glance, for well she knew that Cardo had recognised her, and at the same moment had avoided her eyes, and had turned to make a remark to his neighbour Gwen. She bent her head over some trifling adjustment of her waistband, while the hot flush of wounded love and pride rose to her face, to give place to a deathly pallor as she realised that this was the outcome of all her hopes and longings.

Fortunately the pink tints of the lamp-shade hid her face, and equally it befriended Cardo, for, on seeing before him Valmai in all the beauty with which his imagination and his memory had endowed her, he had felt his heart stand still and his face blanch to the lips. How he gained sufficient self-control to make a casual remark to his neighbour he never could understand, but he did; and while he was recalling the scene in "The Velvet Walk," and his promise to Valmai "that should he ever meet her again she need fear no sign of recognition from him," Gwen chattered on with volubility. All he heard was:

"Oh, you positively must fish, you know, for there is nothing else to be done here. One day you must fish, next day you ride or drive, next day you fish again; and that's all, except tennis. Winnie and I do nothing else. In the evening Beauty sings to us, and there's beautifully she sings. You'll be charmed with her voice—sweet, old Welsh airs, you know—"

"Hush, Gwen; stop that chatter. I want to ask Mr. Wynne something about Dr. Belton."

"Oh, papa! all the way from the station, and you didn't ask him about Dr. Belton!"

Cardo was thankful to have to talk to Colonel Meredith, for it enabled him to turn his head aside, though still he was conscious of that white figure opposite him, with the golden head and the deep blue eyes.

She had regained her composure, and was talking calmly to the curate, who was laying before her his plans for a Sunday school treat. It is one of the bitter trials of humanity that it has to converse about trifles while the heart is breaking. If only the tortured one could rush away to some lonely moor, there to weep and wail to his heart's content, the pain would not be so insufferable; but in life that cannot be, and Valmai smiled and talked platitudes with a martyr's patience.

In the drawing-room, after dinner, she buried herself in the old, red armchair, setting herself to endure her misery to the bitter end. When Cardo entered with Colonel Meredith, Cecil, and the curate, she had passed from agonised suffering to the cold insensibility of a stone. She knew she would wake again when the evening was over, and she was alone with her sorrow; but now she had but to bear and wait.

It would be impossible to describe Cardo's feelings; indeed, he felt, as he entered the room, and saw that white figure in the crimson chair, that he had already passed through the bitterness of death.

"Nothing more can hurt me," he thought; "after this I can defy every evil power to do me harm!" And he stood in his old attitude with his elbow leaning on the mantelpiece, while he answered Gwen's frivolous, and Winifred's sentimental, questions.

"Are you fond of music?" one of them said at last. "Yes? Oh! Beauty, dear, do come and sing to us—that sweet ballad you sing so often, you know—'By Berwen Banks'."

"Not to-night," said a soft voice from the armchair. "I am tired, Gwen. You sing, dear."

"Well, I'll sing that, if you won't."

And she sang it; and Valmai and Cardo, "so near and yet so far," estranged and miserable, listened to every word, which fell on their memories like searing drops of molten lead.

"By Berwen's banks my love has strayed
For many a day in sun and shade;
And when she carolled loud and clear
The little birds flew down to hear.

"By Berwen's banks the storm rode high,
The swollen river rushing by;
And in its waves my love was drowned,
And on its banks my love was found.

"I'll ne'er forget that leafy shade,
I'll ne'er forget that winsome maid;
But there no more she carols free,
So Berwen's banks are sad to me!"

At the last words, during the acclamations of the family, Valmai rose, unable to bear more. There was a little cry and a soft fall by the side of the red chair, and she lay in a white, unconscious heap on the floor.

"Oh! Beauty, darling!" cried Gwen and Winifred, in a breath, while they flew towards her.

Cardo, too, had instinctively rushed towards the fallen figure. He lifted her in his strong arms as though she had been a feather-weight.

"Oh! thank you, Mr. Wynne," said Mrs. Meredith; "this way, please, to her own room at once, where we can lay her on the couch."

And with the whole family forming a *queue* behind them, even the curate standing on the mat at the bottom, Cardo bore her up the staircase and into the room which Mrs. Meredith indicated.

During a little distraction, caused by Gwen's pommelling of the sofa cushions, Cardo for a moment lost control over his feelings, and he pressed Valmai's form convulsively to his breast as he stooped to lay her down on the couch. He was quickly edged away by the fluttering womenkind who pressed round, each with her own restorative; a little sigh from Valmai told him that she was already recovering, and casting one lingering look of love on the white figure, he made his way downstairs, and joined the other gentlemen, who had straggled back into the drawing-room. He listened absently to the different conjectures as to what had caused Valmai's faint.

"Never knew her do such a thing before!" said Colonel Meredith. "Can't think what it was; but I do remember once she burst into tears when she was singing some old Welsh ballad—that very one, I think—yes—'By Berwen Banks'—strange coincidence!"

In a little while the ladies returned also. "She is all right now," they said, "and quite ashamed of herself; she has had a glass of wine and a biscuit, and insisted upon our leaving her—in fact, she turned us all out of the room and bolted the door."

"Isn't she a lovely girl, Mr. Jones?"

"Oh! yes, indeed—yes—very, indeed!" and Mrs. Meredith was delighted to have an excuse for dilating on her visitor's charms of person and character; while Cardo set himself to work to deliver himself of every message which Dr. Belton had entrusted to him.

He bore Colonel Meredith's cross-examination with unflinching patience, and even suggested fresh topics of inquiry, for, while he had carried Valmai up the stairs he had come to the determination to leave the house before he saw her again. The strain of the situation was more than he could bear. To live under the same roof with her, and not to claim her for his own was impossible—to adhere to the terms of his promise, never to allude to his former acquaintance with her was utterly beyond his power. "Base—dishonourable!" Could it have been Valmai who spoke to him in these terms? or was he the victim of some strange hallucination?

When at last the evening came to an end, he thankfully lighted his candle at the hall table, the whole family hovering round with various hopes that "he would sleep well," "that he didn't mind a feather-bed," "that he didn't mind the sun shining in in the morning." "You can close the shutters, you know. Good-night."

"What time does the post come in the morning?" he asked.

"Oh! at seven o'clock; you can have your letters brought up if you wish; but we always like to have them on our plates at breakfast. Bob will bring yours up."

"If it's no trouble," said Cardo.

There was a whole chorus of "certainly not!" "of course not!" under cover of which he made his way safely round the turning on the staircase. He stepped wearily up the second flight of stairs; there was her room! and he groaned almost audibly as he turned into his own.

Inside that bolted door, a listening ear had caught every vibration of his footstep, every tone of his voice, and a tear-stained face was now raised in agonised prayer, over folded hands which held in their clasp a ring hung on a white satin ribbon.

The exclamations of disappointment and regret next morning, when Cardo's empty seat at the breakfast table disclosed their guest's absence, were loud as they were sincere.

"How unfortunate!" said Colonel Meredith. "I meant to have taken him out fishing to-day; there was a little rain in the night and the Ithon would have been perfect for trout to-day. Here's his note:—

"DEAR COLONEL MEREDITH—I am grieved to say that some unexpected circumstances necessitate my leaving your hospitable roof and returning home to Cardiganshire at once. I shall walk to the station and catch the 7.30 train. Please tender my heart-felt thanks to Mrs. Meredith, and all the other members of your family for their kindness and hospitality. I hope to call upon them at another time, and express my regrets and thanks in person.

"With many thanks to you also,

"I remain,

"Yours truly,

"CARADOC WYNNE."

Colonel Meredith was reading the last words as Valmai entered and took her place at the breakfast table.

"Isn't it a shame, Beauty," said Gwen. "Just as I was beginning to make a favourable impression upon him, too! There must have been something in the letter Bob took up to him this morning."

"Oh, of course," said her father; "fine young fellow—very!"

"Awfully handsome, I call him," said Winifred; "such a sparkle in his eyes!"

"Beauty wasn't smitten," said Gwen.

"On the contrary, she was so smitten she fainted," said Winnie; "you are still rather pale, dear. Papa, wouldn't it be a jolly day for a picnic by the Ithon?"

"Yes," said the Colonel; "bring your lunch down in the brake, and we'll light a fire by the carn, and broil the fish, for I am sure we shall get a basketful to-day—eh! eh! Cecil?"

"Yes—and the drive will do Miss Powell good," said the lad, who was in good spirits from having so easily got rid of Cardo.

And after breakfast they all drove off to the picnic, and Cardo's arrival and his departure were forgotten by all save one.

CHAPTER XX.

GWLADYS.

The week that followed Gwynne Ellis's induction to his new living had been too full of business to allow him to call upon his near neighbours, the most influential member of his congregation, Mrs. Besborough Power of Carne Hall; but soon afterwards he began to look around him and make acquaintance with his parishioners.

The Vicarage was large and his ideas of furnishing were limited, so that after arranging and rearranging every room in the house he still looked at them with a dissatisfied air.

"I don't know how it is, father; in spite of all this handsome furniture you have given me, there seems something wanting, doesn't there?"

"Don't see it," said the old man, "unless it is that wonderful piece of furniture—a wife—you want."

"Perhaps, but that will have to wait," and as he drew his handkerchief over the shining face of the sideboard he thought within himself, "Where shall I find one? There are not two Valmai's in the world, and I declare she has spoiled me for every other woman. By the by, I must call on Mrs. Besborough Power, and see if I can't bring her visitor into a better frame of mind."

The next day saw him entering the pleasant drawing-room at Carne Hall, where Mrs. Power was as usual dozing in her arm-chair, with a piece of wool-work in her hand, upon which she sometimes worked a few stitches while she purred a little remark to Gwladys, who sat nearer the window, making believe to work also. She had already remarked, "Auntie, this is the new Vicar, I am sure," when the door opened and Gwynne Ellis entered.

Having shaken hands with Mrs. Power, he turned to Gwladys with a smile of greeting.

"Valmai!" he said, "I beg pardon—Mrs.—"

"No," said Gwladys, drawing herself up, "I am Gwladys Powell, Valmai's sister—but do you know her?"

"Know her? well!" said Gwynne Ellis; "but I have never seen such an extraordinary likeness."

"Yes," said Mrs. Power, "they are twins, and apart, it is almost impossible to distinguish one from the other."

"Where is she?" he asked, "is she here?"

"No," answered Gwladys, "she has been here, but is now staying with some friends of ours in Radnorshire."

"Ah! I see, I am sorry; I should like to have seen her, but I can scarce say I miss her while you are present, for I certainly see no difference between you."

Gwladys was more talkative than usual. She and Mrs. Power were pleasantly impressed, and congratulated themselves upon having gained an agreeable addition to their very limited social circle in the person of their new Vicar.

"This is a charming neighbourhood. I saw by a little glint of sunshine, as

I came up the drive, that you have a pond or lake in that firwood; and that is always tempting to an artist. Do you draw, Miss Powell?"

"Yes," said Gwladys. "My efforts are very humble, but I have one drawing of the lake." And she fetched it from a portfolio.

"Show him all your drawings, dear," said Mrs. Power; "or, better still, would you like to see the lake, Mr Ellis?"

"If it would not tire Miss Powell to show it me—"

"Oh, no! I can take you by it to the west gate, it will shorten your way home."

"But not yet, here is tea," said Mrs. Power; and they were soon chatting over all the parish news.

At last Ellis rose to go, and Gwladys, putting on a broad-brimmed straw hat, passed out before him through the window—Mrs. Power detaining them with endless directions as to where to stop, where to turn to look at the sun through the fir trees, where to look back for a view of the house, etc., etc.

"This walk is lovely," said Ellis, as he watched the graceful movements of his companion, who glided over the velvet carpet of moss with noiseless footsteps, reminding him of a guardian spirit who walked silently beside some hum-drum man of the world.

"I wonder Valmai never mentioned you to me," she said.

"Did she not?" he asked thoughtfully. "Did she never mention Abersethin, Brynderyn, and the Berwen?"

"No, they are all strange names to me, except Abersethin; she lived there after her return from Patagonia."

Ellis was lost in thought again. "I should like to have seen her; I have something important to discuss with her."

"She is coming here the week after next, and then you can speak to her about this interesting subject," said Gwladys.

And Ellis thought he saw a look of displeasure on the lovely face. Certainly he had never seen that in Valmai; but then, on the contrary, there was a high-souled nobility of purpose in his present companion's looks which was absent in Valmai.

"I daresay when I have seen her she will tell you about all these places."

"My sister shall do as she pleases," said Gwladys, a sweet smile chasing away the momentary look of anger; "it will make no difference in our love for each other—she is part of me, and the best part; I am part of her, and the worst part."

When they reached the west gate, both were surprised to find that half-an-hour had slipped away.

"I will bring my portfolio," said Ellis, as he took his leave, "and you will help me to find the best view of the lake."

During the next fortnight, Mrs. Power received frequent calls from the new Vicar; she was delighted with her neighbour, and did everything in her power to make his visits as pleasant to him as they were to herself. His paintings were a never-ending source of interest and admiration to her, and when he proposed to make a sketch of the lake, with its background of fir trees, and glint of blue sky, she was charmed with the idea, and almost every day she and Gwladys accompanied him down the "Velvet Walk" and settled him to his painting, and Gwladys was sent on frequent journeys of inspection during the afternoon.

"Go and see how he is progressing, dear." And she would go and linger over the picture with comments and praise; but it must be confessed that the drawing progressed more rapidly during her absence than during these visits of inspection.

One afternoon she came running down the "Velvet Walk" with an open letter in her hand, and a distressed look in her eyes.

"Oh, Mr. Ellis! such a disappointment! Valmai is not coming this week. She has been feeling unwell lately, and the doctor advises a thorough change for her, so she and Mifanwy Meredith are thinking of going to Switzerland. Hear what she says:—'Mifanwy is longing for the Swiss lakes and mountains, and wishes me to accompany her. I suppose I may as well do so; but I must first make a hurried journey down to Abersethin, and to see you on my way back. I hear from Dr. Francis that dear old Nance is very ill, and it will depend upon how I find her whether I go to Switzerland or not."

"Now, isn't that vexing! You would feel for me if you knew what Valmai is to me! I seem to love her with all the accumulation of love which had missed its object for so many long years before we met."

Gwynne Ellis was looking seriously into the distance.

"I do feel for you, Miss Powell; but don't think me a brute if I say I am not sorry she's gone—something good may come of it."

"I can't understand you," she said, seating herself on a log in front of him. "You have never told me how you became acquainted with her. Have you known her from childhood?"

"Oh, dear, no," said Ellis, laying aside his painting, and stretching himself on the mossy bank. "I will tell you all about it; it is very simple. Being rather out of health about two years ago, I went down to Abersethin to stay at the Vicar's house, he being an old friend of my father's. I found his son, Caradoc Wynne, a fine fellow—a splendid specimen of a Welsh country gentleman—and he and I became great friends during the three months that I spent there."

Gwladys's blue eyes opened in astonishment.

"Caradoc Wynne?" she said, in an anxious tone, which surprised her companion.

"Yes. Generally known as Cardo Wynne at Abersethin. I found him over head and ears in love with Valmai Powell—your sister, it seems, though

I had no idea she had a sister. His rhapsodies about her amused me at first; but when I saw how deeply in earnest he was, I sympathised with him, and took a great interest in the progress of their courtship. His father and her uncle—one being the Vicar of the parish, and the other a Methodist preacher—hated each other with a deadly hatred—but you are looking pale," he said anxiously. "What is it? Am I saying anything to disturb you?"

"Oh, yes! but go on. Tell me about this Cardo Wynne."

"Well, it's a sad story. They were married; I married them without the knowledge of the two opinionated old men—I hope I sha'n't fall too low in your estimation, Miss Powell."

"Oh! no, no! go on, please. Every word you say is like water to a thirsty man. They were married?"

"Yes, safe enough; and straight from the church porch they separated, for he was leaving for Australia that afternoon at his father's earnest request, with the idea of making peace between him and a brother whom he had offended many years ago. Well, I heard no more of Cardo for nearly two years, when I received a letter from him from Australia, telling me of the series of misfortunes which had detained him there so long. First of all, a serious attack of typhoid fever, and a blow on the head which occasioned concussion of the brain. He was carried unconscious to a hospital, and remained there many months, utterly oblivious of all around him, as no operation had been attempted on his skull, nobody knowing of the blow he had received. One of the visiting doctors at the hospital took him home with him as an 'interesting case,' and then he discovered the indented bit of bone which was pressing upon the brain, and causing first the unconsciousness, and afterwards a complete lapse of memory. Poor old Cardo! the jolliest fellow in the world. What must he have felt when memory returned after a successful operation, and he realised that Valmai and his father were utterly ignorant of his whereabouts."

"Oh, stop, stop," said Gwladys, "oh! what shall I do? Mr. Ellis, I dread to hear the end, and yet I must; go on, please."

"Well, it's very sad. Poor old Cardo returned home at once, and finding Valmai gone from Abersethin made his way up here. Did you see him?"

Gwladys could scarcely gasp "Yes!"

"Then no doubt you know how she repulsed him, and taunted him with wilful desertion of her—desertion, indeed! that honest Cardo, whose very soul was bound up in her! Had I not heard it from his own lips, I could never have believed that Valmai would have used the words 'base and dishonourable' to Cardo Wynne. He is broken-hearted, and really, if she perseveres in this unwarranted indignation, I think it will kill him; and that is why I wanted to see her, for I still believe there must be some mistake."

"Mistake! yes, yes, a horrible mistake. She never saw him at all. It was I who spoke those cruel words to him!"

"Miss Powell! you! how can I believe such a thing?"

"Yes, yes, you must believe," she said, wringing her hands, "it is I who have broken my sister's heart—the sister whom I would die to save a moment's pain." And she rose to her feet, though her limbs trembled with excitement. "It is my turn now to tell my story, and when I have finished you will despise me, and you will have good reason."

"Never!" he said, "I can never feel anything towards you but—but—what I must not dare to tell you."

A vivid blush swept over Gwladys's face; but the troubled look returned, as Ellis, gently taking her hand, led her back to the log of wood, and sitting beside her, said:

"Now, tell me everything."

"I must go a long way back," she said, "and begin with my own uninteresting affairs. You know that Mrs. Power looks upon me as her own daughter, and has expressed her intention of leaving me all her money. Money! hateful money! the one thing I never cared about. I should be happier far in a little cottage than I am here surrounded by all these luxuries—it is true, Mr. Ellis, my tastes are simple."

"Certainly, you would grace a cottage or a palace alike," he said, almost under his breath; "but we must all accept the position in which we are placed, and do our best in that."

"Well," resumed Gwladys, "I have had three proposals of marriage, and on each occasion my aunt pressed me to accept the offer. I refused to do so, unless I were allowed time and opportunity to make the most exhaustive inquiries as to my disinterested lover's antecedents. My heart not being touched, I was able to do so dispassionately, and in each case I discovered something dishonourable in their characters. One I found was on the brink of pecuniary ruin, I therefore considered I had a right to think he loved my fortune and not myself. The next, though a man of honour and probity, I found had such an ungovernable temper that his own sisters failed to live with him. The third was a widower. He had broken his wife's heart by his cruelty, and since her death his life had been one long scene of dissipation. Was it any wonder that I rejected them all? and learnt to distrust and almost to hate every man?

"When Valmai came here I soon found out enough of her story to prove to me, as I thought, that she had been weak where I had been strong; that she had given her heart, with all its precious love, to one of the same type of manhood as it had been my ill-fortune to meet; and when, one evening as I walked here by the lake, a young man followed me and addressed me as Valmai, the only feeling that rushed into my mind and possessed my whole being might be expressed in these words—'Here is the murderer of my sister's happiness; at any risk I will keep him from her. She is happy and calm now; he shall never again disturb her peace of mind, if I can help it.'

"He was so completely under the illusion that I was Valmai that I had no occasion to tell a lie, and I only spoke the truth when I told him that I hated him, and that my greatest desire was never to see his face again. He was wounded to the quick. I saw it, I realised it all, and, oh, I felt for him, for there was something open and winsome about him—something that tempted me to trust him; but I hardened my heart, and I added him to my list of unworthy men. I left him here and went into the house, feeling utterly miserable; but I comforted myself with the thought that I had done Valmai good service. And now—oh, now!—I am more miserable than ever; for I see what harm I have done. I meant to do good, Mr. Ellis, believe me. I thought I was doing dear Valmai a real kindness, and now what shall I do? I have ruined her hopes of happiness, and I have lost your good opinion and friendship."

"Never!" said Ellis. "I see exactly how you felt, and can enter into your feelings thoroughly; it only grieves me to think what a low opinion you have formed of men in general."

"You see," said Gwladys, bending her head, "I have led such a retired life, and have known so few men—none intimately, except those three."

"Let me dare, then, to hope that in time you will come to believe that all men are not like the miserable specimens whom you have met. Will you believe that *I*, at least, am only *sorry* to hear you will be so rich? I cannot expect you to believe me, but it is the truth."

"Yes, I believe you," she said.

"Then let us see what we can do to retrieve your mistake. Will you take my word for it that Cardo Wynne is all that is honourable and true?"

"Yes, oh, yes; I am sure he would not be your friend if he were not so."

"Then the path is easy and plain before us. You will write to Valmai, and I will write to Cardo, and the cloud that has darkened their path lately will be swept away, and your hand and mine will be permitted to let in the light."

"I don't deserve such happiness," she said.

Ellis felt tempted to say, "Yes, your deep love for your sister made you do this, and it richly deserves this fulfilment of its endeavours," but he did not, and the omission was noticed by Gwladys, but it did not tell against him.

They sat some time in silent thought, Gwladys's little foot tossing up the moss.

"I have not told auntie, but I should like to do so now."

"I think you are right," said Ellis, gathering his painting paraphernalia together; "let us go and tell her at once."

There was something delightful even in the simple fact of "going together" to tell Mrs. Power the story of Valmai's sorrow and Gwladys's mistake, and when he left it was with the clear understanding that they should not let a day pass without enlightening Cardo and Valmai.

CHAPTER XXI.

INTO THE SUNSHINE,

There was quite a chorus of regrets and good-byes in the quiet little country station from which Valmai started on her journey to Cardiganshire.

"Good-bye, Miss Powell," said Colonel Meredith, who had driven her down to meet the train, accompanied by his whole family. "No one will lament your absence or rejoice at your return more than I shall, not excepting this sentimental young man," and he pointed to Cecil, who was putting on an air of even greater dejection than usual.

He did not deign to answer his father except by a look of indignation that set Gwen and Winifred laughing; but when the train was absolutely moving, he managed to secure the last hand-clasp, and leave a bunch of forget-me-nots in Valmai's hand.

"Good-bye, Beauty, darling," shouted Gwen; while all the others joined in a chorus of "Write soon!"

Valmai placed the flowers in her waistband with an amused smile. "Poor boy," she thought. "What a good thing it rained last night; there will be splendid fishing to-day in the Ithon, and he will forget all about me if he gets his basket full." And she settled herself down comfortably in the corner of the carriage, and proceeded to open a letter which she had found on her plate at breakfast, but which she had hitherto found no time to read. It was from Gwladys, she knew, but she was somewhat astonished at its length, and turning over the leaves once or twice saw it was very closely written and had many words underlined. "What can it be about?" was her thought as she read the first words, "My own beloved sister—"

There was no one in the carriage to notice the varied expressions on her face as she read the closely-written pages; but had anyone been there to see the rapturous happiness which lightened up her features and brightened her eyes as she drew towards the conclusion, they would have wondered what joyful information could have so entranced and delighted the girl who entered the carriage, although with a serene and peaceful countenance, yet with a certain plaintive wistfulness in the shadows of her blue eyes, which betokened no exemption from the ordinary fate of mankind. But now! what unspeakable joy, what ecstatic delight seemed to infuse fresh life and vigour to the fragile, graceful form! For a few moments she crossed her hands on her bosom, and with closed eyes remained silent; then, starting up and pacing backwards and forwards in the limited space of a railway carriage, she gave the rein to her delight and let her thoughts drop out in words of uncontrolled expression.

"Cardo, oh, Cardo! what happiness for me at last, and for you, dearest— it shall be for you, too! Oh, I see it all. He sought me out and found Gwladys, and the strong, strange likeness between us deceived him, though I cannot think how that was possible. Did he not feel the difference? Let me see—what does she say?" And again she read Gwladys's repentant, beseeching words. "Can you ever forgive me, darling? I tried to look as like you as possible, and I tried to be as harsh as I could at the same time. 'If I ever loved you,' I said, 'I have ceased to do so, and my greatest wish is never to see you again.'"

"Oh! how dreadful," said Valmai, "how could he bear it? and how he must have suffered since then; but I will make it all up to him, and now I understand his conduct the other evening. Oh, you slow old puffing engine, make haste, and take me to Blaenos Station, then there will be a whole hour in that crawling coach, and then comes dear Caer Madoc! and oh! it is market day. Cardo always drives in with Dr. Hughes on that day, and walks home in the evening. I will walk! It will be like that dear, happy night when we first met!" And at last her excitement calming down, she settled herself again into her corner, and while she sat silent and immovable, she followed out from beginning to end the incidents of the last few weeks. Although Gwladys's mistaken interference had caused her such deep sorrow, and such a bitter experience as that of Cardo's avoidance of her at the Merediths, she felt nothing but pity for the sister whom she knew would have sacrificed life itself to save her from trouble.

As the train sped onwards, between the blue hills and by the silver streams, her thoughts outran its speed, and in fancy she saw Cardo hurrying along the high road to meet her at Caer Madoc. And he as he drove along beside Dr. Hughes, was full of tender longings and thoughts of her. She seemed to fill the air around him, she seemed to press upon his inner consciousness with such vividness, that he felt it difficult to restrain his voice, and prevent himself from calling her name aloud.

At last, the evening shadows began to fall over sleepy Caer Madoc, and Valmai, alighting from the coach in the "Red Dragon" yard, looked round hurriedly. With her, too, the impression of Cardo's presence had been so vivid, that she almost expected to see him waiting for her; but no Cardo was to be seen! After leaving her luggage in the ostler's charge, she hastened out through the old archway which opened into the High Street.

"No, I prefer walking, thank you; you can send my luggage on to-morrow," she said to the kindly officious man, who followed her to offer his services as driver, and she turned up the street with a heart full of exultant hopes. Here were the last straggling houses that reached up the hilly street, leading to the moor. Her steps were light and springy, as she followed the familiar road, now almost deserted by the last pedestrians returning from the market. The sun had set behind the sea, which she already saw stretching away to the west, a soft grey haze enfolded the hills which rose before her, and the moon was rising to her right and blending her silver light with that of the departed sun, which still left a golden glow over the west. Valmai walked on steadily until she reached the first milestone, and sitting down beside it, she rested awhile, almost hidden by its shadow. It was not one of the modern insignificant, square-cut, stiff stones, but a solid boulder of granite, one of the many strewn about the moor. She listened breathlessly to the different sounds that reached her ears, sounds which seemed to awake in the stillness, as she listened. There was a faint and distant rumbling of wheels in the town behind her, and surely some strains of music, which carried her back in memory to another evening in the past! Down below the cliffs on her left she heard the mysterious whispering of the sea; in the little coppice across the road a wood-pigeon cooed her soft "good-night"; and away in the hay-fields, stretching inland, she heard the corncrakes' grating call; but no human footstep broke the silence of night. Surely Cardo would have gone to market on such a lovely day! or, who knows? perhaps he was too sad to care for town or market? But hark! a footstep on the hard, dry road. She listened breathlessly as it drew nearer in the gathering grey of the twilight. Steadily it tramped, tramped on, and peeping round the milestone, Valmai at last saw a grey figure emerge from the haze. It was Cardo, she felt sure, and rising at once, she hurried some distance on the road in a sudden feeling of nervousness. The steady tramp, tramp came ever nearer, and, looking through the increasing shadows, she saw distinctly the well-remembered form, the broad shoulders, the firmly-knit frame, and in a fresh access of nervousness she hurried on again—putting off the moment of recognition which she longed for, and endeavouring to reach a hollow in the high bank, where she might lie hidden until she had regained courage and calmness.

Meanwhile Cardo, who had driven in to the market with Dr. Hughes in the morning, had started on his homeward journey just as Valmai was leaving the town behind her. It had been a lovely day, he had had pleasant company, and had transacted his business satisfactorily; but a deep and settled gloom seemed to have fallen upon him, which he was powerless to shake off. Through the whole tenor of his life ran the distracting memory of Valmai's unrelenting anger in the Velvet Walk, and of the bitterness of the subsequent meeting at Colonel Meredith's. As he stepped along through the summer twilight, and saw the silver moon which hung above him, his thoughts flew back to the first evening of his acquaintance with her. Ah! how long ago it seemed, and yet how everything pertaining to that evening seemed to repeat itself. There were the strains of the militia band throbbing on the quiet evening air, just as they did on that eventful evening; and there was even a grey female figure hurrying before him as before, and Cardo smiled bitterly as he thought how different everything was, in spite of the curious "harking back" of all the small circumstances. Awaking from a reverie, he missed the grey figure; but forgetting her at once, and again absorbed in thought, he had passed the hollow in the bank, when a soft voice followed him on the breeze.

"Cardo!"

Instantly he turned, and standing still as a statue, watched with eagerness a grey form which seemed to rise from the hedge. He heard his own heart beat loudly, and in the still night air he heard the sough of the sea, and the harsh call of the corncrake. Again the voice said, "Cardo!" very low and trembling. With one bound he was beside the speaker, and in the light of the moon Valmai stood plainly revealed. The sweet eyes glistened as of old, and the night breeze played with the little curls of gold which escaped from their restraining coiffure. She held out her hands, and in a moment Cardo's strong arms were around her.

"My wild sea-bird," he said, in a passionate whisper, "have you flown back to me? Valmai, my darling, what does it mean? Have you forgiven me? Have you repented of those cruel words, dearest? Oh, say it was not my Valmai who called me 'base and dishonourable.' Speak dearest," he said, while he showered kisses upon the uncovered head which leant upon his breast.

"It was not your Valmai, Cardo. How could you think it possible? It was not I whom you saw in the Moss Walk. I did not know till to-day, this very day, that those cruel words were spoken."

"Let us sit here, my beloved; give me your hand; let me try to realise this bewildering joy." And hand in hand they sat on the grassy bank, while the corn-crake called, and the sea heaved and whispered behind them.

There, under the golden moon, with endless questions and reiteration of answers, Valmai told her story and Cardo told his, until the moon rode high in the sky. Again and again Cardo pressed her to his heart, and again and again she took his brown hands in her own and laid her cheek upon them.

"Oh, Cardo! is it true? or is it all a dream? So suddenly to leave my sadness and sorrow behind, and to awake to this blessed reality!" And as they rose to pursue their walk together, Cardo drew her arm through his, as if afraid for a moment to loosen his hold of her.

"But your sister, dearest, is *not* like you! How could I have been deceived? How could I, for one moment, have thought my gentle darling would say such cruel things? No, no! you are utterly unlike each other, though so strangely alike."

"Well, indeed, Cardo bâch! when you know her you will see how sweet and beautiful she is! how much wiser and more noble than I! It was her great love for me, and her desire that I should be happy, that made her act as she did; and to-morrow you must read her penitent letter, and learn to forgive her, and to love her for my sake."

"I will—I will, love; I will forgive anybody, anything, and will love the whole world now that I have you back again. But oh, Valmai, my beloved, how shall I ever make up to you for all you have gone through? I know now you never received my letter written on the *Burrawalla*, and sent by *The Dundee*, for I have heard of her sad fate. In that, dearest, I retracted my request that you should keep our marriage a secret, and you would have been saved all the sorrow you have borne had you received it. But I will make up to you, dearest, if the devotion of a lifetime can do so."

"This is happiness enough to make up for anything," said Valmai; "and I am glad I was able to keep my promise."

"Faithful friend, and trustful wife!" answered Cardo.

"Ah! no," continued Valmai; "I shall never regret having kept my promise! Indeed, I never felt tempted to break it, except one day, when, in the old church, I met your father face to face. Never shall I forget the agonising longing I felt to throw myself at his feet and tell him all, and mingle my tears with his."

"He has told me all about it, love, and how he thought it was an angel, when he first saw you standing there. But let us leave all tales of sorrow for another day; to-night is for love only, for rapturous joy! Are we not together, love? and what does anything else matter?"

"Nothing, nothing," answered Valmai, in words which lost none of their depth of feeling from being spoken in soft, low tones.

In silence, which was more eloquent than words, they pursued their way till they reached the bridge over the Berwen; and as they leant over its side, and looked into the depths of the woods beneath them, they recalled all the circumstances of their first meeting.

"I wish I had bought some gingerbread in the Mwntroyd, Cardo, so that we might eat it here together. Ah! how it all comes back to me!"

And as they leant over the bridge he held her hand in his, and with eyes which sought each other's in the moonlight, they let the time slip by unheeded. The only sound that rose upon the still night air was the babbling of the Berwen.

When at last both had told their story, and every question and answer had again and again been renewed, and all its side bearings and suggestions had been satisfactorily explained, the sweet, lisping sounds of the river flooded their souls with its music.

"Oh, Cardo! to think we can once more sing together. How different to that miserable evening at Colonel Meredith's, when you stood aloof, and Gwen sang the dear old song. I thought it would kill me."

"And I, darling, when I carried you up in my arms, what did I feel?"

"Well, indeed, I don't know; but we have had a dreadful experience, whatever." And presently Valmai began to hum "By Berwen Banks," Cardo irresistibly joining in with his musical bass, and once again the old ballad floated down the valley and filled the night with melody.

"We ought to be going now, or we shall be shut out. I know Nance will be gone to bed already, but, certainly, there is not much distance between her bed and the door."

"Nance!" said Cardo. "No, indeed, my wild sea-bird. I have caught you now, and never again will I part with you. Home to Brynderyn, dearest, with me, where my father is longing to fold you in his arms."

"Anywhere with you, Cardo." And down by the Berwen they took their way, by the old church, where the white owl hooted at them as they passed, and down to the shore, where the waves whispered their happy greetings.

The "Vicare du," as he sat by his study fire that night, was lost in thought. A wonderful change had come over his countenance, the gloom and sternness had disappeared, and a softened and even gentle look had taken their place. A smile of eager interest crossed his face as he heard the crunching of the gravel, which announced his son's return. Betto was already opening the door, and a cry of surprise and gladness woke an echo in the old man's heart as he hurried along the stone passage into the parlour. Cardo came in to meet him, leading Valmai, who hung back a little timidly, looking nervously into the Vicar's pale face. But the look she saw there banished all her fears, and in another moment she was clasped in his arms, and in all Wales no happier family drew round their evening meal that night than the Wynnes of Brynderyn.

There is nothing more to be said, except that Gwynne Ellis's letter awaited Cardo's home-coming, and it shall speak for itself.

"DEAR WYNNE,—I write with such mixed feelings, and at the same time in such a hurry to catch the first possible post, that probably you will think my letter is a little 'mixed' too. You will guess what was my astonishment, when calling upon Mrs. Power, to find—not Valmai, but her twin-sister, Miss Gwladys Powell! My dear Wynne, I was struck dumb by the likeness between them. I waited eagerly for Valmai's arrival, which they were daily expecting, and it was not until I heard she was going to Cardiganshire instead that I mentioned to Gwladys your marriage to her sister, and the cruel manner in which she had received you after your long absence. Then came the explanation, which, no doubt, ere this you have received from Valmai's own lips, for I know that to-morrow she will see you, having received her sister's letter in the morning; and the veil will be lifted, and all your sorrow will disperse like the baseless fabric of a dream. You will see already how Gwladys, dreading your influence upon the sister whom she thought you had deceived and deserted, was tempted, by your mistaking her for Valmai, to impersonate her, and to drive you away from her presence. Her sorrow and repentance are greater than the occasion demands, I think, for, after all, it was her deep love for her sister which made her act in this way; and I am sure that, when you and Valmai have been reunited and all your joys return, you will have no room in your hearts for anger against Gwladys. She is the most lovely girl I have ever seen, except your wife, and her mind and heart are quite worthy of her beautiful face; indeed, my dear Cardo, she is what I once thought was not to be found—a second Valmai! In fact I love her, and I am not without a faint hope that my love is returned. Remember me to Shoni, and tell him I hope to see him again next spring. And what if I bring Gwladys down, and we all roam by the Berwen together?—not Shoni! What can I add more, except that I hope this delicious programme may be carried out?

"Yours as of old,

"GWYNNE ELLIS."